"D
all men on sight!

"What I do with all men is none of your business,
Sir Nicholas. Return to your long line of amours.
They'll be awaiting you."

"When I'm ready." His arm still held her back
against the wall, but his closeness spelled a dangerous
determination, and her act of indifference began to
falter as his warmth reached her face and the bare skin
below her ruff.

This was not the way Adorna wanted to be wooed,
not like his other easy conquests—small talk, gropings
in the dark, a kiss and a fall like ripened fruit into his
lap. She was *not* like the others.

* * *

One Night in Paradise
Harlequin Historical #733—December 2004

Praise for Juliet Landon

The Knight's Conquest
"A feisty heroine, heroic knight, an entertaining battle of
wills and plenty of colorful history flavor this tale,
making it a delightful one-night read."
—*Romantic Times*

ONE NIGHT IN PARADISE

Juliet Landon

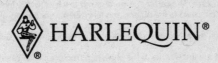

HARLEQUIN®

TORONTO • NEW YORK • LONDON
AMSTERDAM • PARIS • SYDNEY • HAMBURG
STOCKHOLM • ATHENS • TOKYO • MILAN • MADRID
PRAGUE • WARSAW • BUDAPEST • AUCKLAND

ISBN 0-373-29333-X

ONE NIGHT IN PARADISE

First North American Publication 2004

Copyright © 2003 by Juliet Landon

This edition published by arrangement with Harlequin Books S.A.

® and TM are trademarks of the publisher. Trademarks indicated with ® are registered in the United States Patent and Trademark Office, the Canadian Trade Marks Office and in other countries.

www.eHarlequin.com

Printed in U.S.A.

Please address questions and book requests to:
Harlequin Reader Service
U.S.: 3010 Walden Ave., P.O. Box 1325, Buffalo, NY 14269
Canadian: P.O. Box 609, Fort Erie, Ont. L2A 5X3

Chapter One

23 June 1575, Richmond, Surrey

Adorna Pickering's ability to stay calm in the face of adversity was put severely to the test the day that Queen Elizabeth went hawking. They were in the park at Richmond and Adorna was noticed not so much for her superb horsemanship but for her graceful fall backwards into the River Thames and for her pretence that it was nothing, really. Though Adorna managed to impress the Queen, there was one who refused to be impressed in quite the same sympathetic manner.

It had all begun so well, the midsummer sun promising a windless day perfect for hawking, one of Her Majesty's favourite sports in which she always indulged when staying at her palace in Richmond. The park was extensive, well stocked with deer and waterbirds, and a select gathering of the Queen's favourite courtiers made a brilliant splash of colour behind her, quietly vying with each other to show off their finery, their horses, and their popularity.

As the daughter of the Queen's Master of the Revels Office, Adorna's presence in such company was not only accepted but encouraged. Living at Richmond so close to the royal palace had many compensations, as her newly appointed father had only recently pointed out.

Adorna had already attracted smiles and admiring glances, her striking beauty and pale gold hair reflecting the similar pale gold of her new mare in the blue-patterned harness given to her last week for her twentieth birthday. By her side rode Master Peter Fowler, another member of the royal household, a young man on the upward current who privately believed that his future would be enhanced by his association with someone slightly above his station. Not that he was oblivious to Adorna's physical attributes, but Peter was more ambitious than moonstruck, and his appearance by her side this morning was no coincidence.

In a sea of jewel colours, tossing plumes and a speckle of spaniels weaving between hooves, the company waited while the Queen and her Master Falconer cast their falcons up into the sky while down below the beaters flushed ducks from the river, putting them to flight. But, being on the edge of the gathering and not far from the river bank, Adorna's flighty young mare took exception to wings whizzing overhead, squawking loudly. The mare bunched and staggered backwards, quivering with fright, and it was with some difficulty that Adorna controlled her and stopped her barging into nearby horses whose riders were looking skywards. Then, thinking that she was over that semi-crisis, she gave her attention to the falcons, which, in bringing down the ducks, dropped two of them into the river in a flurry of white feathers.

Everyone's attention was now engaged in seeing who would be first to retrieve the flapping quarry for Her Majesty, none of them noticing how Adorna's mare, still restive, had decided to join the retrieving party of her own free will against all her rider's attempts to stop her. Moving backwards instead of forwards despite all that Adorna could do, the mare was beating a determined staccato with her hind hooves into the water around her. Men called, others laughed, including the Queen, some used their swords as fishing hooks, one lad plunged in bodily to earn the Queen's favour, but no one—not even Peter—noticed how Adorna and her pale golden mare were now wallowing, hock deep, into the current.

She yelled to him, 'Peter! Help me!' but his attention was on the ducks like everyone else's, and Adorna was obliged to use her whip to impel the horse forward as the water covered her feet, the hem of her long gown swirling wetly around one knee. But she had left it too late; the whip hit the water instead of the horse, which still refused to respond to her commands. Help came unexpectedly in the form of a large man and horse who plunged into the water ahead of her, grabbing unceremoniously at the mare's bridle only seconds before the current swept over the saddle.

Concerned only with getting on to the bank as a team, she paid no attention to the man's appearance except to note that his horse was very large and that

he himself was powerful enough to drag the reins out
of her hands and over the mare's head and to haul the
creature almost bodily through the muddy water on to
dry firm ground.

Well away from the applauding crowd, Adorna
found her voice. 'Thank you, oh, thank you,' she said,
clutching at the pommel of the saddle as the mare
lurched forward. 'Thank heaven somebody noticed at
last.'

Her thanks were misinterpreted. 'If you think that's
the most effective way to be noticed, mistress, think
again,' the man snapped, devoid of any sympathy.
'The applause you hear is for Her Majesty, not for
your antics. Leave the retrieving to the hounds in future.'

It was not Adorna's way to be speechless for long,
but that piece of calculated rudeness was breathtaking.
What was more, the man's dismounting was far
quicker than hers and, well before she could reply, she
was being hoisted out of the saddle by two strong arms
and set down upon the ground with the hem of her
wet skirts and underclothes sticking nastily to her legs.
His hands were painfully efficient.

'I was referring, sir, to my predicament,' she
snapped back, shaking off his supporting hand. 'If I'd
planned on being noticed, as you appear to think, I'd
not have chosen to back into the river before the
Queen's entire court, believe me. Nor was I in the race
to retrieve a duck. Now, can I rid you of any more
delusions before you go?' Still not looking at him, she
shook the full skirt of her pale blue gown, catching a

glimpse of Peter out of the corner of her eye. He was dismounting. Kneeling. 'Peter,' she said, 'get up off...oh!' Her rescuer was doing the same.

The crowd had parted and, as Adorna sank into a deep wet curtsy, the Queen rode forward on a beautiful dapple grey. 'Geldings make better mounts on these occasions, mistress, so I'm told,' the Queen said. 'Your mount is a beauty, but a little unmannerly perhaps?' The embodiment of graciousness, the Queen exuded a sympathy for Adorna's plight that came as a welcome change from the rescuer's brusqueness.

Yet Adorna could not allow the chance to pass. She stayed in her curtsy, sending a haughty glance towards the man before making her reply. 'Your Majesty is most kind. My mare is still young, though one would have to struggle to find a similarly good excuse for others' unmannerliness.' There was no mistaking the butt of her remark, the man in question glowering at her as if she were a troublesome sparrowhawk on his wrist, while the Queen and her Court's laughter tinkled around them like splinters of breaking ice.

But Adorna's glance had given her the information that she had already suspected, by his imperious manner and cultured voice—he was a self-opinionated witmonger, albeit an extremely good-looking one, whose imposing stature was exactly the kind the Queen liked to have around her. Ill-featured people were anathema to her, especially men. He was dark-eyed and bold-faced with a square clean-shaven jaw, his head now bared to show thick dark waves brushed back off his forehead, a dent showing where his blue velvet bonnet had recently sat. His shoulders were broad enough to take her insult and, as the Queen signalled them to rise, Adorna saw that his legs were long and muscular, outlined in tight canions up to the top of his thighs to where his paned trunk-hose fitted. His deep blue velvet complemented her paler version perfectly, but that appeared to be their only point of compatibility.

The Queen was still amused. 'There now, Sir Nicholas,' she said. 'Apparently it is not so much what one does as the manner in which one does it. I shall expect more from you when I have the misfortune to fall into the river.'

Sir Nicholas had the grace to laugh as he bowed to her. 'Divine Majesty,' he said, 'I believe the Lady Moon will fall into the river before you do.'

'I hope you're right.' She accepted the compliment and turned again to Adorna. 'Mistress Pickering, there are few women who could look as well as you after such a fright. I hope you'll not leave us.'

Adorna knew a command when she heard one. 'I thank Your Majesty. I ask nothing more than to stay.'

'Then stay close, mistress, and let my lord of Leicester's man teach your pretty mare a thing or two about obedience. Sir Nicholas, tend the lady.'

Sir Nicholas bowed again as the Queen moved away to yet another scattering of applause at her graciousness, but Adorna had no intention of being tended by this uncivil creature, whatever the Queen's wishes. She turned to Peter Fowler, but the voice at her back held her attention.

'Mistress Pickering. Sir Thomas's daughter. Well, well.'

Adorna spoke over her shoulder. 'And you are one of the Master of Horse's men, I take it, which would explain why you are more polite to horses than to their riders. What a good thing the same cannot be said of your master.' It was well known that the handsome earl, Her Majesty's Master of Horse, was desperately in love with the Queen.

'My master, lady, has not yet had to drag Her Majesty out of the river in front of her courtiers. It's not your pretty mare that needs a lesson in manners so much as its rider needing lessons in control.' By this time the golden mare was eating something sweet from Sir Nicholas's hand, as docile as a lamb. 'Believe it or not, that is what Her Grace was telling you.'

Furiously, she rounded on him as Peter and two of her friends came to her aid, wringing the water from the hem of her gown. 'Rubbish! There is no one in the world who speaks more candidly than the Queen. If that's what she'd meant she'd have said so. Her Grace commands me to stay close and that is what I must do. I have thanked you for your assistance, Sir Nicholas, but now you are relieved of all further responsibility towards me, despite what Her Grace desires. Go and practise your courtesies on your horses.'

'Mistress!' Peter Fowler's alarm warned her that her own courtesy was fraying around the edges. 'This gentleman is Sir Nicholas Rayne, Deputy to Her Majesty's Master of Horse.'

Before she could find another cutting retort, Sir

Nicholas made a bow to Peter, smiling. 'And you, Master Fowler, are the gentleman with the longest title in Her Majesty's service. Gentleman Controller of All and Every Her Highness's Works. Did I get it right?' He was already laughing.

'To the letter,' said Peter. 'In other words, Head of Security.'

But Adorna was not prepared for any signs of amity. She thanked her two friends and turned to Peter for assistance in remounting, though by now he was diverted by laughter and forestalled by Sir Nicholas who, in one stride, caught her round the waist and hoisted her into the saddle as if she were no more than a child.

For a brief moment, her view of the world turned sideways as her head came into contact with his neck and shoulder, her cheek feeling the softly curling pleats of the tiny white ruff that sat high above the blue doublet. She caught a whiff of musk from his skin and felt the firmness of his hands under her shoulders, and then the world was righted and she was looking down into his face, into two dark unsmiling eyes that held hers, boldly, for a fraction longer than was necessary. Confused by what she saw, she blinked, took the reins from him and waited as he and Peter unstuck the clinging fabric from her legs and arranged it in damp folds around her.

The Queen's party had begun to move away.

'Thank you, Sir Nicholas,' she said, coldly, to the top of his blue velvet bonnet, watching the white and gold plumes lift and settle again. 'I think you should go now.'

He made no reply to that. Instead, he took his own horse from a groom and vaulted into the saddle in one leap, reining the horse over expertly to walk on her other side, his nod to Peter cutting across her stony face.

By the time they reached the wide open fields well away from the river, Adorna's composure was settling into an act which convinced those about her that she was comfortable. This was far from the truth, but showed the level of pretence of which she was capable. The wetness from her beautiful pale blue gown had now seeped up to her saddle, warm, sticky, and chafing her thighs: her golden mare's hindquarters were caked with mud and the shining bells on her harness were clattering instead of tinkling. Far worse than any of that was the disturbing presence of the one who had saved her from a complete soaking, whose inscrutable expression gave her no inkling of his real reason for staying nearby, whether because he wanted to or because he had been commanded to. The pressure of his hands could still be felt, but she would not let him know, even by a sneaking exploration, that he had had the slightest effect.

As the Queen had commanded, Sir Nicholas drew her nearer to the centre of things than she had been before, which did even less for Adorna's comfort. Having changed her peregrine falcon for a rare white gerfalcon, the Queen held it, hooded, on her wrist as a distant heron flew away upwards, ringing into the sky. The gerfalcon was released to pursue it, to climb even higher and then to stoop and dive, bringing the lovely thing down to the retrieving greyhounds whose speed prevented any injury to the precious raptor. Again, there was applause, then the announcement that they would have the picnic.

At this point, Adorna sidled invisibly back to her friends on the edge of the party, accepting whatever morsels of food were brought and passed around by the young pages. She made an effort to dismiss the incident of the river and to make herself affable to Peter, but her eyes had a will of their own, straying disobediently towards the tall well-built figure in deep blue braided with gold whose laughter was bold and teasingly directed towards a group of the Queen's ladies.

Dressed entirely in white, the young Maids of Honour made a perfect foil for the Queen's russet-and-gold that suited her so well. Like Adorna herself, she wore a high-crowned hat with a curl of feathers on the brim, a man's-type doublet that buttoned up to the neck, and a full skirt. But whereas Adorna's outfit was relatively modest in its decoration, the Queen had spared no effort to load herself with braids, chains and rings, frogging across her breast overlaid by pendants, and jewels winking from every surface, even from her neck-ruff of finest white lace.

Adorna's gown had begun to dry by now and they would soon be away again on a search for herons and cranes, perhaps larks for those with smaller raptors. She went to where the mare was tied to a tree, her muzzle dripping with water from a bucket. 'Your legs all right, my beauty?' she whispered, taking a look at the mud-covered rear end. 'We nearly came to grief, you and I, didn't we, eh? Are you going to calm down this afternoon, then?'

'That will depend,' a voice said behind her, 'on her rider more than anything else.'

Refusing to be drawn into another confrontation, Adorna clenched her teeth and slid one hand over the mare's muddy rump, preparing to examine her legs. Sir Nicholas managed the gesture with far more confidence than she, overtaking her hand with his own as he came to stand before her, continuing the examination with all the assurance of a horseman. His hands were strong and brown with flecks of fine dark hair on the backs, his nails clean and workmanlike, and Adorna watched in reluctant admiration how his fingertips pressed and probed almost tenderly. She drew her eyes upwards to his face as he stood, and found that he was already regarding her in some amusement, knowing that the progress of his hands had been marked with an interest of a not altogether objective nature. Against her will, she found that her eyes were locked with his.

'Well?' he said, softly. 'She's still sound after her dunk in the river, and there's nothing wrong with her temperament that a little gentle schooling won't cure. Show her who's master, though.' As he spoke, his hands caressed the mare's satin flanks, which twitched against the sensation, and Adorna knew that his words had as much to do with herself as they did with the mare. 'She's a classy creature,' he said, 'but not for amateurs.' On his last phrase, his eyes left hers and rested directly on Peter Fowler who was just out of earshot, returning to her in time to see a flush of angry pink suffuse her cheeks.

If he wanted to believe that Peter was her lover, even though he was not, she was content for him to do so, for it would afford her some protection, his innuendo being impossible to misunderstand. She was as angry at her own uncontrollable shiver of excitement as at his blatant attempt to flirt with her after his earlier hostility, and the stinging rebuke came out like a rapier.

'Don't concern yourself with my mare's requirements, sir,' she said sharply. 'Nor with mine. We have both managed well enough without your advice so far, so don't think that your one act of bravado makes you indispensable to us. I think you should go back to your master and make yourself *really* useful. I bid you good day.'

She would have walked away on the last word, but his arm came across her, resting on the mare's saddle, and she found herself imprisoned between him and the horse. 'Ah, no, mistress,' he said, without raising his voice. 'That's the third time you've ordered me to go, I believe. There are only a limited number of those who may give me orders, and you will never be one of them. What's more, when the Queen commands me to tend a lady, I will tend her until she gives me leave to stop. If you dislike the idea so, then I suggest you make your objections known to her. Now, mistress, make ready to mount.' And without the slightest warning other than that, he swooped and lifted her into his arms.

She should, of course, have been prepared for this, for he had already shown himself to be a man of immediate action. But strangely enough, she found that she was temporarily immobilised by his overpowering closeness, his refusal to be commanded, his boldness. Now his face was alarmingly close to hers and, instead of tossing her into the saddle as he had before, he was holding her deliberately tightly in his arms, preventing her from struggling.

'You are a stranger, sir,' she whispered, 'and you are insulting me. My father will hear of this.' Yet, as she spoke the words, she knew full well that her father would not hear of it from her lips and that, if this stranger was indeed insulting her, it was making her heart race in the most extraordinary manner that mixed fear with anticipation and a helplessness that made her feel guilty with pleasure. Or was it anger? Any other man, she thought, might have been expected to react with some concern at that threat, her father being Sir Thomas Pickering, Master of the Revels and therefore this man's superior.

His expression showed no such disquiet. 'No, mistress,' he said. 'I think not.'

She could feel his breath upon her face as he spoke, and she knew that he was allowing her to feel his nearness in the same way that an unbroken horse must be given time to get used to a man's closeness, his restraint. His unsmiling mouth was firm and well proportioned and his nose, straight and smooth, led her examining eyes to his own that sparkled beneath high-angled brows, unflinching eyes of brown jasper, dark-lashed and suggesting to her an age of about thirty, by the experience written within them.

'Let me go, I say. Please!'

As he moved to tip her upwards into the saddle, she saw a brief smile cross his face, which had disappeared by the time she looked again. He tapped her riding whip with one finger. 'That's for show, not for use,' he said, severely. 'Stallions need it, mares don't.'

Adorna felt safe enough from that height to pretend unconcern. 'Fillies?' she said. 'And geldings?'

The brief smile reappeared and vanished again as he recognised the return of her courage. 'Remind me to tell you of the first some time. Of geldings I know little that would be of any use to you.' And once again, she knew that neither of them was talking of horses.

The afternoon passed in a daze, though the only one to remark on her unusual quietness was Master Peter Fowler, who said, quite on the wrong tack, 'Did that wetting upset you, mistress? It's a pity you were not allowed to go home and change. You could have been back before Her Majesty noticed.'

That much was true, her home being a mere half-mile away over on the other side of the palace, a convenient place for Sir Thomas and Lady Marion to live when the Queen was at Richmond, and only one of several dotted about the home counties near the other royal residences. Life at court was a great temptation and Lady Marion, Adorna's lovely mother, had no intention of leaving her handsome husband to the attentions of other women with whom he was obliged to come into contact. As Master of Revels, he probably saw more of them than the average household official, being responsible for the special costumes and theatrical effects needed for Her Majesty's entertainment, an element of court life of great importance to balance the weightier matters of state.

Sir Thomas had expected to have Adorna's assistance that day, but then had come Master Fowler's request to take her to the Queen's falconry picnic in the park, and he had not the heart to refuse. All the same, Master Fowler had better not harbour any fancy ideas involving Adorna: she could do far better for herself with her looks and connections.

Adorna's looks were indeed something of which her parents were proud: pale blonde hair and startlingly beautiful features, large grey-blue eyes with sweeping lashes and a full mouth that, as far as her parents knew, had never been tasted by a man. Boys, perhaps, at Christmas, but never a man. Needless to say, there had been plenty of interest, so much so that Sir Thomas and Lady Marion had been criticised by family for being too lenient with her fastidiousness. At twenty years old, the elders said, it was time she was a wife and mother; let her put her high-faluting ideas aside and marry the richest of them, as other women did.

Fortunately for Adorna, her parents had so far ignored this advice, for they knew better than most how the Queen's Court was a notorious hotbed of intrigue, liaisons, broken hearts and broken marriages, deceptions and dismissals. Adorna herself was not one of the Queen's inner circle of courtiers nor had the Queen ever insisted on her regular appearance there, being sympathetic to the Pickerings' views that lovely young women were often targets of men's attractions for all the wrong reasons. Her Majesty had had enough problems in the past with her six young Maids of Honour, some of them losing their honour so quickly that it reflected badly on her, as their moral guardian.

Even so, Her Majesty was well aware of Adorna Pickering's existence and, because she liked Sir Thomas and his wife, she encouraged their talented family to attend her functions. It worked both ways; while the Queen surrounded herself with beautiful and talented people, Adorna's presence went some way towards advertising her father's success as a new office-holder. Even though still part of the Great Wardrobe under Sir John Fortescue, his position carried with it a certain responsibility, one of which was to be seen in the best company.

To have access to Court without actually being sucked into the vortex of it was, Adorna believed, a very pleasant place to be, especially as her home was so conveniently near, with her father always at hand for protection if danger came a mite too close. On more than one occasion, he had been a very efficient tool to use against a too-persistent trespass, and running for cover became Adorna's foolproof defence against over-attentive men, young or old, who would

like to have taken more than was on offer. Though
guests came and went constantly to her home at Sheen
House next door to the palace, there were at least a
dozen places in the fashionably meandering building
where Adorna could remain out of touch until danger
had passed.

True to form, she sought refuge with her father in
the Revels Office for, despite Sir Nicholas's refusal to
be put off by the mention of him, she could think of
no reason why the younger man would venture there
to find her. There was still time left in the day to see
how her father had proceeded without her, nor was it
far for her and her maid to pass from Sheen House
down what had lately become known as Paradise Road
and through the gate in the wall of the palace garden.

To Sir Thomas's annoyance, the Revels Office had
no separate buildings of its own and was therefore
obliged to share limited space with the Great Wardrobe where some of the Queen's clothes were stored,
others being in London itself. Consequently, tailors
and furriers, embroiderers, carpenters and painters,
shoemakers and artificers all worked side by side with
never enough room to manoeuvre. Adorna's creative
talents were often put to good use in the Revels Office
where men with flair and drawing ability were always
in demand to design sets, special effects and costumes
for the many Court entertainments.

Today, she had found a relatively private corner in
which to examine some of the sumptuous and fantastic
creations being prepared for a masque at the palace at
the end of the week. She had helped to design the

costumes and choose the materials and jewels, also to
construct the elaborate head-dresses and wigs, for all
the Court ladies taking part must have abundant
blonde hair. She lifted one of the masks and held it
above a flimsy gown of pale sea-green fringed with
golden tassels, holding her head to one side to judge
its effect.

'Try it on,' her father said. 'That's the best way to
see.'

'That won't help me much, will it, Father?'

'Perhaps not, but it'll help me.' He grinned and, to
please him, she took up the mask and the robe stuck
all over with silver and gold stars and went into a
corner screened off from the rest of the busy room.
Maybelle, her maid, went with her to help, though
Adorna was wearing no farthingale or whalebone bodice to complicate matters. In a few moments she
emerged to confront her father, but found to her surprise that he was not now alone but in the company
of Sir John Fortescue and another officer of the revels
who assisted her father.

This was not what Adorna had intended, for she was
not wearing the correct undergarments, nor was the
pale green robe with stars even finished, and it was
only the papier mâché mask of a Water Maiden covering her face that hid her sudden blush of embarrassment as she held the edges of the fabric together across
her bosom. And there was only one sleeve; her other
arm was bare.

Before she could retreat, they had seen the half-
dressed sea nymph and immediately began an assess-

ment of its cost multiplied by eight, the amount of white-gold sarcenet with Venice gold fringe and the indented kirtles with plaits of silver lawn trailing from the waist. Not to mention the masks, head-dresses, shoes, stockings, tridents and other accessories, multiplied by eight.

'Put the head-dress on, my dear,' Sir Thomas said. 'Which one is it? This one?' He picked up a conch-shell creation covered in silver and draped with dagged green tissue to resemble seaweed and passed it to Maybelle.

'Er…no, Father, if you please,' Adorna protested.

But she was overruled by the three of them, and the thing was placed on her head, pushing down the mask in the process and making it difficult for her to see through the eyeholes. She must alter that before they were used. She heard murmurs of approval. 'I must go,' she mumbled into the claustrophobic space around her mouth. 'Excuse me, if you please.'

Blindly, she turned and was caught by a hand on her arm before bumping into the person who had been standing silently at her back, someone whose familiar voice made her tear quickly at the mask, lifting it and tangling it with her loose hair and the head-dress in an effort to see where she was. The fabric across her front gaped as she let go of it and was snatched together again by Maybelle's quick hand, but not before Adorna had seen the direction of the man's eyes and the unconcealed interest in them.

'Not a good day for water nymphs,' Sir Nicholas

whispered, letting go of her arm and stepping back to allow her to pass.

Summoning all her dignity, Adorna quickly snatched at a length of red tissue from the nearest tabletop and held it up to hide herself from the man's gaze. 'This is the Revels Office,' she snapped, 'not a sideshow.'

Amused, Sir Nicholas merely looked across at her father and Sir John.

Sir Thomas explained. 'It's all right, my dear. Sir Nicholas comes from the Master of Horse. He needs to know about our luggage for the progress to Kenilworth. Don't send the poor man away before he's fulfilled his mission, will you? Or I'll have his lordship to answer to.'

Fuming, Adorna swept past him and returned to the screen, her face burning with annoyance that the man had once again seen her at a disadvantage. That he had seen her at all, damn him!

'It's all right, mistress,' Maybelle whispered. 'He didn't see anything.'

'Damn him!' Adorna repeated, pushing her hair away. 'Here, Belle. Tie my hair up into that net. There, that's better.' Her second emergence from the corner screen was, in a way, as theatrical as the first had been, for now she was not only reclothed in her simple day gown of russet linen but, covering the entire top of her body in an extravagant swathe of glittering red was the tissue she had snatched from the table. It trailed over one shoulder and on to the floor behind her, blending with the russet of her gown and contrasting brilliantly with the gold net caul into which her hair had hurriedly been bundled.

Astounded by the transformation as much as by the sheer impact of her beauty, the four men's conversation dwindled to a stop as she approached, her head held high, and it was her father who spoke, at last. 'Quick change, nymph!' he laughed.

Sir Nicholas was more specific. 'Water into fire,' he murmured.

Sir John cleared his throat. 'Ahem! Yes…well, your designs for the masque appear to be well in hand, Sir Thomas. I trust you'll not leak any of this, Sir Nicholas. The masque theme must be kept secret until its performance.' The Master of the Great Wardrobe looked at the younger man sternly from beneath handsome greying eyebrows.

'I quite understand, sir. No word of the masque will be got from me, I assure you. My lord the Earl of Leicester is planning several for Her Majesty's progress to Kenilworth, and he's just as concerned about secrecy.'

'Ah, yes,' said Sir Thomas, 'you need to know how many waggons and carts we need for the Wardrobe, don't you? Well, why not come and join us for a late dinner on Wednesday? Lady Marion and I are celebrating my appointment with some friends. These two gentlemen will be there, too. Do you have a lady, Sir Nicholas?'

'No, sir. Not yet.' He smiled at their grins, and Adorna was aware that, had she not been there, more might have been said on that subject. But her father had blundered by inviting him to their home, which meant that both her places of refuge were now no longer safe from his intrusion.

Sir Thomas was clearly expecting his daughter's approval of the invitation. He looked at her, eyebrows raised. 'Adorna?' he said.

The expression in her eyes, though fleeting, said it all. 'No lady yet, Sir Nicholas? Perfect. Cousin Hester will be with us by tomorrow and Mother was wondering what to do about a partner for her. Now the problem is solved.'

Sir Nicholas bowed gracefully. 'Thank you, mistress. I look forward to meeting Cousin Hester. Is she…?'

'Yes, the late Sir William Pickering's daughter. The heiress.' That should turn your neat little head, she thought. 'Now, if you will excuse me, gentlemen?'

Moving away from the group at the same time, Sir Nicholas was not inclined to let her go so easily, but strode alongside her, weaving his way in and out of the workers at the tables. By some miracle, he reached the door before her.

She glared at him. 'I do not need lifting on to my horse, sir, I thank you. I left it at home.'

'You're walking? In this?' He indicated the trail of billowing red stuff.

'As long as you are gawping at me, yes. In this.'

'And if I stop…er…gawping?' He gave an impish smile.

She sighed, gustily, and glanced across at her father's group. 'Go back to your business, sir, if you please, and leave me to mine. You are in the wrong department.'

'I'll get used to it,' he said softly, 'and so will you, mistress.'

'No, sir, I think not. See how you fare with Cousin Hester.'

'And will Cousin Hester be in Water or in Fire?'

'In mourning,' she said, sweetly. 'Good day to you, sir.'

Chapter Two

To her father's question of why she had been so ill-disposed towards Sir Nicholas Rayne that afternoon, Adorna had no convincing reply except that she didn't much care for the man.

Sir Thomas agreed that the excuse was a poor one. 'I hope I'm not as short with those I don't much care for, my lass, or I'd not hold on to my office for too long. Is there more to it than that?' He was a shrewd man, tall and elegant with white hair and beard and a reputation for fairness that made him keep friends with all factions.

'No, Father. No more than that.'

'He's a well set-up fellow. The earl speaks highly of him.'

'Yes, Father. I expect Cousin Hester will like him well enough, too.'

'Then perhaps by that time you could pretend to, for everyone's sake.'

'Yes, Father. I'm sorry.'

'He has more about him than Master Fowler, for all his long title.'

'Oh, *Father*!'

'Well, you're twenty now, Adorna, and you can't be chasing them off for ever, you know. There are several who—'

'No...no, Father, I beg you will do no such thing. I shall know the man I want when I see him, and Peter will serve quite well until then.'

'Really? Well then, you'd better start looking a bit harder because it's time your mother and I were grandparents. Perhaps you're being a bit too pernickety, my dear, eh?' He touched her chin gently with one fingertip.

'Yes, Father. I expect I probably am.'

Pernickety was perhaps not the word Adorna would have applied to her thoughts on men and marriage, though she might have agreed that they were somewhat idealised. Having never been in love, she had relied so far on the descriptions given her by friends and those gleaned from romantic tales of King Arthur and Greek mythology. Not the most reliable of sources, but all there were available. Consequently, she believed she would recognise it when it happened, that she would know the man when he appeared. Obnoxious, arrogant and presumptuous men were not on her list of requirements. For all that, she could not have said why, if he were so very unsuitable, Sir Nicholas Rayne was continually on her mind, or why his face and form were before her in the minutest detail.

To her amusement, she had heard in the usual

roundabout manner that she was regarded by some men as being hard to get, not only because of her efficient safety nets, but mainly because she had never yet been prepared to bind herself to any man's exclusive friendship for more than a few weeks. There were men and women among her friends whom she had known as a child, some of whom were parents by now, but she and a few others enjoyed their state of relative freedom too much to let go of it. In the same way, she supposed, that the Queen enjoyed hers. While others involved themselves deeply in the serious business of mate-finding and binding, she was happy to indulge in men's admiration from a distance, sometimes playing one off against the other, but committing herself to none. It was a harmless and delicious game to play in which she took control, rather like the plays her brother wrote where actors acted out a story and then removed the disguise and went home to sleep soundly.

She found her father's sudden concern irritating. It suggested to her that he might cease to be as helpful to her as he had been in the past. It also suggested that he had recognised in Sir Nicholas Rayne a man he might be prepared to consider as son-in-law if she didn't make it absolutely clear that he was not the man she was looking for. Exactly who she *was* looking for would be harder to explain, for while she and her female friends accepted their own conquettish ways as being perfectly normal, none of them felt that fickleness in a man was desirable. A man must be constant, adoring and lover-like, and none of those commendable traits could be ascribed to Sir Nicholas Rayne, Deputy Master of Horse. Let him stick to his horses and she would stick to her ideals.

Sheen House was the most convenient of the Pickerings' houses, the nearest to Sir Thomas's place of work when the Queen was in residence. It was also Adorna's favourite, situated to one side of the old friary built by the Queen's grandfather when he rebuilt the old palace of Sheen, which had been destroyed by fire. Sheen Palace in its new form was then renamed Richmond after the earldom in North Yorkshire that had been Henry VII's favourite home. The palace was massively built on the edge of the River Thames, its gardens enclosing the friary which had its own private garden, known as the paradise, at the eastern end. Since the dissolution of the monasteries almost forty years previously, the friary had been left to disintegrate, its stone reused, its beautiful paradise overgrown, now used by the palace guests for walking in private. The road that led past Sheen House, past the old friary and down the southern wall of the palace garden to the river, had now become Paradise Road. Most of the friary land was visible from the garden of Sir Thomas Pickering's house, providing what appeared to be an extension of their own, the friary orchard and vineyard being used by the palace gardeners. The rest of Richmond's houses spread along the riverbank to the south, most of them timber-framed set amidst spacious gardens and orchards, free from the noise and foul air of London Town.

* * *

Sheen House, however, was built of soft pink brick like the palace itself, originally in the shape of an E for Elizabeth. Sir Thomas's latest addition to the buildings was a banqueting house in the garden, built especially for Lady Marion's entertaining, and it was here on the next day that the call reached Adorna and Maybelle that Cousin Hester had arrived. The small octagonal room was situated in one corner approached by a paved walkway above the fountain-garden, far enough from the house for them to remove their aprons and fling them on to the steps before greeting their guest.

They had fully expected to see some change in Cousin Hester, having last seen her as a mere child of ten on one of her father's rare visits to Sheen House. Hester's father had never been married, not even to Hester's mother, an unknown lady of the Court who had allowed her daughter to be brought up by one of Sir William's married sisters. Consequently, the astonishment felt by both women at the sight of each other was in Adorna's case cleverly concealed, and in Hester's case not so.

'Oh!' she whispered. 'Oh…I…er…Mistress Adorna?' Hester looked from Adorna to Maybelle and back again. Although a year older than her cousin, she was still painfully shy, twisting her black kid gloves together like a dish-clout, her eyes wide and fearful.

Bemused, Lady Marion laid a motherly arm across her guest's shoulders. 'Call her Adorna,' she whispered, kindly. 'And for all you're Sir Thomas's cousin rather than our children's, you must call us all by our

Christian names, you know. Sir Thomas and Seton and Adrian will be in later.'

That announcement did not provoke the delighted anticipation it was intended to, for the young lady looked as if she might have preferred to make a bolt for it rather than meet men and boys.

Adorna took pity on her, smiling with hands outstretched. The wringing hands did not respond. 'Welcome, Cousin Hester. You must be tired after your journey from St Andrews-Underhill.' There was no real reason why she should have been, for her new home was only a stone's throw from St Paul's in the centre of London.

'Yes,' Hester whispered. She looked around her at the white plasterwork and the warm tapestried walls. 'It's cool and quiet here. I remember how I liked it before, long ago.'

'Well,' Lady Marion said, leading her towards the carved oak staircase, 'a lot's happened since then, and now you're a woman of independent means, free to do whatever you wish. You're our guest for as long as you choose to stay.'

There was no corresponding flash of delight at hearing her new status described. On the contrary, the very idea of having to make her own decisions was apparently not something she looked forward to with any relish. Sir William Pickering, Sir Thomas's cousin, had died at the beginning of the year, leaving his fortune and his house in London to Hester.

'Did you bring your maid with you?' said Adorna. 'If not, you shall share Maybelle with me. She knows how to dress hair in the latest fashions. Come, shall we find your room? The men will bring your baggage up.'

Cousin Hester's mourning-garb was only to be expected, in the circumstances, though neither the hostess nor her daughter would have allowed themselves to look quite so dowdy as their guest had the same thing happened to them. While they were not particularly in the forefront of fashion as those at Court were, neither were they ten years behind it as Hester was. Her figure could only be guessed at, concealed beneath a loose-bodied gown closed from neck to hem with fur-edged ties, puffed shoulder-sleeves and tight bead-covered under-sleeves. The hair to which Maybelle may or may not have access was almost completely hidden beneath a black french hood that hung well down at the back, though the bit of hair that showed at the front was brownish and looked, Maybelle thought, as if it needed a washing before it would reveal its true colour.

After her father's reproach the day before, Adorna now exercised all her charity towards her half-cousin, knowing little of the background of experience which had kept Hester inside her protective shell. For a woman of her age, she was impossibly tongue-tied and, for an heiress, she was going to find it difficult to protect herself from fortune-seeking men of whom there were countless hereabouts. Adorna managed it by virtue of her closeness to her parents; Hester would not manage it at all without some help. Yet on their guest list for Saturday, Adorna and her mother had

already paired off this pathetic young lady with Sir
Nicholas Rayne who might, for all they knew, be one
of those sharks from whom she would need protection.
On the other hand, they might suit each other per-
fectly. Strangely, the idea had lost its appeal for
Adorna.

Having helped to unpack Hester's rather inadequate
belongings and a very limited range of clothes, Adorna
conducted her on a tour of the house, which she believed would make her feel more at home. Inside, there
was much of it that Hester remembered, but outside,
the large formal garden had been restructured into a
series of smaller ones bounded by tall hedges, walls,
trellises and stone balustrades, walkways, steps and
spreading trees. The banqueting house was also new
to her.

Adorna opened the double doors to reveal a marble-
floored garden-room with windows on all eight of its
sides. The ceiling was prettily plastered with clouds
and cherubs bearing fruit, and the panels between the
windows were painted to represent views of the garden
beyond. In the centre of the floor was a round marble
table supported by grimacing cherubs.

'For the banquets,' Adorna said, 'the suckets and
marchpanes. I'm making them ready in the stillroom.
We'll come out here after the last course and nibble
while the servants clear the hall ready for the entertainment.'

'Tonight?'

'No, tomorrow. About thirty guests are coming to
dinner. Didn't Mother tell you?'

The colour drained from Hester's face. 'Guests? Oh, dear.' Her hand flew to her mouth. 'Perhaps I should stay in my room. I'm in mourning, you must remember.'

'Hester, dear…' Adorna drew her down to a stone bench fixed to the wall '…being in mourning doesn't mean you have to avoid people. It's nearly seven months since Sir William died, and how often did you see him in your twenty-one years?'

'Two…three times. I don't recall.'

'So, you can still wear black for a full year, if you wish, but Sir William would not have wanted you to hide away for so long, would he? After all, he was a man who lived life to the full, I believe.'

She supposed Hester to know at least as much as she did about Sir William Pickering, who had once believed himself to be in the running for the Queen's hand in the days before the Earl of Leicester. She had shown him every favour and he had exploited that favour to the full, making himself extremely unpopular while he was about it. But the Queen did not marry him and he had retired from Court, permanently unmarried but not chaste.

'Did your aunt never tell you about her brother?' Adorna said. 'By all accounts your father was a remarkable man. In the Queen's Secret Service, a scholar, a fine handsome man. Women adored him, and he must have loved your mother and you very much to have wanted you to inherit his entire wealth. He doesn't sound to me like the kind of man who would want his daughter to hide herself away when she has the chance to meet people. My mother and father will be here, remember. We'll take care of you.'

Hester, who had been gazing at her hands until now, sighed and stared out of the window. 'Yes...but...'

'But what?'

'Well, you're so used to it. You know what to say, and you're so beautiful, and fashionable...and...'

'Nonsense! Some of the most fashionable ladies are not beauties, and some beauties are dowdy. Everyone has at least one good feature, and you have several, Hester.'

'I do?'

'Of course you do. The secret is to make the most of them. Would you like me to help? I can, if you'll allow it. Maybelle and I can do your hair, and we can find something a little prettier to wear?'

'In black?'

'In black, but more flattering. Yes?'

At last a smile hovered and broke through. 'All right. And will you tell me what to say, too?'

'Ah, now that,' Adorna said, 'may take a little longer, but I can certainly try. The first thing to do is to smile.'

By the time Sir Thomas returned to Sheen House in mid-afternoon, the transformation had begun and the outmoded mousy young lady who had been greeted by Lady Pickering was not quite the same one who curtsied gracefully to the master of the house, though the effort of it robbed her of words. Between them, Adorna and Maybelle had worked wonders. The hair had now been washed, burnished and arranged into a small jewelled cap that sat on the back of her head like a ripe hazelnut. Hester's straggly eyebrows had been plucked to form two slim arches, and her faint eyelashes had been darkened with a mixture of soot and saliva, which seemed to work very well. Even those few measures had been enough to convert an ordinary face into a most comely one, but Hester's greatest assets were her teeth. Once she began to show their dazzling whiteness, there was no reason why she should not smile more often, Adorna told her.

Under the loose gown, she was found to be as shapely as most other young women, if somewhat gauche, not knowing what to do with her hands. Or her head, for that matter. But when she tried on Adorna's black taffeta half-gown with the slashed sleeves and the blackwork partlet, then the new Hester began to emerge.

Teaching her how to move with confidence did not produce such instant results, for there were years of awkwardness and tensions to remove, nervous habits and self-conscious fumblings to eradicate which could not even be mentioned for fear of making them worse. So Adorna advised her to listen rather than to talk. 'It's easy enough,' she said. 'Men will talk about themselves until the moon turns blue and then some more. You'll only have to nod and they'll never notice you haven't said a word. You can't fail. They're all the same. Just smile at them, and they'll do the rest.'

Hester did not recognise the cynicism, never having found a pressing need to express herself on any par-

ticular subject, so the advice was well within her ca-
pabilities. She had noticed the palace wall beyond the
Pickerings' garden and wanted to know if that was
where Sir Thomas worked.

'No,' Adorna told her, 'my father's offices and
workrooms are round the back, not far from the tennis
court and bowling alley. That wall is the Queen's Gardens. Would you like to see?' She had noted Hester's
interest in their own.

Predictably, the response was muted. 'Well…er,
might we not be intruding?'

Adorna laughed. 'Meet somebody? Well, probably
the odd courtier or two, or the gardener. Come, let's
show off the new Hester.' The new Hester followed,
dutifully.

The palace itself dominated a large area of the riverside, spreading backwards and upwards in a profu-
sion of towers and turrets that pierced the sky with
golden weather-vanes, shining domes, flags and chim-
neys. The colours of brick and stone mingled joyfully
with flashing panes of glass that caught the sun, and
the patterns that adorned every surface of the façade
never failed to enchant Adorna. But Hester's eyes
were too busy searching for any sign of life to enjoy
them. On a rainy day, Adorna told her, one could still
walk round the magnificent garden beneath the covered walkway that enclosed all four sides, but Hester
was still unsettled. 'What's that shouting?' she whispered, nervously.

'The tennis court, over there at the back. Shall we
go and see?'

'Er...there'll be people.'

'They'll be far too busy watching the players to see us.' Adorna took her arm and drew her gently onwards towards the sound of people and the curious pinging noise that became a hard clattering the nearer they walked.

The tennis court was a roofed building like the one at Hampton Court Palace that the Queen's father had had built. They entered through an arched doorway into a dim passage where suddenly the clatter and men's cries became sharper, and Adorna felt the resistance of Hester's arm as she drew back, already fearing what she might see. Although Adorna could sympathise with her cousin's dilemma, she saw no point in balking at the first hurdle. She placed Hester in front of her and steered her forwards, smiling to herself at each reluctant step.

The light came from windows high up on the two longest sides; the walls built up high had galleries running along them under sloping roofs upon which the hard balls bounced noisily before hitting the paved floor in the centre. A net stretched across the court, visibly sagging in the middle while four men, stripped down to doublets and hose, whacked at the ball with short-handled racquets. The two women sidled into the gallery where men and women leaned over the barrier to watch the play with shouts of, 'Well done, sir!' echoing eerily, laughing at the men's protests, their shouts of jubilation.

They found a space behind the barrier, Adorna nodding silent greetings to a few familiar faces, feeling

Hester flinch occasionally as the ball hit the wooden roof overhead and rolled down again. It was only when she gave her full attention to the players that Adorna realized she was within an arm's length of Sir Nicholas Rayne whose aggressive strokes at the leather ball were causing the marker to call out scores in his favour, though she could not begin to fathom out why.

Almost imperceptibly, she drew back, wishing she had not come, yet fascinated by his strength and agility, his amazing reach that scooped the ball up from the most impossible places, his quickness and accuracy. At one point, as the players changed ends, Sir Nicholas was one of those who pulled off their doublets, undoing the points of their white linen shirts. Rolling up their sleeves, they showed muscular forearms, at which Hester was obviously disturbed. 'Should we go, Adorna?' she whispered.

The name was caught inside a moment of silence, and Sir Nicholas turned, stared, and deliberately came to the barrier where they stood. He rested his hands just beyond Adorna's. 'The Mistresses Pickering. Welcome to Richmond, mistress,' he said to Hester. His appraisal, Adorna thought, must have been practised on many a likely-looking horse, though thankfully Hester would not realise it.

But his narrow-eyed survey of Adorna was of a more challenging variety, and his personal greeting to her was no more than, 'Enjoy the game, mistress,' which she was quite sure did not mean what Hester thought it meant.

She was given no time to find a reply, for he walked quickly away, swinging his racquet, while she was torn between making a quick and dignified exit or staying, hoping to put him off.

It was Hester's astonishing response to the greeting, predictably delayed by nervousness, that decided the course of action. 'Thank you, Sir Nicholas,' she said to his retreating back.

'What?' Adorna whispered, staring at her guest. 'You *know* him?'

Hester nodded. 'Uncle Samuel and Aunt Sarah often invited him to Bishops Standing before he left to join the Earl of Leicester's household. I've not seen him for a year or more. He's always so polite, but I never know what to say to him.'

For someone who didn't know what to say, that was the most Hester had said since her arrival. Which, Adorna thought, meant either that Sir Nicholas was the cause of some interest within the timid little heart or that her own efforts were already bearing fruit. Unlikely, after such a short time. 'Did he visit often?' she probed, watching him.

'Quite often. He and Uncle Samuel used to play chess together, and hunted, and talked about horses.'

Adorna was silenced, overtaken by the combined thudding in her chest and the crash of the ball against the wall. Had he pretended not to know Cousin Hester? Or had he simply not pretended anything? *I look forward to meeting Cousin Hester. Is she…?* Of course, it had not occurred to her to discover any previous acquaintance. So what had been the true purpose of his visit to Sir William Pickering's sister's home? Chess? Horses? 'Is his home near them?' she whispered.

Hester's reply came with an expression that suggested Adorna ought to have known the answer to that. 'His father is Lord Elyot,' she said. 'He *owns* Bishops Standing.'

The astonishment showing so clearly in Adorna's lovely eyes was caught at that moment by the player at the far end of the court whose mind was not entirely on the game. His keen eyes levelled at hers like a hunter stalking a doe, while his partner yelled at him to attend.

'Chase two!' the marker called.

'No. Chase one!' Sir Nicholas said to himself as he sent the ball crashing across the court. The next time he had chance to look, the two Pickering ladies had disappeared.

The full impact of what was happening to her began to take effect at the end of that day, by which time Adorna was too confused to sleep. She and Hester had strolled back to Sheen House, diverting their steps through the friary paradise especially to examine the overgrown roses, the heavily budding lilies, the rue and lady's bedstraw that symbolised the Virgin Mary to whom the garden had probably been dedicated. It was a magical place where, even now, the outlines of the beds could still be seen, providing Hester with a topic for suppertime when Lady Marion asked them where they'd been. It saved Adorna herself from having to reply, her mind being far away on another journey.

As the summer evening drew to a close, she made an excuse to be alone, to walk along the raised pathways to the banqueting house to see that the doors and windows were closed. There was a moon, silvering the pathways and the orchard below, outlining the derelict friary and staring through the glassless east window, lighting the high palace wall. She stared out across the paradise where she had walked earlier, frowning as she caught a movement beyond the shadows. A man passed through the garden door from the palace, leaving it slightly ajar, picking his way carefully across the space to stand under a gnarled pear tree, his broad shoulders well inside the low branches. There was no mistaking the shape of him, the long legs, the easy movement, the carriage of his head. Sir Nicholas Rayne. She was quite sure of it.

He had waited no more than two minutes when another figure came through the door, a woman, looking about her hesitantly. Sir Nicholas made no move to show himself, no rush to greet her or sudden urge to embrace. The woman searched awhile and then saw him, but still there was no laughter stifled by kisses but only a slow advance and the joining of hands indicating, Adorna thought, either a first meeting or a last one. The two stood together talking, his head bent to hers, her hand occasionally touching his chest, her finger once upon his mouth, briefly. The watcher in the banqueting house placed a hand upon her own breast to still the thumping inside, to quell the first awful, sour, bitter, agonising pangs of jealousy so foreign to her that she did not recognise them as such. She thought it might be guilt, or something akin to it, telling herself that the man and his woman mattered nothing to her. Less than nothing.

Do you have a lady, Sir Nicholas?

No, sir. Not yet.

What was this, then? An attempt to acquire one, or to get rid of one? He was a flirt. He was already welcomed by Hester's foster-parents, no doubt as a potential suitor for their niece. There was surely no other good reason for them to encourage his visits, for they had no other family. What did it matter to her, anyway?

The couple was moving apart. The lady was preparing to leave, stretching the last touch of their hands to breaking point. She was weeping. Quickly, he took a stride towards her, reaching out for her shoulders and pulling her with some force towards his bending head. His kiss was short and not gentle, ending with a quick release and a faint cry from her that reached Adorna, wrenching at her heart. She clung to the wall, watching as the woman picked up her skirts and ran to the door, leaving it open behind her.

Sick and dizzy from the impact of a kiss that had not been for her, Adorna stood rooted to the spot, staring at the back of the man she had tried to keep away with her coldness, willing him to turn and come to her here, in the soft shadowy night. He did not move.

A call came to her from the house, her father's call,

loud and unmistakably for her. 'Adorna! Come in now! It's getting late, Adorna!'

She must answer, or he'd come looking for her. 'Yes, Father.'

As she knew he would, Sir Nicholas turned towards the high wall behind him where the banqueting house was built into one corner. She could not leave without him seeing, and her loose blonde hair would show him her exact location. Reluctantly, she closed the double doors with a snap and locked them noisily behind her, tossing her bright hair into the moonlight. If she must reveal herself, then she would do it with aplomb. She did not look below her as she went to meet her father. 'Coming!' she called, merrily.

The reflection in the polished brass mirror kept up a steady and silent conversation with the blue-grey eyes, and the candle flame bent in the light breeze from the window, barely shedding any light on the messages of confusion and soul-searching that refused to untangle. What had now become clear to Adorna, after her reaction to the secret tryst in the garden, was that she had blundered in the wrong direction by her attempts to make Hester more attractive. Even to herself, she could hardly pretend that she had done it for Hester's own sake alone, for at the back of her mind had been the possibility that a young and personable lady with a fortune would surely be of more interest to the man who had behaved with such familiarity towards herself. Then, it had seemed imperative that a way be found to get rid of him or to keep him at a more manageable distance, at least.

But now there had developed within her deepest self a reluctance to exclude this man quite as forcibly as she had been doing, especially now that there seemed to be a real chance of him seeing Hester in a new light. Her foster-parents apparently approved of him, and doubtless Hester herself was impressed by his connections. Another more relaxed and enticing meeting between the two might just be enough to do the trick, and she herself would have helped to bring it about.

Yet she could not like the man. He was too aggressively male, too experienced for her, probably promiscuous, too presumptuous. And rude. And what was he doing speaking so pertly to her when there *was* another woman, in spite of his denials? No doubt he had a long line of mistresses somewhere, all of whom he would deny whenever it suited him. Yes, let him make an offer for Hester, since she had come into her fortune. A man like him would appreciate more wealth, rather than the Master of Revels' daughter.

She lifted the sleeve of her chemise to look once more for the imprint of his fingers on her upper arms. There they were, like a row of shadowy blackberry stains. She caressed them, wondering which part of her he had seen yesterday that the other three men had not. Slowly, she slipped her chemise down to her waist and stood, holding herself sideways to the mirror and raising her arms to enclose him, feeling his imaginary grip upon her shoulders, the hard dizzying kiss upon her mouth. How would it feel? Something deep inside her belly began to quiver and melt.

Guiltily, she folded her arms across herself and tiptoed over the creaky floorboards to her bed where she stretched, aching, seeing him again in the moonlit paradise as he turned to look. No, this could not be what they called falling in love; this was confusing and painful; there was nothing in it to make her happy. In the darkness behind her wide-open eyes she watched him at tennis, saw his appraisal of Hester's new image, saw his hands on her mare's flanks, his control of his own great mount. His bold words and stare had stirred her to anger and excitement as no other man had done. But no, of course, this was not love. How could it be? She was right; this was not the man for her. Let Hester take the field.

Chapter Three

This resolution, nursed by Adorna until she fell asleep, had vanished completely by the time she woke, which meant that the whole argument had to be reconstructed from the beginning in order to establish any reason why Sir Nicholas should have been on her mind in the first place. Which was difficult, in the light of day.

Another disturbing development was that, overnight, Hester had apparently discovered how to smile. Adorna suspected that she must have been practising in front of the mirror, but this newest enchantment showed itself first at breakfast and was then rehearsed at intervals throughout the day so that, by the time the two of them had put the finishing touches to an array of subtleties for the banquet, Adorna was forced to the conclusion that Hester was happy. There was surely no other explanation for it.

Not that Adorna had any objections, as such, to Hester being happy, only a reservation that the reason behind it must mean only one thing. Sir Nicholas. After a year or more, Hester was happy to make contact again.

Even Lady Marion noticed it. 'She'll dazzle the men with that smile,' she said to Adorna. 'They'll be writing sonnets to it before the week's out.'

Adorna stood back to look at the effects of the trailing ivy interlaced with roses hanging in swags across the oak panelling of the great hall. 'She's learning more quickly than I thought,' she said with her head on one side. 'Is that level with the others?'

'More or less. I think she ought to have her own maid though, dearest. Perhaps I'll suggest finding one for her. If she's going to improve as fast as that, we can't let her choose one who doesn't know a farthingale from a martingale, can we?'

Visions of Hester wearing a strap from her chin to her waist to keep her head down caused an undignified halt to the proceedings that lightened Adorna's heart, if only temporarily. Her mother's relief at having an extra male guest to partner Hester had grown to far greater heights once she discovered that the two were already acquainted and from then on, no instruction was too detailed to make sure that Hester and Sir Nicholas were to be regarded as a pair. From which it was obvious to Adorna that her father had made very little of the man's visit to the workshop two days ago. Knowing her parents' tendency to see potential suitors even before they appeared, Adorna was very relieved by this.

Although they had never regarded Master Peter Fowler as a serious contender for Adorna's hand, Peter

himself did, being one of the first to arrive for the
dinner party, bringing a gift for his hostess in the shape
of a tiny silver padlock and key. A symbol, he told
her, of his protection for her most precious jewel.

Smiling courteously, Adorna said nothing to contradict this, for it was precisely this aspect of Peter's
company that had singled him out from other young
men. He was tall and well made, personable, correct,
agreeable and utterly dependable, as his job demanded. Protection was not only his profession but
also the reason for his attraction, for if Adorna could
not be safe with Peter, then who could she be safe
with? Naturally, his lapse at the Queen's hawking
party in Richmond Park had been unusual, but Adorna
did not blame him for that. Brown-eyed and curly-
haired, he offered her a brown satin-clad arm while
expertly assessing the security of the pale pink bodice
that skimmed the swell of her breasts with a hint of
white lace to half-conceal the deepest cleft. A lace pie-
frill ruff clung enticingly to her throat.

She laid the tips of her fingers on his arm. 'Peter,'
she said, 'I want you to meet our house guest. She's
appallingly shy. Will you talk to her?'

Hester curtsied with lowered eyes while Peter, bowing to the shy black-clad figure, thought the contrast
to Adorna could hardly have been greater. Even in
black, the dowdiness had been replaced by a beguiling
vulnerability to which Peter instantly responded, for
Hester's nut-brown hair under a jewelled velvet band
had suffered hours of Maybelle's ministrations and

now, framing her face in a heart-shaped roll, suited her perfectly.

Peter's response to Adorna's introduction was even more immediate. 'Sir William Pickering's daughter?' He beamed. 'Why, mistress, I have admired your late father's exploits since I was so high—' he held a hand level with his waist '—and I even met him, once. Come, will you speak of him to me?' His large fingers closed warmly over the trembling ones and Hester was obliged to abandon Adorna's advice concerning smiles and nods in order to talk of a father she had hardly known. It was good practice, but not exactly what Lady Marion had had in mind.

Sir Thomas's musicians were by now in full swing high up in the gallery at the far end of the hall. Below them, the guests entered from a porch at one side, adding another layer of sound that rose in waves of laughter and drifted away into the great oaken rafters. Even while she chatted, Adorna could identify the booming stage-voice of Master Burbage, their actor friend, followed by the reed-pipe squeak of Master Thomas Tallis whose wife Joan held him up by one elbow as a stool was placed beneath him. Yet, though she was soon surrounded by friends and acquaintances, Adorna felt the effect of someone's eyes on the back of her head that pulled her slowly round and drew her away like a netted fish.

Although Sir Nicholas was part of a newly arrived group, he took no part in their conversation but aimed his narrowed eyes towards Adorna, meeting hers as she turned, throwing out a challenge for her to come and welcome him. To refuse would have been too discourteous.

She lifted the golden pomander that swung on a chain at her waist and went forward, unable to withdraw her eyes from his though, even as they met, there was not the smile of welcome she had given to others.

'Your lady mother bade me welcome,' he said, softly.

'Of course,' said Adorna. 'She would see no reason to do otherwise.' Her heart beat loudly under her straight pink bodice, making her breathless.

'And you, mistress? Do you see a reason to do otherwise?'

'I see several reasons, sir, but don't concern yourself with them. It cannot be the first time a woman has taken an aversion to you. But then, perhaps it is.'

He glanced around him as if to find an example, but saw Hester instead. 'Ah, Cousin Hester. Was it your doing that transformed the lady, or had it already begun? Quite remarkable. She's learning to speak, too, I see. Well, well.'

Coming from another, she might have smiled at this sarcasm, but a mixture of pride and protection quelled it. 'I was not aware,' she said, 'that you and she knew each other. She tells me that you found the hunting good at Bishops Standing.'

'Is that all she told you?'

His blunt question made her pause, not knowing how to learn more without betraying her interest. Mercifully, she was prevented from saying anything by the Yeoman of the Ewery's arrival, whose invitation to dip their fingers into the silver bowl of scented water signalled an end to most conversations. She dried hers on the linen towel and handed it to Sir Nicholas. 'I am expected to take you to her,' she said. 'Will you come, sir?'

'Gladly,' he said, smiling. 'I can hardly wait.'

For some reason, she would have preferred a token show of reluctance, but now there was just time, before the procession to the table, to present Sir Nicholas to Mistress Hester Pickering and to watch like a hawk as his eyes smiled into hers and quickly roamed, approving or amused, over the new image. By this time, the effect of conversation and the warmth of the hall had brought a most becoming flush to Hester's cheeks and a sparkle to her eyes and, though she kept the latter modestly lowered, the newly darkened lashes made alluring crescents upon her skin. This show of mutual pleasure left no doubt in Adorna's mind that Lady Marion would be delighted to see how her plan was falling into place so neatly.

Peter took Adorna's arm to steer her to one side, noting the direction of her interest. 'I thought you said she was shy,' he said.

Adorna looked puzzled. 'Did she tell you of her father, then?'

'Only a little. She talked of Sir Nicholas, mostly.'

Once again, the conversation was curtailed by the ceremonial observed by every noble household at meal-times, the waiting, the seating, the ritual carving and presenting, by which time there were obligatory gasps of delight at the array of dishes, their colours, variety and decoration. Lady Marion had, for this event, brought out the best silver dishes, bowls and ewers, the great salts, the best spoons and knives, the finest monogrammed linen. On the two-tiered court-cupboard stood the best Venetian glasses, while an army of liveried servers attended diligently to every guest's needs.

Adorna tried to avoid looking at Hester and Sir Nicholas, but her curiosity got the better of her, her sneaking looks between mouthfuls and words feeding her snippets of information as to Hester's responsiveness to Sir Nicholas's attentions. His attention was required from other quarters, too, for the table of over thirty guests was merry and light-hearted, and Sir Nicholas was an excellent conversationalist. Adorna would have been blind not to see how the women, young and old, glowed when he spoke to them, prompting her to recall his uncivil manner as he had hauled her out of the river, his familiarity afterwards, even when he had discovered whose daughter she was.

With renewed assiduity she turned all her attention towards the other end of the table and to her partner, taking what pleasure she could from the safe predictability of Peter's good manners and to the chatter of her friends, all the while straining to single out the deep cultured voice of Sir Nicholas Rayne. At the end of two courses, they were led into the garden where the double doors of the banqueting house had been thrown open to receive the slow trickle of guests. Here was laid out an astonishing selection of tiny sweetmeats on silver trays, candied fruits, chunks of orange

marmalade, sweet wafers and gingerbreads, march-
pane and sugar-paste dainties covered with gold leaf.
Jellies and syllabubs were served in tiny glasses, and
biscuits were placed on wooden roundels, each guest
nibbling, exclaiming, and moving outside to admire
the formal flower-beds, the view over the friary orchard and the river in the distance.

Purposely, Adorna kept some distance between herself and Sir Nicholas while she spoke to many of the
guests, laughing at their jokes and listening to their
opinions, never straying far from Peter's side. From
there, she could signal to Sir Nicholas that she had no
wish for his company. Her mother, however, had already begun to waver on this point.

She whispered in Adorna's ear, 'You didn't *tell*
me!'

'Tell you what, Mother?' Acting total innocence
came quite easily to her.

'That he was so handsome. And distinguished. If
I'd understood that he was my lord of Leicester's deputy, I'd have had him instead of Master Fowler partner
you. Is Sir Nicholas the one who helped you out of
the river?'

Adorna's eyes strayed once more to the midnight-
blue taffeta doublet, velvet breeches and black silk
hose, to his elegant bearing, to the gold buckles and
jewels on his swordbelt and scabbard. His hand rested
on one hip while with the other he held up his wooden
roundel, reversed, from which he read the poem
painted on the rim.

'Lord Elyot's eldest son,' her mother continued, 'I

think, dearest, that you ought to be making yourself a little more agreeable to Sir Nicholas. He's going to be wasted on Cousin Hester.'

'I'd much rather he played the part you invited him for,' Adorna replied. 'Though I think Hester's wasted on *him*.'

But Lady Marion was only half-listening. 'Don't be difficult, dear. Come along!' she called to Sir Nicholas's group. 'You must sing your roundelays, you know. I think you should be the one to start them off, Sir Nicholas, if you please. Show them how it should be done.'

The idea of having guests to sing for their suppers was not a new one, each one expecting to contribute to the others' entertainment in some way either by singing or by playing an instrument. At thirteen, Adorna's youngest brother Adrian usually had to be held back forcibly from being the first to perform, but this time he added his voice to his mother's. Although Sir Nicholas's roundelay was short, he made it last longer by singing it several times over to a simple tune of his own devising.

And so my love protesting came, but yet I made her mine.

His voice was true and vibrant, but Adorna refused to watch him perform, not wishing to see who he looked at while he sang. Yet as soon as the applause died down and another guest followed, a whispered comment at her back closed her ears to everything except the exchange of riveting gossip.

'Pity he doesn't make them his for longer than three

months,' a man's voice said, half-laughing. 'He goes through 'em faster than his master.'

'Hah! Is that how long the last one was?'

'Lady Celia. Traverson's lass. Handsome woman, too, but ditched after three months. Penelope Mountjoy afore that and heaven knows how many afore her. He has 'em queueing up for him.'

'But he's only been in his post for a year or so.'

The voice chuckled. 'Trying out the new mares.'

'They're happy to assist, eh?'

'Aye, but not so happy to be left, apparently. Still, if he's after old Pickering's heiress, he'll probably not find any protesting there.'

The two men joined in the applause though they had not listened to the song, but Adorna's blood ran cold as she sidled away to the back of the crowd to avoid an invitation to sing, shivering with unease at the sickening words. Even among men it seemed that Sir Nicholas's reputation as a rake was chuckled over, envied, plotted and predicted, his victims pitied. From the corner of her eye, she identified one of the gossips as her father's colleague, the Master of the Queen's Jewels, the other as a superior linen-draper who held a royal warrant.

Ditched after three months? Trying out the new mares? It was as she had suspected; the man had been amusing himself, teasing her to make her respond to him, despite her obvious antagonism. Then he would blithely go on to the next before choosing how, when and where to include Cousin Hester in his schemes, sure that she would defer to his convenience more than any other. For the hundredth time, she heard the woman's sob echo through the evening, saw again her last slow touch, her hurried departure into oblivion. Her heart ached for the woman's pain and for Hester, too, who would have no experience of how to deal with a man's inconstancy, being unused to dalliance and light-hearted love affairs. Hester would not recognise insincerity if it was branded on a man's forehead.

That much was true, though at that precise moment Hester was having no problems with her own brand of innocence or with other people's kindness, whether the latter was sincerely meant or not. Dear Adorna and Lady Marion had identified her deficiencies, which were many, and had offered her every assistance to overcome them, and it would be both churlish and unnecessary to deprive them of the pleasure of success. Moreover, the pleasure was not all theirs. She practised her smile once more on a young gentleman who offered her a heart-shaped biscuit and saw how his eyes lit up with pleasure, as Sir Nicholas's had done.

What a pity Aunt Sarah had not made her aware of such delights, but then, her foster parents were much older than Adorna's and had had neither the time, experience nor patience to be plunged into parenthood with a ready-made child. They had provided her with an elderly nurse and tutor, shelter and food, a good education and firm discipline and, if she wanted company, there were always the horses. Uncle Samuel was a passionate horse-breeder: Aunt Sarah was not passionate about anything. Passion, she had once told Hester, was a shocking waste of energy.

Hester was satisfied, almost pleased, that Sir Nicholas had noticed the changes enough to compliment her. He had always been most kind, and it was quite obvious that Lady Marion had asked him here especially to put her at her ease. The least she could do in return was to remember what they had told her about smiling, listening and keeping her hands still.

She glanced across the long shadows that now striped the lawn, seeing Adorna talking animatedly to a group of men, her expressions so graceful, her hands and head articulate, her back curving and set firmly against Sir Nicholas from whom she had made no attempt to conceal her indifference. They had scarcely spoken to each other at the tennis court, nor had Adorna joined the ladies who surrounded him, but Hester supposed that the gentlemanly Master Fowler was Adorna's special friend and that she preferred his company to anyone's. Which Hester could well understand, though for their sakes she would make herself most agreeable to Sir Nicholas since that was clearly what they wished.

Her aunt and uncle had, naturally, warned her that once she was on her own, there would be fortune-hunters, but her mind was at rest as far as Sir Nicholas was concerned, he having a fortune of his own. Apart from that, if he had ever entertained thoughts along those lines, he had had plenty of chances during the six years or more he had been visiting Uncle Samuel.

The guests were beginning to move back into the house again, Adorna firmly linked to Master Fowler. To Hester a dear gentleman offered his arm, which she daintily laid her hand upon, smiling at him, picking up her skirts over the grass and thinking how much easier this was than she had once believed.

In the great hall, the tables and benches had been cleared to leave a space for the entertainments, and here Hester was happy to watch as sheets of music were handed to those guests who were prepared to perform on viol, flute and lute. Nothing could have been lovelier than when Adorna played a beautiful melody by William Byrd on the virginals, for she was able to sing at the same time in a voice so sweet that the guests were spellbound, making Hester appreciate even more how much she herself had to learn.

There was dancing, too, which had never been Hester's strongest point, so she remained at one side in the company of yet another gentleman who talked non-stop about his fishing visits to Scotland when she would rather have listened to the music. She did, however, notice how Adorna kept her eyes lowered whenever she went forward to take Sir Nicholas's hand, and how he looked at her without the smile that he had bestowed upon herself, which seemed to indicate that he was as little interested in Adorna as she appeared to be in him.

Then there was the play, written by seventeen-year-old Seton, Adorna's brother. He had persuaded some of his friends from the theatre company known as Leicester's Men to join him in this short and extremely

funny performance, made all the funnier because it
was entirely unrehearsed. Master Burbage, their leading actor, kept it all together somehow, but even he
could not keep his face straight when Adrian, who had
begged on his knees for a part, began to *ad lib* most
dangerously, throwing the other characters off track.
It brought the house down, the evening to a close, and
Hester to the conclusion that, if it got no worse than
this, she might begin to get used to dinner parties.

As duty demanded, Adorna stood with the rest of
her family to bid each of the guests farewell, promising Master Burbage that she would rectify one glaring omission by attending one of the Leicester's Men's
performances at their London venue before long. With
a quick squeeze of her mother's hand, she slipped
away from the family group, along the passageway
leading to the back of the house and out into the
walled herb-garden. Here she waited until the calls of
farewell had begun to fade. This was another of her
refuges, used on this occasion as an escape from Peter
who had earlier left her in no doubt that tonight a
formal kiss on the knuckles would not be enough.
Without seeking to argue about it, Adorna was convinced that anything more than that would be too
much. It was better, she had whispered to her mother,
if she disappeared and explained tomorrow, if need be.
Lady Marion had had experience at making excuses.

It was almost dark, but still she could just see the
brick pathway leading through the garden door on to
the lawn where the guests had strolled earlier. There

was the walkway that led to the banqueting house in
the corner, the fountain still tinkling. Distant bursts of
laughter and chatter still floated through the open windows, shapes moving in and out of soft candlelight.

Keeping to the shadows, she entered the small room
with a feeling of relief that the evening was over, that
she had escaped Peter's personal leave-taking and that
the act she had kept up all evening could now be
dropped. The banqueting-house floor was still littered
with crumbs in the light of a single candle that the
servants had left burning, and a heap of wooden roundels, painted side uppermost, lay discarded on the table, their rhymes sung and forgotten. Holding them
towards the candle flame, she went through the stack
one by one until she found the one she wanted, peering
to make out the words and touching them with the tips
of her fingers.

'And so my love protesting came,' she whispered,
reading as she turned it.

'But yet I made her mine,' came the reply from the
doorway.

She half-leapt in fright, clutching the plate to her
bodice and whirling to face him, angered by the intrusion. 'I came here...' she began, ready to resume the
act. But the lines had already faded from memory, and
she could only glare, defensively.

'I know why you came here.' Sir Nicholas closed
the door quietly behind him. 'You came here to escape
Master Fowler's attentions, in the first place. Isn't that
so? Poor Adorna. Saddling yourself all evening with

him to keep yourself out of my way. Was it worth it, then?'

'It worked well enough until now, sir!' she snapped.

'Tch, tch!' He shook his handsome head, smiling with his eyes. His hair and the deep blue of his clothes blended into the shadowy room, but could not conceal the width of his shoulders or the deep swell of his chest. Though he made no move towards her, Adorna found his presence disconcerting after a whole evening of trying to avoid him. He held out a hand for the plate. 'May I?' he said.

Evading his eyes, she placed it back on the pile. 'A silly jingle,' she said. 'Quite meaningless. I must not be seen with you here alone, Sir Nicholas. We have nothing to say to each other, and my father will—'

Before she could say what her father would do, he had stepped forward a pace and nipped the candle flame with his fingers, plunging the room into darkness except for the lambent glow from a rising moon. At the same time, Adorna's neat sidesteps towards the door was anticipated by the intimidating bulk of his body. 'Then we must make sure,' he said, 'that we are not seen here alone, mistress. But I cannot agree that we have nothing to say to each other when you said so little to me earlier in the evening. Do you not recall the moments when you could have spoken but chose not to? Shall we reconstruct the dance to ease the flow of conversation?' In the darkness, he held out his hand.

She had noticed his graceful dancing, but this was a game she did not intend to play, nor was she by any means ready to fall into his flirtatious trap, as she was

sure many others had done. Far from queueing up for
his attentions, she wanted nothing to do with him, especially after what she had heard that evening. It was
time someone taught him a lesson.

Taking up the act where she had left off, she let out
an exaggerated sigh and turned away from him to stare
out of the same window where, two nights ago, she
had watched him kiss a woman in the friary paradise.
'Sir Nicholas, I have had a busy day and I have little
inclination to wake all Richmond with my screams.
But I am prepared to do so if it's the only way to get
out of here. Now, please will you go and make your
courtesies to my parents and leave me in peace? Others may find your ways diverting, but I don't.'

In one step, he came to stand close behind her with
his knees enveloped in her wide bell-shaped skirts.
'For one so unmoved by my diverting ways, mistress,
you send out some strangely contradicting signals,' he
said, his voice suddenly devoid of his former playful-
ness. 'You came in here to seek my—'

'I did not come in here to *seek* anything!' she
snarled at him over her shoulder. 'The poem was one
that caught my eye.'

'I see.' He allowed the explanation to go unchal-
lenged. 'So perhaps you came here to remind yourself
of something you saw out there. Eh?'

'I saw noth—' She bit her words off, remembering
that he had seen her. She started again. 'What I caught
the merest glimpse of, Sir Nicholas, in no way concerned me. If you choose to tell my father that you
have no lady, that's entirely your own affair. I care

not if you have a different lady for each day of the week. All I ask is that you don't *ever* consider me to be one of them.'

'You may be a marginally better actor than your brothers, Adorna, but I still say that your signals are in a tangle. Shall I tell you why?'

Again, she made a move towards the door, but her skirts hampered her and this time his arm came across her to form a solid barrier. She willed herself to maintain an indifference that had nothing to do with the facts, to make her voice obey her head instead of her heart. It was not easy.

'No,' she said. 'Don't. If you find my signals conflicting, then you are obviously not reading them correctly, sir. Master Fowler finds them easy enough to understand, and so do other men. When I keep out of their way it means that I do not want their company. Now, what part of that message do *you* not understand? Shall I put it in French for you? Or Latin?'

Even in the darkness, she could feel the changes that crossed his face, his silence verifying that she had scored at last, checked his cocksureness. For once, he was nonplussed. But it did not last long. 'You mean it, don't you?' he whispered. 'Do you flee from all men on sight, just for the fun of the ride?'

His temporary unsureness gave her courage. 'What I do with all men is none of your business, Sir Nicholas. But one thing I *will* tell you is that any man who compares me to a horse, however delicately, may as well take himself off to the other side of the Christendom. And if you've finally understood that I mean what I say, then I shall sleep better at nights. Now, return to your long line of *amours*, sir. They'll be awaiting you.'

'When I'm ready. I find it interesting that you feel able to indulge in equine double-talk when you are looking down at the top of my bonnet, but it's a different matter when your feet are level with mine, isn't it? Now, that can mean only one thing.'

His arm still held her back against the wall, but his closeness spelt a dangerous determination, and her act of indifference began to falter as his warmth reached her face and the bare skin below her ruff. She gulped, moistening her mouth.

'You are obviously about to tell me,' she whispered, 'though you must have performed this jaded ritual so many times before.' She turned her head to one side. 'Tell me, if you must, and then allow me to go in. I'm getting chilled here.'

It was a blunder she could hardly have bettered, but in one way it prepared her as nothing else would for what he might do. Although there was a part of her that wanted him with a desperate longing, she had never anticipated yielding to a man in the middle of an argument about the exact meaning of her signals. If she herself didn't know what they meant for certain, how could he, for all his experience? No, this was not the way she wanted to be wooed, not like his other easy conquests; small talk, gropings in the dark, a kiss and a fall like ripened fruit into his lap. She was *not* like the others.

Before he could take hold of her, she had knocked

his hands sideways and rammed one elbow into his
doublet, swinging herself away into the darkened room
to find the table as a barrier. Caught by the side of her
hand, the pile of wooden roundels clattered onto the
floor, halting her long enough for Sir Nicholas to reach
her again with a soft laugh and an infuriating gentling
tone that she was sure he used on restive horses.
'Steady…steady, my beauty. You're new to this,
aren't you, eh? I knew it. Scared as a new fill—'

Her hand found its target with a terrifying crack on
the side of his head that shocked Adorna far more than
him. Never in her life had she done such a thing before, nor had she ever needed to. The success of her
assault, however, gave her no real advantage except to
reinforce her anger and fear, which Sir Nicholas was
already aware of. Even in the dark, he was able to
catch both her wrists and pull them to his chest, holding her firmly to him, panicking her by his closeness
and by her own unusual helplessness. This was not
how she wanted to be wooed, either. She had never
thought that fighting might be a part of it.

To fight and twist away was one thing, but a whalebone corset beneath the pink fabric of her bodice was
quite another and, though she might have screamed,
the breath was not in place before he spoke without a
trace of the facetiousness she had dreaded.

'Adorna…hush now. You've got it wrong. Listen
to me.'

'I don't want to…be here… Let me go!'

'I cannot let you go.'

'Words…words!' she hissed. 'I'll *not* be your latest conquest!'

'Adorna, what is all this about my conquests, my long line of *amours*? What is it that you've heard? Give me a chance to refute it. I'll not deny that I enjoy women's company, but it's not the way you think.'

'I don't think anything!' She pushed at him, angrily.

'Yes, you do, or you'd not be so fierce. I'm not trying to force you into a relationship. Did you think I was?'

'Then what are you doing with my wrists in your hands, sir?'

'Persuading you to listen to me, for you'll not listen any other way. There, I've released you, see. Now, you can do whatever you wish with your hands while I tell you how lovely you are.'

'Oh, for pity's sake!' she yelped. 'Tell me that my hair is like the moon's rays, my mouth is like a rose-bud, my eyes are like—'

'Adorna!'

'Like two faded periwinkles, my nose…oh… whatever the best noses are like nowadays, but spare me the rest, I beg you. I've had all that and more, and you can have nothing to add that I've not already—'

Apparently there *was* something that he could add that, so far, no one else had ever succeeded in doing, something that stopped the flow of scorn as effectively as a gag. She tried to talk through it, but he was no amateur like the one he had identified at the Queen's picnic, and his was not the kind of kiss that pushed and hoped for the best. Knowing that she would try to avoid him, he caught her head and turned it sideways on to his chest, wedging her there while he cut off the scolding words with a sweet tenderness that dried up her thoughts, too. This, he was telling her, was more potent than words, beyond argument, and totally beyond her experience.

Her hands, now freed, could have torn at him but lay unhelpfully upon his doublet instead, feeling nothing. She had sometimes wondered how a woman was supposed to return a man's kiss when he was doing all that needed to be done, and now she stopped thinking altogether for, after the first startling invasion of his mouth on hers, her mind closed as effectively as her eyes, and she was swept away into the deepest, darkest, most overpowering sensation she could ever have imagined. And she *had* imagined, often.

Drunk with the new experience, her mind was slow to adjust and, when he paused, just touching her lips with his, her pretences had deserted her. Without any prompting, her hands knew what to do, reaching up through the darkness to touch his face and to find their own way over his ears and hair that parted under her fingers. Shadows of shattered conscience warned her of some former conflict, some contradiction, but it was too dark to identify them before they fled, and his lips returned to take what, this time, she was yielding up without protest. He was tender, carefully disturbing the surface of her desire until a moan began to rise in her throat.

Then he released her, easing her upright and supporting her in his arms while her head drooped, almost touching his chin. 'You were saying?' he whispered, eventually.

She shook her head, saying nothing, thinking nothing.

'Then will you listen to me awhile?'

'Another time,' she whispered. 'Please? Another time? My father…the servants will be here soon to…' she peered about her and disengaged herself from his arms '…to clear up, to lock the doors.' Unsteadily, she stepped aside, hearing a loud crack from beneath her skirts. 'Oh, no!'

Sir Nicholas bent to lift her foot and to retrieve two halves of a roundel, placing them on the table. 'Can't be helped,' he said. 'Adorna, just one thing before I take you back.' He took her hand and held it against his chest. 'Whatever you've been hearing of me, and you know how people gossip at Court, don't allow it to prejudice you against me. If there is no scandal, people will invent it. It's gossip, Adorna.'

There was nothing she could reply to that except to remove her hand and hope that her cheeks and lips would be cooled by the night air before she entered the house. The last remaining guests were departing as they appeared together, though one who lingered was, to Adorna's consternation, Master Peter Fowler. He came to greet them with some eagerness, his expression as he looked from one to the other showing that he recognised what Adorna had hoped to conceal.

'Peter,' she said, reading his face.

'There you are!' Peter said, breezily. 'Sir Nicholas, I was hoping to catch you, sir.'

'Me? Whatever for?'

'I've been across to the palace just now. The keys, you know. Bedtime.' He smiled apologetically. The handing over of the keys of Her Majesty's chamber at bedtime was a ritual he could not evade. 'And I've been given two messages for you. You're a popular man, sir.' His expression, Adorna thought, held a glint of sheer mischief as he came to her side, ready to lead her away. 'One from his lordship's man to say that he'd be glad if you'd take a look at the bay stallion again before you retire.'

'Certainly. And the other?'

'Oh, from Lady Celia Traverson's maid. It appears her mistress was expecting you to visit her this evening in the east tower room, sir. Seemed a bit upset. I said I'd see you got the message.' He glanced again at Adorna with a suggestion of triumph in his merry eyes. 'Wonderful evening,' he said.

'Yes,' she agreed, taking the arm he offered. 'Wonderful.'

As if to verify the effect of Peter's ill-timed messages, she met the eyes of her former companion as he made her a formal bow and saw the anger that washed briefly across them, drooping the lids with a stifled frown. Their glances agreed that there was no explanation that he could offer to which she would want to listen, and that Adorna's former hostility, far from being lessened, had now increased. Her coldness turned to a relentless freeze. She did not need to ask who Lady Celia Traverson was, having heard the same name that evening in connection with his last love affair. Nor was there any doubt in her mind that Lady Celia was the woman he had met in the friary paradise while she had watched, yearning for such a kiss. And now, her first kiss had turned bitter upon her lips.

Chapter Four

Sir Nicholas straightened, dropping the stallion's hoof gently into the deep straw. He patted the sleek brown rump and looked across at his noble employer over the top of it. 'Perfect,' he said. 'It was the same last night. He's sound enough, sir.' He leaned back against the stall.

The Earl of Leicester, the Queen's favourite and the handsomest man at Court, some said, leaned against the other side of the stall and folded his arms across his wide chest. 'Samuel Manning certainly taught you a thing or two, Nicholas,' he said. 'You believe it was the mare, then?'

Sir Nicholas smiled. 'Almost certainly, sir. They can do a fair amount of damage when they're new to it, as you know.'

'Then we shall have to make sure he's well padded next time, eh?'

The laughter was mutually rueful. The earl looked pointedly at the reddened skin along the left side of Sir Nicholas's eyebrow, unable to conceal his interest.

'Don't tell me,' he said, 'that you need some padding, too. I'll not believe it. Was that the problem?'

A hand went up to comfort the tender place. 'Nothing to speak of, sir,' Sir Nicholas smiled. 'A misunderstanding.'

'Not Lady Celia, surely?' the earl said gently. He was as tall as Sir Nicholas and, even with his sleeves rolled up to his elbows, his graceful bearing and proud head showed him to be a man of considerable importance. He crossed his long elegant legs, well muscled and encased in brown leather thigh-boots.

'Lord, no, sir.' He sighed, taking hold of the stallion's tail and slipping his hand down its silky length. 'No, Lady Celia departs from Portsmouth today. She and her mother and sister will embark as soon as they get a fair wind, and she's distraught, naturally.'

'At leaving England, or you?'

'Both, sir. Nor does she like the idea of marrying her Spanish duke.'

'Mmm…I heard about that. Her Majesty's not keen on the connection, but Lord Traverson is adamant about it. Says it's too good an opportunity to miss.'

'He would, being of a Roman Catholic family. We ended our relationship weeks ago, but she asked me to meet her, for a last goodbye. Except that it wasn't the last, of course.'

'Hah! Never is, man. They say a last goodbye at least three times; I could have told you that. Recriminations, then?'

'Oh, no, sir. No bad feeling. Just a sadness. Our

parting was mutual, but I'd not have wanted her to go all that way, just the same. We were friends.'

'Sad,' the earl said. 'So who's the unwilling one?'

'Sir Thomas Pickering's daughter, sir.'

'Ah! The Palomino!' A slow grin spread across his face. 'The one you hauled out of the river the other day? Well, you'll not get that one eating out of your hand so easily. Nor will you be the first to try.'

Nicholas was, however, reasonably sure that he had been the first to succeed in areas where others had failed. 'No, sir. That's what I heard, but I think now's the time for some schooling.' He grinned back at the earl. 'I also think I'm in for a rough ride.'

Studying the stallion's beautiful hindquarters, the earl leaned forward and rested his arms across the broad satin back. 'Then you may be glad of a word of advice, my friend.'

'Sir?'

'Keep her guessing. You'll get nowhere with a woman if you're too predictable. They can second-guess you every time. And don't be too kind too soon. Fillies like *that* one need to know who's master from the start.' To his surprise, he saw that his deputy's chest was heaving with laughter. 'You don't believe me?' he said.

'Certainly I believe you, sir, but maybe I should tell you what this was for.' He placed a palm upon his temple.

'I was hoping you would.'

'For talking to her as if she were a horse.'

Their laughter made the stallion look round, his

muzzle caught by the earl's hand. 'So then you began
to praise her beauty, I suppose?'

'Yes, as a matter of fact…'

'Lost your wits of a sudden, man? Tch! You know
better than that.'

'I do now, sir. But I shall have to move fast if I'm
to make any headway. There's Her Majesty's progress
to your castle at Kenilworth in a few days, and young
Fowler has got a foothold already.'

'Argh! She'll not be serious about him, man. He's
only for show. Nor would her father consider him.
Anyway…' his voice brightened '…she can come up
to Kenilworth with Sir Thomas, if you wish. Would
that help?'

'Indeed it would, sir, I thank you.'

The earl smacked the stallion's back and ran a hand
down its tail, fanning it like tissue. 'I'll see she gets a
royal command, then. You need to keep your hands
on the reins and stay firmly in control at this stage. As
for young Fowler, if he'd been attending to his business, he'd not have let her slip into the river in the
first place, would he? Think on it, man. Now, let's go
and take a look at those new Irish geldings. They're
supposed to be fast-goers, too.'

There was probably no other man of Nicholas's acquaintance from whom he would have accepted advice
on such a delicate issue, never having been the kind
of man to discuss his love life with others, as many
did. But Lord Leicester was as experienced with
women as he was with horses, though his stormy relationship with the Queen had been one of the most

talked-about since her accession seventeen years ago.
At forty-two, they were both as enamoured as ever,
though hardly a month passed without some compli-
cation arising to set her snarling at him like a wildcat.
The earl's invitation to the Queen to make a royal
progress to his magnificent castle at Kenilworth was,
as Sir Nicholas knew, a last major attempt to remain
permanently high in her favour after so many serious
indiscretions, though if the Queen had known what
Nicholas knew about his master's extra-marital activities, she would probably have decided on a progress
in the opposite direction instead. His lordship had a
huge capacity for intrigue and a magnetism that few
women could resist, a combination which seemed to
Nicholas like a recipe for disaster.

Had he been faint-hearted, Nicholas might have
viewed his own predicament in the same light, last
night's ending being as close as one comes to disaster,
thanks to the help of a certain Master Fowler who
knew exactly what he was doing. Although he had
never before encountered the same relentless resistance in a woman as in Mistress Adorna Pickering, his
experience told him that she was certainly not as im-
mune to him as she pretended to be and that her act
last evening had been impossible for her to maintain
until the end. Then, she had lost it in his kiss, after
which he discovered what she had been trying to conceal, even from herself. She wanted him.

With that satisfying knowledge firmly in place, he
mused over his master's advice about the tight rein
and decided that a little variation on that theme would

not come amiss. She had eaten out of his hand once;
she would do it again. Eventually.

Adorna would not at that moment have agreed with
this theory if she had known of it. Having wept with
anger and other unidentifiable emotions, she had slept
badly, waking up to the same reflection of how little
regard men paid to the truth in order to win a woman.
The truth, she told herself, would have been easier to
deal with. At least it would not have left the same sour
taste in her mouth as his pathetic lies had done, especially after…no…she would not think about that.
But she did. What did it matter, anyway, except that
she had given her first kiss to a man to whom it would
mean very little except yet another trophy?

Lady Marion could not help but notice her daughter's swollen eyelids and pink nose. 'A cold?' she said,
looking doubtfully sideways. 'Come here, child. I
know a tearful daughter when I see one. What is it?'
She took Adorna's hand and led her back to the cushioned stool she had just vacated. 'You've had no
breakfast, and it's no good saying it's nothing. It's
men, isn't it?'

Adorna nodded.

'Ah! Well, if it's any comfort, love, there's probably
not a woman in the whole world who hasn't wept over
a man, one way or another. Which one, Sir Nicholas?'
She didn't wait for a reply, having guessed it already.
'Yes, well, I admit I got it wrong about having him
partner Hester when it's obvious he's more interested
in you. We can't tell her so now, of course; that would

do her confidence no good at all. But we can soon put it right. I'll get your father to invite him—'

'No, Mother!' Adorna objected. 'Please, I don't want him to. I don't like the man. I prefer Peter.'

'Don't like him, love? What is there not to like? I thought he was perfectly charming.' She scrutinised her daughter's face for signs, and found them. 'Ah, I see. So he kissed you.' Her eyes strayed through the sunlit window where the wobble of green glass distorted the banqueting house grotesquely. 'So that's how my best wooden roundels found their way on to the floor. We thought a fox must have got in.'

Adorna laid a hand over her mother's puffed pink sleeve. 'I'm sorry about that, Mother. It was my fault, I shall have to find a better hiding place next time.'

Lady Marion's hand enclosed hers in sympathy, but not too much. 'Well, you know, love, I'm not so sure that hiding is the answer any more. It served well enough while you were a lass, but your father and I think it's about time—'

'Oh, Mother! Not *you*, too!'

'Listen to me, love. A determined man is not going to be put off because he can't find you. And what are you going to do when he *does* find you alone, as he did last night? You cannot blame him for getting the wrong idea.'

'Yes, I can, Mother. He should learn to take no for an answer.'

'Did you mean no?'

Coming from her mother, the question was a surprise, and Adorna didn't know how to answer it.

Since the calamity was not quite as serious as she had expected, Lady Marion saw no need to hide her smile. 'One day,' she chuckled, 'you will see how unreasonable that is. Since when did a man ever take no for an answer? I'm glad your father didn't.'

'Didn't he?'

'Lord, no, child. Four times he asked me to marry him. I only said no just to see how long he'd keep on, but it was me who cracked, not him. Did Sir Nicholas ask you to…?'

'To marry him?' Dramatically, Adorna's voice was loaded with scorn. 'No, of course not. Men like him are not looking for marriage. He has a reputation to uphold.'

Slowly, her mother stood up as Hester entered the sunny parlour. 'If that's so,' she said, 'then I think, my child, that you could easily put an end to it. And what's more…' she lowered her voice for Adorna alone '…he might have it in mind to put an end to yours.' She smiled at Hester.

'My…?' Adorna's eyebrows squirmed, but Hester was close, having no thoughts about an intrusion on a private moment, and the intriguing subject of Adorna's reputation had to be shelved until Maybelle was obliged to continue it in the privacy of the bedchamber.

'Your reputation, mistress?' Maybelle said, giving the full pink skirt a shake. 'Well, everyone has some kind of—'

'Oh, don't hedge, Belle. Just tell me what you've heard.'

Maybelle sat on the carved pine linen-chest, deflating the pink silk like a balloon upon her knees. 'Well, you know what the Court ladies' maids are like.'

'And?' She waited for Maybelle to verify what she herself had already heard.

'And, yes, they say that you're hard to catch. But,' she added hastily, 'it could be much worse. Better than being easy to catch, isn't it?'

Adorna had no ready answer to that as she pondered yet again on the apparent ease of her capture by a known master of the art and then, to crown it all, on her capture by default by the one she had been trying to avoid. There was no comparison, Peter's amateurish goodnight peck being nothing like the earlier sensuous experience from which she had not, at the time, recovered. In that moment, as Maybelle watched for her seemingly artless observation to filter through, the question itself seemed to crystallise Adorna's dilemma more quickly than all her nightly cogitations. She *did* want to be caught. She wanted, more than anything in the world, to be crushed against him and to feel his hard arm across her back, his lips touching hers, making her taste his and forget how to protest. *And so my love protesting came…*

'Yes,' she said, finally. 'I suppose so.' With one finger, she traced the sinuously entwined frond embroidered on her coverlet.

Maybelle, aged eighteen, prettily dark-eyed and as sharp as a knife, placed the pink bundle to one side and came to sit next to her mistress on the bed. 'You suppose so?' she whispered with her neatly coiffed head on one side. 'Look, if you've discovered he has something you want, you can still have it and give him a run for his money at the same time. Why not slow down a bit and let him think he's caught up with you? Then, when you've had enough of him, you sprint off again. You're good at putting on a show when you need to, mistress. You can act your way through that, easy. You take what you want and then you can go back to Master Fowler. He'll always be there to help you out.'

'But that would be, well, asking for a different kind of reputation, wouldn't it?'

'Who'd notice? He'd hardly be likely to brag about the fact that you'd dropped him before he could do the same to you, would he? Bad for his image.'

The conversation had rested there, with just enough of an idea to keep Adorna's thoughts occupied all that day while employing herself in her father's Revels Office with Hester who, they discovered, was more than content to assist with the embroidery. Before supper, they rode together across Richmond Park with friends, Hester surprising them once again by her excellent horsemanship.

Like words that turn up on a daily basis after an absence of years, Sir Nicholas and some of the men from the Royal Mews were seen in the distance studying the paces of some large greys. Although her party watched them awhile, Adorna trotted off smartly in the opposite direction as soon as Sir Nicholas approached. It was, she told herself, too soon for unrehearsed pleasantries.

She was still unrehearsed when she was presented with another chance on the following day while keeping her promise to Master Burbage, principal actor with Leicester's Men, the ones who had caused such merriment at the dinner party.

For almost a year, Adorna's brother Seton had been one of their members, chiefly as a writer of plays, at which he excelled, and more recently as an actor, at which he did not. It was one thing to cavort about at home when all of them were equally inept, but it was quite another to perform professionally when all of them except him were very good.

At seventeen, Seton Pickering was so remarkably like his elder sister that some said, in private, that he ought to have been born a girl. They had the same colouring, the same classic features, the same willowy grace, but Seton's ability to write plays had brought him, through family friendships, to the attention of James Burbage, who instantly recruited young Seton to write for his company under the patronage of the great Earl of Leicester, no less.

Unfortunately for Seton, the unknown side-effects of his acceptance concerned the company's constant shortage of suitable young men to play the female roles, a tradition that for reasons of modesty were never allowed to women themselves. So, as one who knew the whole cast's lines by heart and who had a head start when it came to disguising as a woman, poor Seton was exploited in a direction he would have preferred not to go, having no wish to perform the way his younger brother did. At thirteen-and-a-half, Adrian was rarely *not* performing.

Adorna's decision to visit the specially built playhouse at the sign of the Red Lion at Whitechapel did not meet with Seton's immediate approval, in spite of her promise to Master Burbage. 'You won't like it,' he told her, pettishly. 'It's noisy. Hester won't like it, either.'

'But it's you we want to see,' Adorna said. 'And Master Fowler will be there to see to our safety. I know you'll be good.'

'I won't,' he grumbled. 'I never am.' All the same, he gave her a hug and a watery smile.

They made the journey on horseback from Richmond to the city, and it was two hours after noon when they were eventually allowed into the building with the eager crowds paying their shillings for seats in an upper gallery supported by scaffolding. Hester, already uncomfortable, was unsure about the wisdom of the whole venture, but Peter's protective instincts were already alert, for this kind of place was well known to swarm with pickpockets. He shepherded them into a shady corner and did his best to divert Hester's attention from the press of bodies.

'Look down there,' he shouted, pointing to the stage. 'If we'd paid more we'd have been allowed to sit on the stage itself, as those gallants are doing. I hope they don't stop the performance.' The clamour made any attempt at conversation quite impossible, and it was Hester's nudge that made Adorna turn to where she was looking, not at the stage but to the gallery at one side of it.

A group of fashionably dressed people had just entered and were arranging themselves along the benches, laughing and chattering with excitement, one of whom Hester had already recognised. The sunlight fell on him as he waited to be seated, dressed elegantly in dark green and red, his small white ruff open at the neck to accentuate the strong angle of his jaw. Sir Nicholas Rayne.

Holding her breath, Adorna pulled herself back from the edge of the gallery wondering why, of all times and places, they would be obliged to sit within sight of each other to remind her of a moment she was trying to forget. The trumpets sounded for the start of the play, the audience turned to face the stage, but Adorna was sure that, if she could hear the beating of her heart, then surely everyone else could. She would not, *could* not look at him.

'He waved,' Hester said as the din settled.

'Did he?' said Adorna. Indirectly, she had scrutinised every one of his companions, two other men and three young, pretty and vivacious women whose chatter was unaffected by the arrival of the first actor. But then, nor were others until at least five minutes had passed by which time the words could be heard. All the way through, there was a continuous upstaging from the rowdy group of young gallants who had paid well to sit on stools within reach of the actors, and when Seton made his entrance as a lovely young woman, their loud comments would have made a sailor blush.

Adorna's glance across at Sir Nicholas's group showed that some of them thought it was hilarious while she squirmed for her brother's predicament, having to suffer that kind of thing each day in a different role. Though his acting was not quite as bad as he had told her it was, it became clear to her, knowing him as she did, that this sensitive young man was enjoying the performance even less than she was. She applauded loudly and enthusiastically at each of his speeches, ceasing to care whether Sir Nicholas was watching her or not, determined to make Seton aware of her support.

As the actors took their bows, Adorna shouted to Peter that she was going backstage to find her brother. 'I know where the horses are,' she called to him in the pandemonium. 'You take Hester and wait for me. I'll be all right. I can look after myself.'

'No, don't go!' Peter yelled back. 'You'll be trampled to death.'

'Don't be dramatic.' She smiled, squeezing Hester's arm. 'I must have a word with Seton. See you outside.' Slipping past them, she climbed over the bench and found her way at last into the dark shaky stairway that led her in the direction of the stage, elbowing her way against the crowds. To her consternation, she came face to face with those in Sir Nicholas's group who, although not known to her personally, had been aware of her presence in the gallery. She smiled and squeezed past, seeing Sir Nicholas's concerned expression over their heads, fortunately too far away to make contact.

His eyes followed her, disapproving. 'Mistress Pickering,' he called.

But Adorna pressed forward, ignoring him, finding herself in a shabby wooden passageway where actors, their faces grotesque with thick sweating paint, squeezed past her on their way to curtained cubicles. She peeped into two before she found Seton.

Beneath the pale pink face-paint, the ridiculously red cheeks and painted lips, Seton was beaded with sweat. His eyes were wide and sad, his fair lashes blackened, his head still covered by a massive blonde wig that fell in luxurious curls over his lace ruff. From a distance he had looked convincing; now, he looked absurd. His sweat had made dark stains under each arm and the two bulges on his chest had been trussed until they almost met his chin. The jug of ale in his hand shook uncontrollably.

Miserably, he placed it on the small littered table. 'Dorna!' he said, croaking. 'I saw you.'

They fell into each other's arms, swaying in mutual comfort, Adorna as pained to see her brother in this state as he was to be seen. He had not wanted it. His malformed shape reeked of sheep's wool, and she could not tell whether his shaking was for relief, distress, or laughter. 'Shh!' she crooned. 'You were very good.' Then, hearing the inadequate words, she added, 'Well done, love. Even Master Burbage didn't know his lines as well as you.'

'I should do,' he said. 'I wrote them.'

'By far the best play I've ever seen. Wonderful story.'

'Thank you…thank you, love.' He turned them both to the sheet of polished brass on the wall that served as a mirror. 'Look, Dorna. Look at us both.'

Still clinging, they saw two sisters, identical in so many respects that they might have been twins.

'Well!' Adorna smiled at his reflection. 'Shall I call you sister now?'

Seton broke away, eager to be rid of the stifling disguise. 'Not for the world,' he said. 'As soon as my voice breaks, I'll do this no more. I'm counting the days.'

'It won't be long, love. It's going already.'

'You heard the squeaks?' He gave a rasp of laughter. 'Yes, I know. I shan't be able to keep it up in that register much longer, thank heaven. It hurts with the strain.' Seton's voice had been late to change, though there had been those, Master Burbage, for instance, who hoped it never would. Such things were by no means unusual. 'Here, help me off with this thing.' He put a hand to his forehead to peel away the wig.

But before Adorna could comply, the curtain rattled to one side to reveal an unknown figure who stood swaying on the threshold, his face bloated and purple with drink, his eyes swivelling from one female figure to the other. 'Eh?' he said, thickly. 'Two…*two* of you?' He swept a hand over his face. 'Can't be. I'm seeing things again.' He kept hold of the curtain for

support while he fell into the cubicle with an outstretched hand ready to grab at Adorna's bodice.

She lashed out, yanking at the man's hair as he
came within range while Seton, in the confined space,
picked up the jug of ale to hit him over the head. The
curtain and its flimsy pole came down with a splin-
tering crash as the intruder was yanked firmly backwards by a dark green arm across his throat and, above
the mesh of curtain and limbs, Adorna identified the
green-and-red-paned breeches of Sir Nicholas. Standing astride the prostrate drunkard, his eyes switched
from brother to sister and back again, his expression
less than sympathetic.

'Congratulations on your performance, Master Pickering. Are you hurt, mistress?' he said to Adorna.

There had not been time for any injury except to
her composure, which had suffered even before her
meeting with Seton. 'No, I'm not hurt, I thank you,'
she said. Curious faces had appeared behind Sir Nicholas, and a pair of stage-hands came to drag the man
away by his feet, still parcelled. The curtain rail lay
smashed across the passageway. 'Who was he, Seton?'
she asked.

'The usual kind of backstage caller with his congratulations. It's quite a common occurrence, love.'

'You mean they come here to…?'

Seton smiled and pulled off his wig, making himself
look, in one swift movement, utterly bizarre. 'Yes, all
part of the business. You have to get the wig off first.
That usually stops 'em.' He took Adorna's hand. 'Now
you must go. Let Sir Nicholas take you home. He

appears to be more security-conscious than your Master Fowler. Sir...' he turned to Sir Nicholas '...we were glad to have your assistance. I thank you. Could you see my sister safely home, please? She should never have been allowed to come backstage on her own.' His voice wavered over an octave.

'Your sister didn't come here alone, Master Pickering. I was waiting at the other end of the passage for her. And you may rest assured, I intend to see that she gets home safely.'

On that issue, there seemed no more for Adorna to say except to hug Seton once again and assure him that she would give good reports of the play to their parents. Outside, however, in the emptying space of the shadowy theatre, she began her objections, suddenly realising how impossible it would be to follow Maybelle's advice at a time like this. 'Sir Nicholas,' she said, slowing down, 'I came with Master Fowler and Cousin Hester and our servants. We shall be quite safe enough, I assure you. I thank you, but—'

'No need to thank me, mistress,' he said, coldly formal with his use of her title. 'You will be going home with Master Fowler, as you came. But I told your brother I would give you my personal protection, and that is what you'll get, whether you want it or not.'

She stopped in her tracks. 'You came here, sir, with your own friends and I came with mine. I prefer not to join you.'

Unmoved, he stopped ahead of her with a loud sigh, only half-turning to explain as if to a difficult child.

'You are not joining me,' he said, wearily. 'I'm joining you. My friends have gone home. They are Lon-
doners. Now, can we proceed? The horses will be getting restive and your cousin Hester will be worrying,
I expect.' Whether about Adorna or the horses he did
not specify.

She could not explain why she preferred Peter's
company to his, nor why she felt embarrassed that he
had seen her brother at less than his best and unable
to shield her from harm, the way *he* had done. The
afternoon had not lived up to her expectations, and her
heart bled for Seton, whose discomforts had been far
more acute than any of theirs.

Rather like the play itself, the journey home was
long, uncomfortably hot, and tense with an act which,
as far as some of the characters were concerned, made
them relieved to reach the end. Whether she would
admit it to herself or not, she had been further nettled
by this latest display of Sir Nicholas in the company
of women, though the thought no more than skirted
the labyrinth of her mind that there was no good reason why he should not be at a playhouse with friends
of either sex. New to jealousy, she still did not recognise its insidious tentacles.

Just as bad was the small howling voice of reason
that reminded her, at every glance, of the prejudice he
had pleaded with her not to hold. A dozen times on
that journey from London to Richmond, she watched
him and listened to his deep voice as he talked easily
with both Peter and Hester, and she wondered whether
this unpredictable return to his original abruptness sig-

nalled an end to his efforts to win her interest and, if it did, then why had he followed her when she went to see Seton? She recalled her father's persistence, his four times of asking, and wondered how her mother's nerves had stood up to the uncertainty.

On reflection, it could only have been by design that, as they entered the courtyard of Sheen House in the early evening, Sir Nicholas manoeuvred his horse near enough to hers for him to be the one to lift her down from the saddle, leaving Peter to assist Hester. As her feet touched the ground, she would have removed her hands from his shoulders as quickly as she could, but he caught them tightly and held her back, unsmiling.

After miles of contemplation, Adorna would have pulled away, angrily, her hurts being multiple and confused and not to be easily soothed. Certainly not in the temporary shelter of her horse in a crowded courtyard. But she was surprised enough to wait as he touched both her knuckles with his lips, sending her at the same time the quickest whispered message she had ever heard. 'At bedtime. In the banqueting house.' Then he released her, turning away so fast that she might even have imagined it.

Her first reaction was of an overwhelming relief that, like her father, he had not given up too soon. Hard on its heels came the heady thrill of fear and promise; already she could feel his arms, his mouth on hers. Then, what if she refused to meet him, to show him once and for all that she had no intention of being added to his list, whether at the bottom or the top? How that would teach him a lesson more swiftly than Maybelle's version, though it would leave her longing for something she had tasted and would never taste again? Was she experienced enough to deal with that?

As she had half-expected, Peter and Sir Nicholas were both invited to supper and, since it was already an hour later than supper-time, they readily accepted. Hester, exhausted by the three-day effort of being sociable, left the conversation to the others and retired to her bed soon after the meal. Adorna, however, was compelled by the circumstances and by her own confusion to maintain a pretence of indifference towards Sir Nicholas, which, she believed, would give him no hope that she would accept his invitation. At times she came close to being sure that she would never do so, for that would be to walk into his trap like a drugged hare. Her resolution veered by the hour.

Peter and Sir Nicholas took their leave of the Pickerings together, the duties of Her Majesty's Chamber coming before pleasure and, whether for friendship or to make sure of the competition, Sir Nicholas rode with him back to the palace, presumably to return later, unseen.

'I do wish you would try to unbend to Sir Nicholas a little, Adorna,' Sir Thomas said as they watched the guests depart. 'He's a most pleasing and competent chap. Knows his job, too, by all accounts.'

'You've been making enquiries, Father?'

'Yes,' he said, taking her arm. 'Of course I have.

He's Lord Elyot's son and he's gleaned most of his
horse skills from Samuel Manning, Hester's uncle.
Good connections.'

'And what about his connections with Lord Traverson, Father? Do you know anything of those?'

'Traverson? No, nothing at all. All I know about
Traverson, the old fool, is that he's sent his eldest
daughter off to Spain to marry some duke or other.
That's as near to being a royal as he'll ever get, for
all his efforts. What do you know about him, then?'

'Nothing at all, except that he's one of the Roman
Catholics that Her Majesty objects to.'

'So that's why he's sent his wife and daughters off
to Spain, I expect, to get them to safety. No Protestant
would risk the Queen's anger by taking the daughters
on, her views being what they are, and nor would
Traverson allow it, either. So much for religious tol-
erance. Come on in, love. Time for bed. You've had
a busy day.'

'Yes, Father. I'll go and lock up the banqueting
house.'

'Eh?' he frowned. 'Lock up the—?'

His arm was caught, quite firmly, by his wife's
hand; she pulled him back and closed his mouth at the
same time.

Chapter Five

Reciting her opening lines, Adorna opened the door and went inside, sure in the pit of her stomach that this was not a sensible thing to do, and certainly not the way to show a man how consistently unaffected she could be. It was not so much that a well-bred young woman would not have done this kind of thing; she would, there being few enough places where one could be private, let alone with a lover. Every nook and cranny had to be made use of. But having acted the hard-to-get with such force, this would seem to him like a remarkably sudden capitulation after so little effort on his part. Even her mother had put up more resistance than this, apparently.

On the other hand, the invitation may have been no more than a cruel jest. The thought sent shivers of fear across her like an icy draught.

The place had been swept and tidied with the sun's warmth still locked inside, the first deep shadows of night clothing the painted walls and blackening the windows. She waited, straining her ears towards every sound, picking up the distant hoot of an owl and wondering vaguely how she could be at such odds with herself that she could do the exact opposite of what she had planned to do. Could she be in love against her will? Was that what love did?

From the palace courtyard a clock chimed the hour, then the half-hour. She sat, stood, and sat again, starting at every sound, watching the lights go down in the house, one by one. Another hour chimed. Numb with anger and cold, she closed the doors behind her, quietly, this time. One last look towards the wall where the door led from the paradise into the palace garden, then she picked up her skirts and went into the house with a painful knot burning in her throat, knowing that this must be the snub she had predicted, though not quite so soon. That, and the coolness since his appearance at the theatre, would be his way of teaching her that it was he who had the upper hand.

There was one thing, however, that this fiasco had taught her; that she would never be caught like this again, that it had mercifully prevented her from continuing from where they left off and that, in effect, she had had a narrow escape. She should be thankful. This time, she would not weep or admit that her pride had taken a fall. She could act, as Maybelle had reminded her. Let them see how well she could perform.

Yet in her dark bed, the act was abandoned and the mask of nonchalance removed, and she gave way to the surge of uncontrollable longing that his kisses had awakened in her. After that, she fumed with anger at the man's arrogance, his sureness that she would come willingly to his hand. Never again. Never! She would die rather than become one of his discarded lovers.

The timing of it could not have been better even if Dr John Dee, the Queen's astrologer, had looked into his scrying-glass and forecast the best day for forgetting, this being the day of the masque in the royal palace for which she and her father's men had put in weeks of preparation. To have every prop ready on time, they would have to work nonstop.

Hester went with Adorna to the Revels Office, insisting that, although neither of them would be taking part in the masque, she could assist with the embroidery. 'Is this the *bodice*?' she whispered to Adorna, her eyes widening at a mere handful of tissue. 'This bit here?'

'Yes, that's it.' Adorna smiled. 'Many of the Court ladies show their breasts nowadays at this kind of event. This is modest compared to some.'

'You designed it?'

'Yes, four like this and four with a silk lining. This one's for Lady Mary Allsop. She likes to be seen.'

'But you can *see* through it!' Hester didn't know whether to laugh or to appear shocked. 'What does Her Majesty say to this?'

'Her Majesty is very careful not to let anyone outshine her,' Adorna whispered, laughing. 'She bares almost as much herself, occasionally.'

Only a few days ago, the idea of Cousin Hester sewing spangles on semi-transparent masque-costumes for ladies of the Court would have been unthinkable.

But there she was, beavering away with her shining brown head bent over a heap of sparkling sea-green sarcenet at five shillings the yard, actually enjoying the experience. Even the apparent contradiction of women taking part in a masque while not being allowed to act on stage had been accepted by Hester without question. Adorna had also noticed how the men made any small excuse to attract Hester's attention and how she was now able to speak to an occasional stranger without blushing. Cousin Hester was taking them all by surprise.

Sir Thomas smiled at his daughter, lifting an eyebrow knowingly.

By evening his smiles had become strained as he supervised the magnificent costumes being packed into crates for their short journey across several courtyards to the Royal Apartments at the front of the palace, along corridors, up stairs, through antechambers and into a far-too-small tiring-chamber. As the one who knew how the costumes were to be fitted, Adorna went with them to assist the tiring-women amidst a jostle of bodies, clothes, maids, yapping pets, crates and wig-stands.

'Here's the wig-box, Belle,' Adorna called above the din. 'Keep that safe, for heaven's sake.' The wigs were precious golden affairs of long silken tresses weighing over two pounds each, obligatory for female masquers.

She checked her lists, ticking off each item as it was passed to the wearer's maid, waiting with suppressed impatience for the inevitable late arrival. 'Where's Lady Mary?' she asked one of the ladies.

The woman wriggled out of her whalebone bodice with some regret. 'Don't know how I'll stay together now,' she giggled, happy with her pun. 'Lady Mary? She wasn't feeling well earlier, mistress. Anne!' she called to the back of the room. 'Anne! Where's Mary?'

'Which Mary?' came the muffled reply.

'Mary Allsop!'

'Not coming. Indisposed.'

Adorna's heart sank. 'What?' she said. 'She can't—'

'Indisposed my foot,' the courtier simpered. 'I expect she's chickened out at the last minute.' She glanced at the costume Adorna held.

'As usual,' someone else chimed in.

'But we can't have seven,' Adorna said. 'There have to be eight Water Maidens in four pairs. There are eight men expecting to partner you.'

The courtier held her breasts while her maid pulled a silky kirtle upwards to cover her nakedness, fastening it at the waist. 'This is like wearing a cobweb,' she grinned. 'Well then, Mistress Pickering, you'll have to take her part. You'll fit that thing better than anyone, I imagine.'

Adorna was not going to imagine any such thing. 'Er…no. Look, one of your maids can do it. Now, who is the nearest in height to…?'

There was a sudden surge of protest as Adorna's

suggestion was rejected out of hand. 'Oh, no! Not a maid. No, mistress.'

'The masquers must be from noble families.'

'Or Her Majesty would be insulted, in her own Court.'

'Adorna, come on, you can do it.'

'Yes, you're the obvious stand-in, and you won't need to wear the wig, either. Come on, mistress.'

'I cannot. I've never worn…well…no, I can't!' Even as she refused she knew the battle to be lost, that there had to be eight and that she would have to take the place of the inconsiderate absconder. At the same time, she could still remember what pleasure she had derived from designing each costume which, although slightly different in colour, style and decoration, had made up the eight Water Maidens. She had imagined herself wearing each costume, floating in a semi-transparent froth that swirled like water a few daring inches above the ankle. She had tried some of them on when only herself and Maybelle had seen, sure that no one would ever see as much of her as they would of the Queen's ladies.

The masks had been adjusted to hide the wearers' identities from all but the most astute observer. No one would know it was her except, perhaps, by her hair.

'Wear the wig,' said Maybelle, 'then they'll not know till later that you're not Lady Mary.'

But Adorna knew how unbearably hot the wigs were. 'Not if I can avoid it,' she said. 'I'll risk my own hair. I'm only one of eight, after all.'

'Then you'll do it?'

'I think I'll have to, Belle. But…oh, no!'

'What?'

'This is the one with the…oh, lord! What would Cousin Hester say?'

'She's not going to know unless someone tells her. It's what Sir Nicholas will say that's more interesting,' she said, cheekily. 'Think of that, mistress. This'll show him what he's missed better than anything could.'

'I had thought of that, Belle.'

'Well then, step out of this lot. Stand still and let me undo you.' She spoke with a mouthful of pins as she detached the sleeves, bodice and skirts while Adorna still ticked off her list and handed out silver kid slippers, silk stockings, tridents and masks to the ladies' maids.

There was only the smallest mirror available for her to see the effect of her disguise as it was assembled, piece by piece, upon her slender figure. But both maid and mistress noticed the women's admiration as the silver-blue tissue was girdled beneath her breasts, neither fully exposing nor hiding the perfect roundness that strained against the fabric at each movement. Others were more daringly exposed, but not one was more beautiful than Adorna, so Maybelle told her as she placed the silver mask over her face and teased the pale hair over her shoulders.

'There now,' Maybelle said, placing the papier-mâché conch-shell on Adorna's head. 'It'll take 'em a while to recognise you in that.' Not for a moment did she believe her words, for there was dancing to be got through before the masquers could be revealed, and Adorna's shimmering pale gold waves were far love-lier than the wigs.

'So this,' Adorna muttered, 'is what Seton means by stage fright.'

With the last checks in place and the head-dresses imposing an unnatural silence upon the eight Water Maidens, they waited for the trumpet-call to herald the entry of the masquers. Then the door was opened, as-sailing them at once with a blaze of light and jewels, colourful and glittering clothes, eager faces and the dying hum of laughter. Blinkered by the small open-ings in the masks, they saw little except the immediate foreground, but now Adorna realised how this hid their blushes as well as so many leering eyes that strained to examine every detail.

Surrounded by her favourite courtiers, tall and hand-some men, the Queen was seated on a large cushioned chair at the far end of the imposingly decorated cham-ber that glowed warmly with tapestries from ceiling to floor. The latter, clear of rushes, had been polished for dancing and now reflected the colours like a lake through which the eight glamorous masquers glided in pairs, each pair led by a semi-naked child torch-bearer with wings.

One child, mounted on a wheeled seahorse, asked the Queen to approve of the masque, but Adorna's eyes had rarely been so busy in trying to seek out, without moving her head, someone she recognised. Her father would be otherwise engaged with the props behind the scenes, the organisation and mechanics of the clouds, the little Water Droplets, the noise of the thunder and the giant sun's face that smiled and winked. While she paraded and danced a graceful pavane she could not help wondering what he would say when he knew.

The doubt about his approval nagged at her, blunting the pleasure of seeing Sir Nicholas's reaction to what she intended to deny him. The pleasure waned even further as she became quite certain that Sir Nicholas was not present. Some of the other masquers were having no such qualms, for they had already made some minor adjustments to reveal more than had originally been intended, but it was after the pavane that a shriek and a sudden parting of the crowd indicated that there had been an invasion of sorts. A group of tall silver-clad men, glittering in satin-beaded doublets and silver-paned breeches, strode fiercely through the open door, yelling and whirling white fishing-nets about their half-masked heads.

'Ho-ho!' they called. 'What treasures do these fair Water Maidens bring? Yield them up, Maidens! Yield up, we say!'

This was the part of the masque about which Adorna had been kept in the dark, being concerned only with the women's department, but now she recognised at a glance both the Earl of Leicester and Sir Christopher Hatton by the shape and colour of their beards. They threw their nets about with gusto, making the women guests yelp with excitement, but it was the Water Maidens who had to be netted, and it was they who fled furthest.

There were some, naturally, who did not make it too difficult for the fabulously dressed Fishermen with the white ostrich-plumed caps, but Adorna was not one of them, suspecting that Sir Nicholas was probably a Fisherman with his sights on one of the others. This was her perfect chance to be netted by someone else, to let him see, as Maybelle had said, what he was missing.

'Here, my lady,' she laughed, removing her conch-shell head-piece and handing it to a courtier old enough to be her mother. 'You could be netted, if you wish it.'

Willingly, the lady held it above her head, drawing the Fishermen's attention while Adorna skipped aside to find one of the eight who looked least like Sir Nicholas, a ploy that misfired when, as she dodged Sir Christopher's net, she whirled round to find that the man she had hoped to evade had spotted her. His wide shoulders, proud bearing and dark hair could not be concealed by the silver half-mask any more than she was by her complete one.

Across the long room they surveyed each other, one with legs apart, menacing and determined, the other equally adamant that any man would be preferable to this one, at this moment. She slipped away to where guests shoaled like fish, but it was too late to mingle with them before his net flew through the air towards her.

She threw up a hand to ward it off, catching it and hurling it aside scornfully, feeling a surge of triumph as she planted both feet firmly on it, glaring at the

Fisherman. The guests, unused to anything but a token show of resistance, roared their approval of her clever ruse and turned to watch what would happen next while, at the far end of the room, the Queen's head appeared above all the others to see what was going on.

Ready to sprint off again at the first hint of approach, Adorna was not prepared for the sudden shift under her feet as Sir Nicholas yanked hard at the net, pulling it on the slippery floor to unbalance her and bring her down on to her side with a sharp slap. Then, laughing softly, he hauled his net back and shook it out unhurriedly, his voice challenging and strong. 'Come on, Water Maiden!' he called. 'You should be as used to this performance as I am by now. Come, let's have a look at your bounty, eh?'

The men yelled and clapped, but Adorna's expression was well hidden behind her mask, though her voice betrayed enough to suggest that this was not all an act. 'I'm a cloud, Sir Fisherman! A mist. A waterfall. I have no fish, no bounty. You'll get nothing from me. Go and seek your bounty elsewhere.' Quickly, she scrambled to her feet, vexed that her flimsy bodice had not been designed for this kind of activity and that her legs, usually concealed, were now perfectly outlined for all to see. Hoping once more to hide in the arms of the guests, she turned towards them. But they were far too occupied in cheering her bravado and in ogling her charms to move aside and, before she could think of an alternative, the net came swinging towards her once more to fall neatly over her head and shoulders.

A roar of approval went up in the crowded room, the men calling for Sir Nicholas, the women calling for Adorna to do something. But it was obvious who would win with the net tightening about her, pinning her arms helplessly to her sides and, unlike the others who had been carefully drawn towards their captors, she was hauled unceremoniously across the floor to the slow clap of the guests, totally unable to resist the strength of his arms.

'Now, my beauty,' Sir Nicholas said loudly as she drew nearer, 'are you going to reward my efforts? What's it to be this time?'

In the Queen's presence, her answer would have been totally inappropriate. His taunts infuriated her, as did the guests' enjoyment, nor did the concealing comfort of her mask last long when he pulled her close and lifted it to reveal her flushed and angry face.

'Mistress Adorna Pickering,' he laughed. 'I would have recognised your...er...face anywhere.' His eyes were not on her face. Then, as if she had indeed been a netted mermaid, he picked her up in his arms and brought her head slowly up to his and, before his lips met hers in this public and humiliating display of mastery, she saw the gleam of exultation in his eyes, the white flash of his teeth.

'No!' she whispered, angrily struggling against his wicked grip. 'You are making it look as if I am...we are...'

'Yes,' he said. 'I am, aren't I?'

Even here, in the worst of circumstances, when his kiss was the very last thing she wanted, there was a moment when she became deaf to the yells of approval and heard only the way her heart danced to a rhythm of its own. He kissed her through the net as if no one else had been there, as if the reward he took was no paltry thing but worth all the discernment he could give to it, and it was only when the kiss ended that her other senses returned, with her anger. By then, it mattered nothing to anyone except herself, for the crowd were dispersing and making ready for the dance, still laughing at the rough diversion, both men and women envying the two masquers.

The Earl of Leicester slapped Sir Nicholas on the back as Adorna was carried to one side, his lazy and open examination of her dishevelled attire adding to her chagrin by his unconcealed approval of the contest. 'I see what you mean, man,' he murmured into his ear. 'Time for some lungeing then, eh?'

'Put me down!' Adorna snarled, hating them. 'How dare you manhandle me in this way before Her Majesty, sir?'

He placed her upright within the shadowy window-recess that opened immediately on to the River Thames, admitting the night air that helped to cool her flushed face and neck.

'Her Majesty is as much amused as everyone else.'

'Except me!'

'And you cannot go before she does. That would be a breach of etiquette. Besides,' he said, easing the net away from the tangle of fringes and stars, 'the masquers have to dance together first.'

She tried to step away, but he pulled her back and

held her against the wall while he untangled her hair. 'Stand still,' he said, 'or I'll have to hobble you.'

'Don't *dare* to speak to me as if—'

His kiss was meant to be a gag and, in that, it was more effective than even he had expected, given Adorna's fury. He did not allow her to recover herself, but seemed intent on keeping a firm hold on the authority he had won. 'As if you were a filly?' he said, holding her eyes and beating them down with the unflinching brown jasper of his own. 'You believed that a box on my ears would bring me up short, did you, lass? Well then, just recall that day you sat up there so safely in your saddle and asked me about fillies, and I said I'd tell you someday. Ah, I see you remember that. Well, I'm telling you now, Mistress Adorna Pickering, and we'll take it in easy stages, shall we?' He removed his mask at last. 'The introductions are over. Your education begins here. Now, the musicians are starting up again, the galliard, and you must dance with your captor.' He stood back to release her, holding out his hand.

She shook with outrage, more than ever aware that, for all her plans, this was going disastrously wrong. She would not give him the satisfaction of her immediate obedience; instead, a myriad of schemes fought for the right to make her as difficult, rebellious, intransigent and downright impossible as any woman had ever been or could ever be, just to show the arrogant savage what he was up against. Seething with vexation at her own lack of opportunity, she ignored his hand just long enough to see a slight movement of his body, a warning that she had better give in.

Haughtily, she placed her hand in his and felt his warm fingers close over hers. She had never seen him look so handsome. Or so dangerous. 'My captor only for this dance, Sir Fisherman,' she said, darkly. 'A net is not the best means of catching water, you know. You'll have to do better than that before you start your self-imposed role as tutor.'

'Oh, I will, Maiden. I will,' he whispered. 'I'll do much better than that, believe me. I won't even need half a chance.'

'Not a ghost of a chance.' She allowed herself to be led into the formation for a galliard, though her mind was churning over the fact that so far he had offered no explanation or apology for last night, not even a reference to it. Which showed him to be both heartless and mannerless, a man to whom Hester was more than welcome, if she wanted him. From now on, she vowed to herself, she would not only place Hester in his path, she would hurl her bodily into it, whether she wanted him or not.

He was, as she had seen before, an excellent dancer, and more than once during the lively galliard, she felt the Queen's scrutiny as she received whispered information into one diamond-weighted ear. As a partner, he could not have been bettered; graceful, sure of his movements, strong and athletic, and during those brief moments of physical contact, she could almost believe that their animosity was a thing of fiction. He would not let her go, but kept hold of her for the next dance, and she was too close to Her Majesty to make a fuss.

The coranto, with its leaps and little running steps, was one in which the Queen herself was an expert, an even more intricate measure than the gay galliard. Here the man could vary the steps at will, taking his partner with him as long as she concentrated. Adorna came close to containing her anger in the heat of the exercise, particularly when he held her above him with his hands around her waist, both of them in complete unison, at one with the rhythm, the steps, the lifts, as if they had rehearsed together. None of which should have been possible between two people so incompatible on every other level.

For the sake of good manners, not to mention the Queen's presence, she was obliged to swallow further biting comments with the dainty tid-bits he offered her from the banquet prepared in the chamber next door, though it was she who drank liberally of the wine being offered. More than once he reminded her that it was undiluted, that the Queen herself always took water with it, but the impulse to gainsay him at every opportunity had now taken on the dimensions of a crusade against his tyranny, and she took far more of the wine than she needed to quench her thirst, just to thwart him. He need not treat her like a schoolboy. Education, indeed!

It was at the informal banquet that she saw Master Peter Fowler from the opposite side of the chamber. She could have sworn he had not been there earlier, but then his duties could have been the reason for that.

All the same, she was relieved that he had not seen the undignified duel between herself and Sir Nicholas, though it appeared to be the presence of the latter at her side that prevented Peter from coming to speak to her. She smiled at him, but her smile was acknowledged only by a bleak expression of discontent that slid from her to Sir Nicholas and back again. She made a move to go to him, but found that the firm hand on her waist was manoeuvring her round to speak to other guests, as if on purpose to deflect her interest, and she knew then that the rivalry between the two had begun in earnest with neither her consent nor approval. It looked as if Peter had been warned off and that he had accepted the instruction, being in no position to do otherwise. She made a note to herself to reverse the situation as quickly as possible, but when she next looked, Peter was nowhere to be seen.

More than once, in the hours that followed, the idea of seeking her father's protection came and went. It had always been a useful gambit, always successful. But for once, and for a medley of strange and disturbing reasons, she was glad that her father had not been present, the same reasons telling her that, this time, it would be best for her to handle the problem alone.

'You've had enough,' Sir Nicholas said, in a low voice, returning the full glass to the server.

Adorna tossed her pale hair over her head and reached out to retrieve the wine from the man's hand, downing it at one go before he could move away. She handed him the empty glass with a smile. 'I think I'm the best judge of that, Sir Shiffer…shiff…Fisherman,' she said. 'Or had you intended to instruct me on what to eat and drink, too?'

His reply was lost as the room fell silent, the ladies sinking into billowing clouds of lace, feathers, silk and jewels, the men to their knees like dwarves in a rainbowed forest. The Queen was leaving. She halted in front of Adorna.

'But for you, Mistress Pickering,' she said, 'one of our Fishermen would have had an empty net. We have you to thank for stepping into Lady Mary's shoes. That was courageous, as it turned out. You are not hurt, I hope?'

Adorna looked at the forty-two-year-old face, still remarkably handsome and shining with intelligence through piercing topaz eyes. 'Your Majesty is most gracious,' she said. 'I'm not in the least hurt, I thank you, though I do seem to be perpetually wet these days.'

The Queen's laugh was merry and tinkling. 'But I notice that you made it a little more difficult for Sir Nicholas to haul you up, this time. Was that because you do not care for the mode of capture or because you do not care to be netted by Sir Nicholas?'

'I am not yet ready, Your Grace, for any man to capture me.'

'I'm glad to hear that.' The Queen nodded. 'Then we are of the same mind on that score, mistress. I agree that we should not make it too easy for them.' She walked on, smiling until the doors closed quietly behind her.

Sir Nicholas placed a hand on the small of her back, continuing from where he had left off. 'No,' he replied to her facetious question. 'Anyone who can converse so clearly with the Sovereign after as much neat wine as you've had needs no instructions from me. Even if it *was* nonsense.'

'It was *not* nonsense, sir, it was…'

'Yes, it was. You *are* ready for a man.'

'Now who's talking nonsense? You know as much about that, sir, as you know about fishing. Nothing at all. I bid you goodnight.' She kissed several friends on the way to the door, as was usual, but Sir Nicholas was not one of them. Indeed, she was relieved to find herself at last in the peace of the tiring-room where only Maybelle and a handsome young man were having a quiet conversation in a dimly lit corner. The clothes were all in order, and her own garments had been laid out ready for her. The young man bowed courteously and left. 'Is he waiting for you, Belle?' Adorna asked.

'Yes, mistress.'

'Then just help me out of this thing and into my kirtle and chemise. If I throw that cloak around me I'll not look any different in the dark. Get your young man to go home with you and take my other things at the same time. I'll slip through the palace garden as soon as I've gathered my wits together.'

'Didn't you enjoy it, then, after all? Lift your arms.'

'Slip it downwards, Belle. No, I didn't. And my head's reeling. I need to sit still a moment.'

'Too much wine?'

'Too much everything.' Her tongue's usual agility had begun to fail her, suddenly. 'Hurry up. No, leave my loos and shippers.'

'Stockings and slippers?'

'Tha's what I said. Now, get me into my…there, that'll do.'

'But you can't go home only half-dressed.'

''Course I can. Who's to see me? There, you go and take these with you.' She bundled the heavy skirt, bodice and stays, sleeves and ruff into the maid's arms. 'Don't be late back, Belle. Who is he?'

'His name is David, only he says it Daveed. He's French.'

'One of the French mission to the Queen?'

'Yes, mistress. You be all right alone? You sure?'

'Better than I've been all evening, Belle. Go.'

Alone, she pulled her cloak closer around her shoulders, sitting down suddenly on a clothes-chest as the room swayed dangerously. Fresh air was what she needed, and sleep.

The door opened, disturbing the beginning of a dream. Her heart sent drumming beats into her throat, but she was immediately defensive. 'What?' she said. 'Advice on how to dress?'

'Come,' said Sir Nicholas, holding the door. 'I'll see you home.'

'Why? You think I may have an assignation with Faster Mowler? Fowler. If so, you may well be correct.'

'There is no assignation and you should be in bed.'

'Whose?'

'Can you walk, or shall I carry you?'

She stood up, hearing her words take on a boister-ous life of their own. 'Neither, I thank you. I can carry myself home.'

'Yes, I'm sure you can. Sooner or later.' He lifted her heavy hand and pulled gently, and Adorna saw a flicker of surprise as her cloak fell open to show that her full overgown was missing.

Wearily, she pulled the cloak back into place, snap-ping at his helping hand. 'No more than you've seen already, and no different from all the others.' Walking without legs was something new to her, although she placed the experience together with all the others of that unforgettable evening. The shock of the cool night air reeled like gunpowder through her head, making her clutch at the door-frame as they passed from the Queen's Apartments into the covered walkway sur-rounding the royal garden.

She felt his arm go around her, supporting, and the events of the evening fell about like skittles in her mind while her body responded in the only way it knew how, instinctively and uncontrolled. Blindly, she turned to him, reaching up with her hands to search him in the darkness, understanding the reason for his hesitation but knowing that here she could taunt him and take his response in private without the act she had been forced to adopt before the Court. Here, she could fight him with knives unsheathed and be damned to the consequences.

Holding his head only a whisper away from hers, she whipped him with her scorn, oblivious to the danger. 'So what was all that about the lungeing-rein, Sir Nicholas? You think you can school every filly, do you? Well, sir, I believe you might have bitten off more than you can chew this time, because I don't stand around waiting for—'

His hesitation was shorter than she had predicted before his mouth closed over hers, the scathing words she had just delivered wiped from her memory in a ravenous avalanche of kisses that buried them for ever. She was never able to recall what she had said to provoke him, only that it might have seemed that he was waiting for just such a provocation.

The loss of her words was nothing to her gains in other respects for, despite her taunts that she was equal to his experience, she had no idea what she was talking about except kisses and mild caresses of the kind she and her gossip-friends had giggled over. Going to bed with a man, according to their information, was what some unmarried women did, but exactly what this entailed was still something of a mystery, and the sex acts they had witnessed between animals could surely bear little relation to humans.

But now her body burst into flame at his touch, urging her to press herself against him while revelling in the hard restraint of his arm across her back, the width of his shoulders, all those details she had unwillingly watched this evening while hating his strength, his mastery, his arrogance.

In the enclosing darkness, she was only dimly aware of being lifted into his arms and laid upon the pine bench that lined the walls, their cloaks beneath them.

His weight lay half over her, his legs heavy upon her own sending new shockwaves upwards through her body as the imprint of every contour made its way through the soft linen of her kirtle. His mouth came again to hold hers captive while his hand moved carefully over her embroidered chemise, coming to rest, at last, over her breast.

'No!' She pulled her head aside, breaking his kiss and expecting the amazing sensation to stop. 'No,' she gasped, when it did not.

His lips stayed in contact with hers, just short of a kiss, just close enough for her to expect it at any moment. 'Steady...steady,' he whispered. 'It's all right...steady!' Moving his hand over the full roundness, he kept her lips waiting and her awareness flitting between hand and mouth. Then, as she stilled, he slipped his hand beneath the fabric while claiming her mouth just as a gasp filled her lungs, ready to protest again. The shock turned to a moan of ecstasy and the hand that had grabbed at his wrist slackened its hold, allowing him to explore, softly, slowly, tenderly raking her nipple as his lips nibbled hers. She gave a cry, unaware of its precise meaning. 'That's good,' he whispered. 'Very good. Now, what else are you going to teach me, eh? About this...?'

Her breathing quailed under his hand that plotted the next unfamiliar warm voyage across the skin of her ribs and stomach, sliding over her hips and making her cry out again with the unbearable suspense of it. 'No,' she whispered, meaning yes. Reaching up with her free arm, she slipped her fingers into his hair and pulled his head down to meet hers, her words and needs no longer in unison. His dizzying kiss made her moan with desire, but she heard it only from a distance, like the denials she had voiced since their first meeting, fading at his command.

'More?' he said. 'This is but the beginning.' His lips moved downwards on a different course over her neck and breast, straying across to her other side to torment her nipple with his tongue and teeth, taking her hand and holding it firmly away as she writhed and arched, pinning her down. 'Now, my beauty,' he said, kissing the taut skin, 'is there something else you wanted to show me? What was it you had in mind, back there, that I haven't a ghost of a chance of getting? Eh?' His deep voice vibrated across her lips.

But a slow and exquisite ache that began somewhere in her thighs had now centred in a mysterious place, telling her that things were happening that she could never have dreamed of, that she had started something of which she had never been in control from the start, that he had the power to mould her with his touch. As to what she had meant by her riposte, her mind was a blank as she shook with the impact of her own body's responses. She was silent and trembling as his teasing hand made a slow and inexorable progress over her breast and stomach, reaching down until it came to rest on the soft mound between her legs. By which time he had claimed her lips once more with a kiss that was intended to make protests difficult, but not impossible.

However, he was more aware than Adorna that

some kind of protest was necessary, for although he intended that she should remember this first chastening lesson, there would be far better times and places to continue it when her senses would be clear instead of dulled by wine. Her contrariness had served his purpose well, but she would blame herself as much as him for this memorable episode before she would be tempted to return for more.

'Well?' he said, caressing. 'Have you remembered?' When she made no answer, he understood that she was already on the verge of surrender and so, to provoke her, he tightened his grip on her wrist and shifted his weight.

'No...no! Please...don't!' Her voice shook itself into a whisper, full of the premonition that, whatever his next move was to be, it was up to her to make him understand that no matter whether this was what he did with other women, he could not do it with her. She could not have said why, having no experience to go on, but the certainty was there.

Instantly, he withdrew his hand, gently pulling her clothes back into their proper place. 'Shh...shh...all right. I've stopped. That's enough for now, I think.' Carefully, he swung himself away, easing her upright to rest in his arms until her trembling was under control.

Even in her fuddled and confused state, she could not have denied that the capitulation already begun in the banqueting house was now well under way in the Queen's garden. But though her fear of being added to his conquests remained as great as ever, he had shown her with appalling ease how close she had come to ignoring every one of her objections. The thought was terrifying.

'Let me go home,' she whispered, shakily. 'You have taken advantage of me, sir.' She stood, clinging to one of the wooden pillars for support.

He came to stand behind her, his hands beneath her cloak covering her breasts and pulling her back to him, possessively. 'Oh, no,' he said into her ear. 'Oh, no, sweet maid. That I did not, and you know it. If I had truly taken advantage of you, I could have plied you with more wine instead of telling you to stop. I could have taken you into any one of a dozen dark rooms. I could still have you stark naked and on your back right now, if that's what—'

'No!' she panted. 'That you will *never* do! Now release me.' For all its apparent fervour, her plea lacked momentum under his persuasive hands that cleverly drew her mind from resentment towards the breathtaking response of her body. Still tingling from his attentions, she had no will to protest as his wandering hands reinforced his first lesson.

'You started this, my beauty, and now you're in it up to your pretty little hocks again, aren't you. And no guardians to run to.'

'Master Fowler will…be my…' Her mouth was taken over by his kiss.

'Yes,' he said at last, 'run to your Gentleman Controller as often as you wish, but he'll never have control of you as I shall. You can stop playing your game of run-and-hide now, Adorna. It's time to face reality.'

He caught her wrist and swung her round to face him, taking a fistful of her golden hair to tilt her face under his. 'I want you and I shall have you. Fume and fight as much as you like; your opposition will make my winning and your losing all the sweeter.'

'Fine words,' she snarled, 'from one who makes a secret assignation with no intention of keeping it. If that's the reality you intend me to face, sir, I'll stick with my so-called games a while longer, I thank you.'

'So that's niggling at you, is it? Well, if I'd thought you'd have accepted my explanation any earlier, I'd have given it to you, though there's hardly been a good moment for apologies, has there? I was foaling a mare. A first foal. Premature.'

'And you could not have sent a message?'

His voice softened with an invisible smile. 'Oh, yes. Yes, I could have. I could have sent your Master Fowler. He was with me in the courtyard when the stable-lad came to tell me that the mare had started. I could have asked him to go to the banqueting house where you'd be waiting for me and tell you not to. Should I have done that, do you think?'

The idea was absurd, she realised that now. He could not have sent anyone with such a message. 'I was *not* waiting for you,' she said, angrily pulling at his grip on her wrist. 'I went in.'

'Ah, I see.' He smiled, releasing her. 'Then there is no real harm done after all, is there? And no apology needed. Now, anything else before I take you home?'

'Yes, there is. Have you warned him to stay away from me?'

'Who? Master Fowler?' His smile grew into a soft laugh. 'No, mistress. I do not warn men off. I don't need to. Our Gentleman Controller will get the message soon enough without any extra help from me. I think you've already seen that tonight.'

'And I think, sir, that the less I remember of this night the happier I shall be. I choose my own friends and I shall choose my own lovers when I'm ready. And you will not be among them. Master Fowler would never have behaved as you have.'

'In which case, Mistress Adorna Pickering,' he said, pulling her to him once more, 'you would not have behaved the way *you* just have, would you? And that would have been a pity.' Like his first kiss, he gentled her lips with his own, reminding her of how she had responded to him and luring her into another betrayal of her slumbering protests. It also made her aware that this theory, though probably sound, was way beyond her understanding at that moment and had better be analysed on the morrow.

Chapter Six

Fortunately, Lady Marion was entertaining some friends when Adorna arrived home like a sleeping child in Sir Nicholas's arms, and Sir Thomas had not yet returned from the palace. Consequently, no one except Maybelle and the Pickerings' chamberlain were there to see how carefully she was deposited on the bed from which she did not wake until well past dawn. And then she wished she had not.

It was not so much her head that pained her, though that was worse than anything she could remember, but the shattering burden of self-reproach that grew with each of her searching questions to Maybelle about her behaviour, her clothes—or lack of them—and about Sir Nicholas's part in getting her home. The pain worsened as her mother kindly lectured her on the dangers of allowing a man too much familiarity. How did she know about the journey home? 'Because I pay my chamberlain to tell me what's going on in my own house,' she replied. Unfortunately, it was not possible for Adorna to discover exactly what the chamberlain had implied, or how much her mother suspected, or indeed how far Sir Nicholas had gone. And having no one but herself to blame for her determination to drink too much undiluted wine, she realised that she must get herself out of this situation with the same defiance she had used to get into it.

Neither the pain nor her temper was improved by Hester's somewhat ill-timed opinion that Sir Nicholas would make a good husband. 'For you?' Adorna said, wincing at the sunlit garden.

'Well, yes. My inherited wealth and his inherited title would go together rather well, I think. And Sir Nicholas has noticed how much I've changed. Isn't that nice?'

'Very nice,' Adorna murmured, watching a butterfly head off towards a gaudy marigold. 'That makes all our efforts worthwhile.' Secretly, it rankled that the plan she had been so eager to put into action only a short time ago had now begun to look as if it had Hester's approval and, what was worse, that it might actually work. The only comforting thought she could find was that, one day quite soon, Sir Nicholas and Peter would both be gone up to Kenilworth with the Earl of Leicester to prepare to welcome the Queen.

Adorna had missed the Sunday-morning service in the Queen's royal chapel, but felt obliged to attend the evening one at which she hoped Sir Nicholas would not be present. Her hopes were soon sent packing. He came in with the earl's household only moments before the Queen herself, fitting into a space on the bench immediately behind her. It was Hester and Lady

Pickering who turned to smile at him, but the unkind lurch of Adorna's heart had already responded to some strange telepathy, and from then on it was all she could do to keep her mind on course instead of on his presence at her back, his hands so close, his eyes taking in every detail.

She devised a series of strategies for evading him afterwards, but her father and Hester demolished them by keeping her between them as they turned to speak to Sir Nicholas, compelling her to respond to his query about her health. His 'You are well, I hope?' was accompanied by a lack of gravity in his eyes that suggested he might already know the answer.

She had no intention of telling him the truth. 'Well enough, I thank you, sir.' Against her will, her eyes evaluated the impeccable green silk doublet and matching trunk-hose, its surfaces slashed to show long puffs of pale gold silk beneath. A small white ruff sat neatly beneath his chin, but her examination stopped at his mouth, lacking the courage to meet the laughter in his eyes.

Hester, apparently, felt that Adorna's response was sadly wanting in detail. 'She is *now*,' she said, in the awkward silence that followed. 'She's been unwell all morning with a terrible headache. Poor Adorna.' She looked pityingly at her cousin, trying to imagine what a headache felt like.

'Hester!' Adorna said through her teeth. But the damage was done.

'Really?' Sir Nicholas replied, adopting an expres-

sion of extreme concern. 'Is that so, mistress? Now
what could possibly have caused that, I wonder?'

Sir Thomas came to the rescue, dismissing the problem with his usual bluffness. 'Well,' he said, 'anyone
who has to dress eight noblewomen as Water Maidens
all at the same time is entitled to a headache, I'd say.
It gave me one just to think about it. Hah! Now, Sir
Nicholas, I believe I owe you our thanks for escorting
Mistress Adorna home last night. Very thoughtful.
Mighty good of you. I was tied up till the early hours,
you know.'

Sir Nicholas's response was a slight bow, though
his eyes and voice still denied a proper seriousness.
'No thanks are necessary, Sir Thomas, I assure you. It
was a great pleasure to escort your daughter to her
bed…er…room. In fact, it was the highlight of the
evening for me.'

But any deeper meaning of Sir Nicholas's words
was quite lost upon Sir Thomas as his attention was
caught by another friend, and he began to move away.
Not so with Hester, who appeared to be getting the
hang of social chit-chat with a remarkable degree of
clumsiness. 'Oh, you didn't tell me that,' she said to
Adorna, ignoring the bright pink flush that had risen
in her cousin's cheeks. 'Did Sir Nicholas…er…did
you really…?'

'Sir Nicholas is *jesting*, Hester dear,' Adorna almost
snarled, looking daggers at the man to warn him not
to say another word. 'Remind me to tell you how some
men enjoy making ladies blush, will you?' She took
Hester's arm in a firm grip to steer her away.

Hester, however, had taken the bit firmly between her teeth. 'But Sir Nicholas would not do that, would you, Sir Nicholas?' she said, resisting the pressure.

'Yes, he would,' Adorna said, under her breath. Her glance across at her parents gave her even more cause for concern, for now there were eyes flickering in her direction as snippets of gossip were passed back and forth by their friends, heads nodding, smiles of surprise, grimaces of shock. She could not doubt that she and Sir Nicholas were the topic of their conversation.

Sir Nicholas himself offered her little consolation. 'Yes, I would,' he said to Hester. 'But you should also ask Mistress Adorna to explain that a blush of embarrassment doesn't necessarily imply guilt. Ask her about it, Mistress Hester.'

This was getting too deep for her. 'Yes, sir,' she said, looking as if she had already lost the thread. 'Yes, I will.' She bobbed a curtsy, glanced once more at the rosy signs of Adorna's extreme vexation, and moved away to join Lady Pickering, presumably to hear the details with which Adorna had not supplied her.

Adorna herself would have left Sir Nicholas at that point had he not kept hold of her arm. 'No, sir,' she hissed. 'Let me go now. How could you have begun such a conversation before my father and Hester? Now they'll think—'

'What will they think?' he said, close to her ear. 'Are you pretending that your parents will never hear that we were together at the masque? That they'll never know how you stood in for Lady Mary? Of

course they will. Look at that crowd. They can hardly
wait to talk about it. What d'ye think they're saying,
then?'

The temptation to look was strong, but she could
not do it while the embarrassment was so plainly written upon her face. She could not even meet Sir Nicholas's eyes as she replied, 'How could I possibly know
what they're saying?'

'Well, I'll tell you.'

'Don't.'

'They're talking about the Water Maiden who refused to be caught. About how she—'

'Stop!'

'How she wore a gauzy bodice everyone could see
through and—'

'Please!'

'And how the Deputy Master of Horse kissed her
there before them all, while she struggled in his arms.
Then they danced with each other and no one else.
Can you hear that roar of laughter? Your father. Your
mother and Hester are looking shocked. Well? Would
you prefer to go and join them and be invited to explain, or would you rather leave with me and not have
to explain anything?'

There appeared to be no choice left to her. The
blush, now intensified, was certainly not what she
wanted to exhibit to anyone, nor did she wish to see
their expressions of shock and amusement. She could
guess what they would be saying. 'Adorna Pickering
caught at last? Do explain…she *what*?'

Without bothering to answer, she followed him

quickly out through the small north door into a courtyard and from there through a maze of passageways,
smaller courtyards and doors that led on to Paradise
Road. 'I can find my own way from here, sir,' she
said, looking to see if anyone else was about. The
track was deserted.

He began to walk with her. 'You couldn't find it
last night though, could you?'

'Sir Nicholas, it really is most discourteous of you
to insist on reminding me of an incident I would rather
forget. Now that there is no one to see, there is no
point in continuing to embarrass me. Whatever happened last night is past and gone. It will never happen
again. Never. I regret the whole incident and, most of
all, I regret the part you played in it. It's a mercy to
me that I cannot recall much of what happened, which
you will no doubt see as a chance to make up whatever
you like and tell all your gossipy friends. Now, please
will you go and leave me to walk home alone.'

'You have little choice in the matter, my girl,' he
said with his arm across her back. 'You can either
walk sedately by my side to Sheen House or you can
be carried there as you were last night. Make up your
mind. Which is it to be?'

'You are insufferable, sir!'

He smiled at her fury, urging her forward. 'Pity you
remember so little, you in your flimsy kirtle in the
garden afterwards, and me wrapping you in my—'

She drew back a hand to hit him, to put a stop to
the shameful picture she had no wish to see. But this
time he was prepared, and she was slowed by the dull

thudding in her head. He caught her hand well before it made contact, pulling her uncomfortably close to him in a restricting embrace. 'That's enough!' he said, sternly. 'So I shall not give you any more details except for one reminder that you must have missed.'

'And that, sir?'

'That the game of chase has ended and that you had better start to regard yourself as mine. Which is exactly how those people in there...' he tipped his head towards the palace wall '...are seeing you, whether you like it or not. Far better to go along with it. Less confusing for everybody.'

Only a week or so ago, she would have argued herself in circles at his arrogant assertion that she belonged to anybody. To be held in his arms was something kept only for the night's secrets, but to be added to his list of conquests was quite a different thing. Yet the appalling headache of the morning had left her feeling distinctly unsteady, and now she was unable to summon up enough strength to continue the contest. 'Let me go, sir, please, just let me go. We can finish this conversation another time. Tomorrow, perhaps.' The fields and trees swirled dizzily into a black void as a tingling sensation froze her arms and legs. She had had nothing to eat all day. 'Please,' she whispered, 'I need to sit...down...'

And so it was that Adorna Pickering, against every resolution to keep this man at a distance, was carried once more up Paradise Road, this time in broad daylight, to Sheen House where Maybelle and the Pickerings' loyal chamberlain were there to take receipt of her yet again.

It was not the most dignified way to end the day, but at least it gave her an excuse to avoid the interrogation that her parents had intended for her after church.

By Monday morning, when they had had time to put the events into some perspective, they had agreed that, all in all, Sir Nicholas's appropriation of their beloved daughter at the masque was probably no bad thing, even if she had suffered some embarrassment by it. After all, they reasoned, she could have been even more embarrassed *without* his protection, and he had, apart from the horseplay, behaved in a careful fashion. A storm in a wineglass, one might say.

Sir Thomas returned to Sheen House from the palace, mid-morning, waving a letter he had just received from the Queen thanking him for his efforts last evening. He found Adorna in the still-room preparing some rosewater, her hands deep in a bowl of petals. 'Well, my lass,' he said. 'Her Majesty must have approved of your performance at the masque enough to invite you to go up to Kenilworth with me on Wednesday. I shall have to go with the Wardrobe, even though his lordship is doing his own entertainments, but I shall need all the help I can get with the robes. Are you interested?'

No, she thought, Sir Nicholas will be there. Travelling with us, too. I must stay well away from him now. Far better if I remain here, beyond his reach. But the Queen's invitation was not something one could decline. It was a royal command. 'Yes,' she said. 'Of course I am, Father.'

'Good,' he said, picking up a handful of the petals and smelling at them. 'You must take Maybelle and Hester, too. Seton will be there with the players to put on a couple of performances at his lordship's request, so now we only have to remind your mother that you're twenty years old instead of fourteen. Eh?' He laughed, replacing the petals in the wrong bowl. 'Perhaps if I tell her that Sir Nicholas will be sure to keep an eye on you, she'll feel easier about it.'

Adorna scooped up the petals and replaced them with the rest. 'Father,' she said, 'I don't want her to get any ideas about a connection simply because he's escorted me home a few times. It was not looked for, I assure you. It's no more than a coincidence.'

'Ideas about Sir Nicholas, love? Too late, she's already got them. Look,' he said, removing her hands from the bowl and taking them in his own, 'stop worrying about it. I shall be there, too, with hundreds of others. Safety in numbers. So why not go in and start packing? If you and Hester need some extra gowns, I'll borrow some from the Wardrobe for you. Now, go in and tell your mother and Hester.'

'Is the earl's household to go up to Kenilworth with us at the same time?' She tried to sound only mildly interested.

'Ah no, lass. They've gone. Early this morning.'

'What—*all* of them?'

Sir Thomas looked intently at her expression of surprise. 'Well, the earl is the host at Kenilworth, you know, and he'll be escorting the Queen. But his men have had to take the horses up ahead of them. Didn't Sir Nicholas tell you?'

For all she knew, he might have done while she, once again, had been in no position to remember much of what he'd said, though she found it strange that the memory of his hands upon her was sharp enough to send waves of weakness into her legs. 'No, he didn't,' she said. 'But it doesn't matter.' By the time I arrive, she thought, he'll have found others to keep his mind off me. Yet the picture she painted did not give her the satisfaction she had expected it to, nor did Hester's controlled enthusiasm for the venture convince her that this was the right course to follow.

One who did come to make a more specific farewell was Master Peter Fowler, who felt it to be his duty whilst barely concealing his dismay at the part she had played at the masque. He had little time, for his party was ready to move off, and there were many venues where the locks on the doors must be changed, *en route*, for Her Majesty's security.

As kindly as she could, Adorna reminded him that she was free to choose her own companions and that to meet them however she wished was of no concern to anyone but herself.

'And presumably Sir Nicholas Rayne's?' he said, coldly, before immediately relenting. He took her arm. 'Can we talk reasonably for a moment? I have to join the party before we cross the river. Will you walk with me?'

Adorna lifted her golden-yellow skirts, placing her fingers briefly over his. 'Peter,' she said, 'we must not quarrel over this. I'm not responsible for what Sir Nicholas says to me. He probably says exactly the same things to many other women. But nor am I answerable to anyone except my parents for what I do or don't do. If you cannot accept that, then I shall be sorry for it, after being your friend since Easter.'

He trapped her hand over his sober grey sleeve. 'I had hoped to be allowed more of a place in your life than merely a friend of three months, Adorna, but I suppose I shall have to either accept your terms or lose you altogether. I'm prepared to wait. It's too soon, I see that now.'

'Yes, Peter. Much too soon. Despite what you believe, I am no nearer committing myself to a man than I was when we first met.'

'Yet you appeared to be approaching some kind of relationship with Sir Nicholas after Lady Marion's dinner party,' he said softly. 'Or was that my imagination, too? And again at the masque. Does he know of your attitude towards non-commitment?'

She removed her hand. 'You have no right to ask me that, Peter. Sir Nicholas knows of my friendship with you and yes, if you must know, he has been told that I am not available. But I'm having as hard a time convincing him of it as I am you.'

'From what I've heard, Adorna, his purpose in pursuing a woman is not the same as mine. He is not best known for his fidelity with women, you know. Perhaps it's as well that he'll be away from you for a few weeks, too.'

'Neither of you will, Peter. I go up to Kenilworth with my father on Wednesday.'

He stopped abruptly, leaning one hand on the gateway to the courtyard. 'You…you're going?' he blinked. 'Oh, I had no idea.'

'I've only just found out myself. Will you look out for me? I shall be glad of an escort.'

'Of course I will. So Sir Nicholas doesn't expect you?'

'No,' she said, airily, already seeing the handsome figure leading the Queen's horses, glancing in her direction, keeping company with her father, no doubt.

When Peter had departed, however, she felt a pang of regret that she would not have the pleasure of his company on the journey, for it would have been a comfort to her. Not only that, but the effect of arriving at Kenilworth with Peter would have gone some way towards getting her own back on the one who had, apparently, taken some kind of liberty with her and then left her to think about it while he went off to enjoy the company of other women for several weeks. And if that was what she had secretly predicted, dreaded, and warned herself of, she had only herself to blame for allowing it.

Alternative plans immediately began to form before it was too late. She could change her mind, refuse the Queen's invitation, stay well out of the way here in Richmond. That would be discourteous but by far the safest course. She could follow Maybelle's advice and her own inclination, go to Kenilworth and ignore the man, stick to Peter, flirt, and enjoy herself; all the things she would normally have done when pursued too hard by any pushy young man. But perhaps what she dreaded most of all was the look on his face when she arrived, unexpected, at Kenilworth. That was something she did not know how she would be able to bear.

8 July 1575. Kenilworth Castle, Warwickshire

Shading his eyes against the glare of the afternoon sun, Sir Nicholas Rayne watched the distant progress of yet another advance party towards the Earl of Leicester's castle at Kenilworth, probably the last to arrive before the Queen herself on the morrow. The bluish heat haze shimmered over the mere where a line of ducks fled in alarm at the splash of wading men hammering stakes of fluttering pennants into the water, the clack-clack of their mallets sounding like castanets between the blaring of trumpets.

To his left, along the Warwick road, the cavalcade wound like a gaudy ribbon accompanied by the barking of dogs and the excited yelling of children who could not be convinced that this was merely the Royal Removing Wardrobe with her Majesty's articles of daily living. Chests of robes, fan-cases, hatboxes, crates of shoes, leather coffers, linen cloak-bags, her feathers and jewel-cases, cases for her parrot and her monkey, curtained to keep them quiet by the order of Sir John Fortescue. With them rode her tailor and shoemaker, her silk-woman and their assistants, ushers, maids, grooms and pages, musicians and messengers.

Behind Sir Nicholas in the castle's outer courtyard, known as the bailey, men tangled with carts, waggons, packhorses and suppliers that would seem to leave little space for yet another incursion. Every summer the Queen went on progress to see and be seen by her countrymen and, even though the cost of accommodating and entertaining hundreds of people for a few days often crippled them, the townspeople believed that the honour was worth it.

Those who were forced to bear the burden alone, the grand houses, the castles, the favoured courtiers, were not so sure. She had been to Kenilworth Castle once before to please her favourite, the Earl of Leicester, but never had the preparations been so extensive. This time, the earl had almost beggared himself to impress her, and Sir Nicholas had no doubt that she would take it as no more than her due when she arrived to an extravaganza of adoration.

His eyes, however, were not presently focussed on the preparations or on the state of the castle, but on anything in the cavalcade that might reveal the presence of a pale golden horse with a fair-haired beauty in the saddle. She would be there somewhere, he was sure of it. No, correction. He was not sure of it. He smiled, briefly.

'A fine sight, sir,' said the liveried man at his side, picking up the expression of approval.

'Yes, Watt. A fine sight, indeed. Keep the stable

area clear, though. We don't want them round there, only those on the list. Send for me if there are any arguments.'

'Yes, sir.' The man turned his horse and trotted away.

No, he could not be sure, only reasonably confident. Her curiosity had come alive from the start, with her resentment of him, but now it was more than curiosity she had revealed. Now it was an untapped well of desire that had probably surprised her more than it had surprised him. He smiled again, remembering. Not that she would recall much of it except the headache and the anger, but not even an excess of wine could have released something which had not been there in the first place.

He could imagine her reaction to the Queen's invitation, how she would first have refused, accepted, refused again and then thought of all the ways to pay him back for revealing something she had wanted to keep to herself. Her own passionate womanhood. She would not pass up a chance like this. She would put on an act of coolness, as before. Ignore him. Flirt outrageously. She would cling for safety to young Fowler who wanted high connections, and to her father. She would use all her old tricks to avoid any suggestion of a serious involvement although by now she must have realised that she *was* involved, like it or not. And that was why she would come. The Palomino, the earl had called her, teasing him.

A moment later, the bright toss of a pale cream mane showed through the mass of riders, the young woman behind it sitting like a lance poised for her first sighting of him, her first attempt to put him in his place. His smile turned into a huff of laughter. He would bring her back to him when he was ready. There was Mistress Hester, too; a useful ally to him in more ways than one.

He moved his bay gelding forward to meet the leaders at the gatehouse beyond which a raised artificial causeway banked up on one side of the great lake that seemed to float the moated castle upon shimmering water. 'Welcome, Sir John,' he called. 'Welcome, Sir Thomas. On behalf of my lord the earl, welcome to Kenilworth.' As the earl's deputy, it fell upon Sir Nicholas to take the place of his master who was at this moment escorting the Queen to his home. He turned his most complaisant smile in Adorna's direction, intentionally showing no trace of surprise. 'And to the Mistresses Pickering, welcome to you both. Your rooms will be here at the castle. They are ready for you. Master Swifferton will show you the way.'

A young man stepped forward as Sir Nicholas dismounted to take the bridle of Adorna's mare while Hester's mount was led behind. By now, the outer bailey was rapidly filling with the huge body of guests, household servants, horses and waggons, only those in the earl's company knowing exactly where to go. The rivalry for accommodation at the castle itself was intense, everyone preferring to be lodged near to the Queen, though many were billeted at houses in the town, at inns, in tents, or even miles away in the large houses of the gentry. No one was allowed to refuse the Queen's guests.

Both Hester and Adorna had expected to be amongst the latter category, at a safe distance from the action, but it was Adorna whose curiosity surfaced first. 'Here?' she said to the top of Sir Nicholas's black velvet cap. 'Are you sure? I don't think we were expected.'

'I think you will find, mistress, that you are both on Master Swifferton's list. Is that not so, John?' he called over his shoulder. 'In the Swan Tower, is it?'

'That's correct, Sir Nicholas. The top two chambers. Bit of a squash but better than most. Overlooks the water. Lovely views.'

Sir Nicholas released the mare's bridle at the corner of the great keep and pointed to the round tower on the furthest corner of the bailey set into the battlemented walls. 'Swan Tower,' he said, smiling at her with the same complaisancy he had shown earlier. 'Nest up there, Palomino.' He ran his hand over the mare's golden rump and stood back, laughing inwardly at her stubborn refusal to ask what he meant, though a dozen questions showed so clearly on her lovely face.

Turning back to the other guests, he prepared himself to explain why they had been given accommodation in town. 'Sir John, Sir Thomas and Master Seton, you're at the sign of the Laurels in Kenilworth,' he told them, heartily. 'The whole inn has been taken over for you and your men. It's as near to the castle as any building in town. Plenty of room there. I shall

take you over myself, if you will kindly follow me?'
He extended an arm, asking so sincerely after their
welfare that their temporary annoyance was forgotten.

The removal of Adorna from his side was, however,
something of a set-back for Sir Thomas Pickering,
who had assured his wife that he would be with their
daughter and cousin at Kenilworth. It had not occurred
to him that he might not be, yet he was aware that to
be given one of the castle towers was a mark of es-
pecial favour, set as it was at the corner of the earl's
newly-built magnificent garden. With the moat and the
lake on the other two sides, it would have been fit for
a princess, but for its smallness.

Lady Marion's exhortation came to him sharply as
he followed the handsome horsemaster through the
gatehouse and over the moat bridge. 'Find out exactly
what he has in mind,' she had said the night before
he left. 'If his intentions are serious, we ought to be
knowing about it. If they're not, then Adorna must be
warned. I fear he may already have taken her too far.'

'You mean…?'

'No…no, not *that*. Just…well, too far. She's confused, Thomas.'

Sir Thomas had snorted. 'Confused, is she? She's
had 'em all confused for years, love. Us, too, for that
matter. Time someone confused her for a change.'

'Don't be unsympathetic, dear. You know what I
mean.'

'Stop worrying. I'll find out what he's up to. She'll
be all right with me.' He had given some thought to
the timing of such an interview, to the tone of it, for-

mal or informal, and then, as usual, had decided that the manner of it would be dictated by the circumstances.

The time came after supper that same evening when not even he could have helped noticing the distinct coolness of his daughter towards Sir Nicholas, or the man's apparent indifference to Adorna's icy demeanour. To other eyes there seemed to be nothing amiss, not even Master Fowler's unusual buoyancy, but Sir Thomas tended to see things from a typical father's viewpoint where matters were either positive or negative, even affairs of the heart. He tapped Sir Nicholas on the arm as the tables were cleared in the great hall. 'A word, sir, if I may?' he said.

As if knowing the subject in advance, Sir Nicholas obligingly led the Master of Revels towards the large oriel window at one end of the hall that looked westwards over the castle wall and to the water beyond. It was more like a small private chamber where the Queen herself would be sitting at this time tomorrow. The two men stood, their amiable regard lit by the pink evening sky.

'Sir Nicholas, there is a matter, a private matter, that concerns me and my wife regarding your relationship with our daughter.' Sir Thomas watched carefully for a sign, but found none. 'There *is* some kind of relationship, I take it?'

It would, after all, have been difficult to pretend otherwise after the days of gossip from courtiers who had little else to say. Sir Nicholas made no attempt to deny it. 'There is, as you say, sir, some kind of relationship between myself and Mistress Adorna, though it is not easy to define, at present, exactly what it consists of, except admiration on one hand and deep distrust on the other.'

'Admiration, Sir Nicholas? No more than that?'

'*Much* more than that, sir.'

'I see. And the deep distrust? Is there a particular reason for that, do you think?'

'No reason other than gossip, sir, and a couple of misunderstandings. You know how things are at Court. An unattached male comes on the scene and before you know it he's saddled with a reputation whether it's deserved or not, simply because he spends some time playing the field. Which I believe is what Mistress Adorna has been doing these last few years.'

The older man pulled in his chin and rubbed his nose as the truth of it could hardly be contradicted. That was exactly what she had been doing, of course. 'Well, I suppose you have a point there, Sir Nicholas, although my daughter has been most careful not to encourage one man's attentions more than another's.'

'Except Master Fowler's?'

Sir Thomas made a gesture of dismissal. 'Oh, that young man can hardly be counted, Sir Nicholas. He must know that he'll never be in the running. He's her companion for safety's sake, that's all. I'm talking about men like yourself. Aristocrats. She's never allowed a serious relationship. Won't entertain the idea of marriage.' There was a note of resignation in his voice that Sir Nicholas was quick to detect.

'And you and Lady Marion believe it's about time she did, sir?'

The sigh was released slowly. 'Her mother says she's being careful,' Sir Thomas said, looking far out across the pink satin water, 'which I suppose it not a particularly bad thing in this day and age when so many young women rush into relationships as if it were their last chance. They seem to have forgotten how to say no,' he added, thoughtfully.

'I can assure you, sir, that Mistress Adorna has made good use of the word recently.'

'Hah! Lady Marion gave me a no five times until she tired of the game.' His mouth twitched inside the white beard as he added an extra no for effect. 'However,' he said, pulling himself back into the discussion with a jolt, 'there's a difference between being careful and making oneself unattainable, and we're neither of us unaware that Adorna has been steering towards the latter position this last year or more.'

'Which, I feel sure, Sir Thomas, must have its basis in some very sound reasoning, even if we don't quite understand it. For a lovely young woman at the centre of men's attention, it would be quite unrealistic and a waste if she were prevented from enjoying it while it lasted. And yet...'

'Well? And yet what?' Sir Thomas swung his head attentively.

Sir Nicholas came to stand beside the tall stone mullion that supported the window as far as the ceiling, his arms folded across his embroidered doublet. The sun caught the top of his dark shining head and washed it with pink. 'I've been doing the same, sir, as I'm sure you did. Yet there comes a time when a man sees a woman he *knows* is the one he wants. For life, not simply for the chase.'

'I see. And have you told my daughter of this?'

There were dimples of tension around Sir Nicholas's mouth as he replied, recalling the poor timing and Adorna's disbelief. 'Yes, sir. But I fear the lady is more preoccupied with my so-called reputation than with what I said to her on one occasion. The other, she will probably not remember.'

'Ah, the masque, you mean. Yes, she's headstrong, and wine is not her usual tipple. I suppose, as a father, I should ask you exactly what happened afterwards.' He looked uncomfortable, this being a new role to him. 'Did anything happen…you know…er…that…?' The rest of his breath blew itself away between pursed lips.

'Nothing that Mistress Adorna did not initiate herself, sir. And nothing that happened against her will.'

'That's not quite what I asked, Sir Nicholas.'

Sir Thomas had not asked anything specific, but Sir Nicholas let it go. 'No, Sir Thomas. Mistress Adorna is quite unharmed, you have my word on it. She may have been compelled at the time to face a few facts about herself and her feelings towards me, but that won't do her any harm. Naturally, she's angry with me and with herself, and I expect some heavy opposition from her while she's here, but I believe my patience will last longer than hers.'

'You'll have to have more than bloody patience,

man!' Sir Thomas growled, leaning one hand against the carved stone tracery. 'I've had patience, and I can tell you it's wearing a bit thin. I want the very best for my daughter, Sir Nicholas, but if Adorna can't see it when it's staring her in the face, then perhaps I ought to—'

'I beg you to leave it to me, sir.' Sir Nicholas had not missed the reference to his being among the best. 'If I have your approval, I'd like to go about winning her in my own way. Any sign of pressure from… elsewhere…might be a hindrance rather than a help. As you say, she's headstrong.'

Sir Thomas studied his foot. 'So your attentions are honourable, then?'

'Entirely, sir.'

'And you have marriage in mind, do you?'

'I do, sir. I intend to win her, however long it takes.'

The flash of grey eyes from beneath dark eyebrows held a glint of both approval and relief. 'Hmm! You'll have your work cut out, you know. She's always been free, never one to hanker after bairns. Might lead you a merry dance, eh?'

Sir Nicholas smiled at the picture. 'Yes, sir. I have your permission?'

'Well, you've already started, by the look o' things, so you might as well carry on. If you want any help, tell me. It's just as well I brought her with me, then, isn't it? What would you have done if the Queen had not invited her? Hoped for the best for six or seven weeks?' He looked over his shoulder to see that Sir Nicholas was almost laughing. 'Ah, I see,' he said, stopping. 'So *you* had something to do with this, did you? Hence the Swan Tower and its closeness to the Royal Stables. Well, well. Friends in high places.' He laughed, slapping Sir Nicholas on the back. 'Well then, perhaps you'll be good enough to show me the new stable-block before I see where you've put my daughter?'

'Certainly, sir. There's a good hour of light left yet. Come.'

Chapter Seven

Ever vigilant for anything which might affect her mistress's chance of happiness, Maybelle moved sharply away from the double-lancet window of the high chamber in the Swan Tower to confront Adorna, ostensibly to begin removing her lace ruff. 'Look out there,' she murmured, flicking her eyes towards the fading light. 'Your father and someone else.'

The someone else hardly needed a name, especially not here before Hester and her new maid Ellie, a young woman who was as irritatingly eager to please as a month-old pup. Adorna had no intention of appearing too interested. She moved without haste to the window-seat and glanced to the right where, outside the large stable-block built against the castle wall, her father and brother stood in deep conversation with Sir Nicholas Rayne. Still talking, they began a leisured approach towards the Swan Tower.

'Leave it on, Belle,' she said in an undertone. 'They're coming up.'

'Who's coming?' said Hester, pricking her ears, her

hands already clenched upon her skirts, ready to scuttle away down the spiral staircase.

'Only Sir Thomas and Seton,' Adorna said, turning away from the window. 'No need for you to go, Hester. I expect they want to see how we fare up here.' There was a tightness in her seemingly nonchalant reply that she knew sounded strange. 'Move these gowns, Ellie. Are they Mistress Hester's or mine?'

'We haven't yet decided, mistress,' Ellie said, gathering the colourful silks up off the canopied bed. 'These are the ones from the Wardrobe department for both of you.'

Four heads swung in unison as a knock sounded on the heavy bolt-studded door, the click of the latch and the appearance of a snowy head happening almost simultaneously. 'May we come in?' Sir Thomas said, stooping to avoid the low pointed arch. Seton squeezed in behind him, suddenly crowding the small chamber and immediately dashing Adorna's expectations that Sir Nicholas would be with them.

Reproving herself for caring one way or the other, she reacted with self-possession. 'Of course, Father. Maybelle, you and Ellie take those below to Mistress Hester's room and hang them in the garderobe to air. There,' she said, watching them go, 'that gives us a bit more space. Come over to the window and take a look at this garden. You can see the knot-pattern from up here, and there's a raised walk across on the far side with an aviary in the centre of it. You can hear the birds if you listen.' It was an impressively large garden surrounded by high walls, one of which housed the Swan Tower in a corner. Adorna's gaze, however, had already shifted sideways to the ground between the garden and the castle walls to search for a figure she had hoped—expected—to see at closer quarters.

Her father peered down, pointing to the end of the stable-block. 'Your palomino's at this end,' he told her. 'Sir Nicholas asked if you'd like to go down and see her before you retire. And Mistress Hester, too, of course.'

Once so hesitant and indecisive, Hester now needed no persuasion. 'Yes, we'd love…er…well, I'd love to go and see.'

'You go down by all means,' Adorna said. 'I'm sure the mare's seen enough of me for one day.' But she could hardly keep her surprise from showing when Hester slipped out of the room, apparently happy enough to see more of Sir Nicholas and the horses. 'You'll send a message to Mother, won't you, to say we've arrived safely?' she said to her father.

Sir Thomas placed an arm about her shoulders as he closed the little door. 'I shall write it tonight and tell her everything, love. Tomorrow will be far too busy.'

'The Queen will be here,' Seton said, 'and then the fun will begin. Why didn't you want to go down and meet Sir Nicholas, Dorna? You're not too tired, are you?'

Unwilling to answer directly, Adorna asked one of her own. 'What's a palomino, Father? Is it a new breed?'

Her father's arm dropped as he went to test the

bed's resilience, patting the soft yellow brocade cover
and lifting up the hem to study the deep twisted fringe.
'Hmm! Very nice. Not so much a breed as a colour,'
he said, dropping it. 'Called after a certain Juan de
Palomino who was given one by Cortés when he became governor of Mexico. Still highly prized because
they don't breed true, so Sir Nicholas tells me. You
never quite know when you're going to get one, even
with two golden parents. He'd like to breed from your
mare, he tells me.'

A warmth stole up Adorna's neck to her cheeks,
forcing her to seek the deepest shadow in the room.
'I'm sure he would,' she whispered. 'I hope you've
not agreed to it, Father.'

'Of course not,' he said, standing up and pulling out
the crumpled panels of his breeches. 'I would never
interfere in a young lady's love-life. The mare is yours
to mate as you please. Or not.'

'Not,' Adorna said, with finality. 'Definitely not.'

Reverting to a less controversial topic, Sir Thomas
pointed out to her the layout of the town from the
northern side of the tower, and the inn where he and
the Wardrobe were quartered, the moat already reflecting the earliest lights. She followed her father and
brother down the staircase as darkness fell, meeting a
breathless Hester and her maid on the way up, the
heiress glowing with the familiar talk of horses. Apparently, the company of Sir Nicholas had brought a
healthy pink flush to her cheeks and a twinkle to her
eyes. 'He asked after my aunt and uncle,' she said.

At the outer door, Seton laid a hand on his sister's

arm to hold her back while her father spoke to Hester. 'Dorna,' he said, 'have you read it yet?'

'Yes, love. Well, most of it. It's very good.'

'You wouldn't like to go through it with me, would you?'

She blinked. 'That's not like you. You know everybody's lines.'

'I know. I just wish…'

'Wish that you didn't have to perform?'

The misery clouded his face like a sudden rainstorm. 'Yes,' he said, looking beyond her shoulder. 'It's in four days' time and I don't know how I'll perform in front of…oh, never mind. In front of Father, too.' Loaded with gloom, he dropped his hand into hers as he had often done when they were children. 'I'm a man, Dorna. I wish they'd understand that.' His voice squeaked in protest.

Adorna's hand squeezed. 'First thing in the morning, love. We'll find a quiet spot in the garden and go through it together. The Queen won't arrive until midday. She's already reached Warwick, so Peter says.'

Seton's face cleared. 'Right. Bring your copy. I'll be through the gates as soon as they're open.' He lifted her knuckles to his lips. 'Thanks, love.'

'Sleep well, and stop worrying. Father wouldn't be Master of Revels if he minded men dressing up as women.'

His eyebrows bounced, wickedly. 'Or women dressing up as fighting Water Maidens?'

'You've heard about *that*?' she whispered.

'I'd have to be deaf not to. The whole Court must

know by now.' His voice chortled up and down an octave. 'In fact, they seem to be waiting for Act Two.'

'Well, there isn't an Act Two,' she snapped.

'You mean, that was *it*? So what d'ye think *he*'s after, then?'

Frowning, Adorna turned to look where her brother's eyes rested and saw, to her confusion, that Sir Nicholas was strolling towards them down the path from the royal stables. There was no way round him.

'Goodnight, Seton,' she said. 'See you tomorrow.' Three yards behind her, she took her father by surprise with a quick peck on his cheek. 'G'night, Father,' she said. Her vanishing act would have been the envy of William Shenton, the Queen's Fool.

Still sure that Sir Nicholas could not have anticipated her arrival that day, Adorna was as puzzled as Hester at their luxurious accommodation, though it had crossed her mind more than once that it might have been more to do with Hester herself than with Sir Thomas's high office that had gained them this distinction. By now the whole Court would know that the heiress was not only available but amongst them. One had only to see how, on this first evening, the men had sought Hester's attention as well as Adorna's, though the former's colour had not been so high then as on her later return from the stables. Adorna nevertheless congratulated herself on avoiding Sir Nicholas, though the manner of it had perhaps been a little more obvious than she had intended. She would do better tomorrow.

The stillness of the night and the sweetly scented

air from the garden below did less than she had hoped
to quell the excitement that had mounted over each
day of their journey, each stop-over hardening her resolution to take matters into her own hands after her
shameful submission on the evening of the masque. If
the man believed that she would now succumb at the
next snap of his fingers, he would soon discover his
mistake. Nor would there be any more problems with
Peter after their talk. As for Hester, she would be easy
enough to steer into Sir Nicholas's path, for Adorna
believed that her readiness to talk of him and his superb horsemanship had teetered on the brink of hero-
worship at times.

By the light of a candle, she lay next to Maybelle
and read to her the last scene of Seton's play, one of
two he had written for this visit to Kenilworth. 'Wake
me at daybreak,' she whispered, closing the pages. But
Maybelle was already asleep and Adorna was left to
wonder how safe this ivory tower would be in comparison to her Richmond refuge, and whether her father would be as willing to assume his usual protec-
tiveness from an office so inconveniently situated. The
contradictions within these hopes failed to register
with her when, only an hour ago, she had actually
hoped Sir Nicholas *would* invade her privacy. But
then, she had been consistent in wanting to have her
cake and to eat it, too.

The early sun cast deep shadows across the garden
and set light to canopies of diamond-dusted spiders'
webs from leaf to leaf that trembled as Adorna walked

carefully past, lifting her skirts so as not to disturb them. Silently over the grassy pathway, she stalked the darting wrens and shy thrushes, always the first to begin feasting. Situated on the north side of the castle, the symmetrical beds of fragrant herbs were divided by walks that led towards a circular fountain in the centre, while the exotic birds chirping in the aviary added yet another element to the garden's magic.

Seton hardly noticed her arrival, his head almost hidden behind a sheaf of papers that flailed the air in time to his whispered narrative. He lowered the script with a sigh as she approached, looking down at her from the high-terraced walk. 'It's no good,' he said in a loud whisper. 'It sounds worse every time I read it.'

'How do I get up there?' Adorna said, looking for a flight of steps.

He pointed to the far end. 'That way. Steps. Be careful, they're slippery.'

Joining him, she was able to see his troubled face. 'You've not slept, have you?' she said. 'What on earth is it? You're not usually so worried.'

'I don't usually perform before the Queen and her Court, do I?' he said, wearily. 'And these performances are so important to the earl. He's our patron, and all this palaver is meant to impress the love of his life, you know. Nobody believes he'll get another chance. Nor does he, either.'

'To get her to accept him? After all these years?' Adorna looked out across the formal, static, ordered enclosure and saw in her mind's eye how it hid a seething mass of life, just like the Court, full of complications, competition and dependency. 'And you want the plays to be the best ever. Yes, I can see how you think it will reflect on the earl if they're not, but Father obviously thinks they're acceptable.' It was the wrong thing to say; as Master of the Revels, their father was obliged to censure everything performed before the Queen, but he was no critic of good writing.

'I don't want acceptable, love,' Seton said. 'I want brilliant.'

The silence was broken by a distant clamour of ducks out on the mere. A line of swans honked softly across the castle and disappeared.

'Show me what's bothering you,' said Adorna, turning her pages.

Seton turned to the last scene. 'I'm supposed to be the beautiful Beatrice who finally admits her love for Benedict. The trouble is, I can say it in my head as if I'm her, but I'll never be able to say it out loud to a hundred people or more. It's so private.'

'It's the loveliest part of the whole play,' Adorna said. 'Here, you be Benedict for a change, and I'll be her. Let's see if that helps.' She pointed to the beginning of their dialogue. 'Shall you start there?'

Seton began, unconvincingly.

And is your heart of the same mind, sweet Beatrice,
Or are the twins conjoined as close as ever in dislike
of me?
Or perhaps it is your fear that freezes them in per-
petual winter
And makes you less than bold to look at summer in
the face.

Adorna replied:

Nay, my lord, I pray you let me speak
Of how once my heart refused to thaw or bend to
thine,
Of how since then my yearning's like a flower grown,
Opening its petals to the sun, the dew, the day's long
hours
And every nourishing thing that Nature owns.
Now I am persuaded to accept, to love, to be no more
aloof,
To say that what was mine shall now be yours, for-
sooth.

There was disbelief and scorn in Seton's Benedict:

Thou'lt not find me so easy to persuade, though all—

He stopped abruptly as a quiet voice interrupted to
remonstrate, as if he had been the director.

'Oh, no, Master Seton. No, that would be too discourteous by far.'

'What?' Seton's papers hit his knees with a slap.
'Sir Nicholas, my sister and I were hoping for—'

'For some privacy. Yes, I know. Don't go, Mistress
Adorna, please.' From the shadow of the gilded aviary
the tall figure of the knight emerged to lean against
one side of the trellis and look down upon the two
fair-haired players. 'Forgive me, do, but I was unable
to ignore the poetry. It's very moving,' he said, obviously sincere, 'but Benedict's reply to that wonderful confession is unworthy. No gentle man could dis-
believe such a genuine submission. Your Benedict
would have to have a heart of stone, surely?'

'And you would know about such things, would you, sir?' Adorna said, coolly.

'Of a man's reaction to a longed-for declaration of love? Certainly I would. None better. May I suggest a change there, Master Seton? It may help you to feel more comfortable as Beatrice.'

'Well…er…yes, if you think so, Sir Nicholas.' Seton placed a hand over Adorna's arm as she stood and laid her script on the bench. 'Stay, Dorna. You said that far more convincingly than I could do. Stay and see what Sir Nicholas has to suggest.'

She resumed her seat, placing Seton between them yet unable to tear her eyes away from the countless differences between the two males that could not be explained by age alone: Seton's delicate white fingers against the strong brown hands with a dusting of dark hair on their backs, the knight's solid wide frame and muscular neck against Seton's slightness, the size of their heads, the length of thigh, the sheer bulk of Sir Nicholas against the young man who looked and sounded so much like herself.

Her eyes were drawn to the powerful hunch of his shoulders under a sleeveless blue velvet doublet, to the thick dark hair that touched against the high collar of his white shirt, hair that she believed she may have fingered, somewhere, some time. She watched, under the pretext of following their discussion, how the skin stretched over his cheekbones, how the muscles in his jaw rippled, his eyes and eyelids moved beneath angled brows, the mobile mouth that had so expertly taken hers, and more. What more?

Catching her examination, he held her eyes and read them. 'Do you not agree, mistress?' he said, watching the colour flood into her cheeks.

'Er...yes, if Seton agrees. He's the author.' Her eyes dropped to the script, now written upon in his large bold hand. Of all the people in the world, she would rather it had been anyone but he who had heard her speak Beatrice's lines, for now he was sure to be hearing them as if they were her own. 'May I see?' she said.

Seton sounded relieved. 'It's much better like this, Dorna. My Benedict was too ill-natured, whereas this one keeps his authority but is more kindly. Thank you, Sir Nicholas. Shall you read the new bit, sir? Please?'

Sir Nicholas took the page from him. 'If you wish. Mistress Adorna? You will be Beatrice again, for the moment?'

She felt trapped. 'Who is this Beatrice, Seton?' she said, suddenly irritated. 'And what has this Benedict done to deserve such a climb-down?'

'They're nobody, love. Just people. Read it.'

As soon as they began, sharing the amended script, the two characters became stand-ins for Adorna and Nicholas, who were saying to each other what they might have said in real life if things had been different, if she could have been convinced that his intentions were serious and that she was not simply the latest in a long line of potential conquests. This time, Benedict's scepticism was exchanged for loving acceptance with a hint of teasing, a far more credible ending than Seton's. Adorna's hands were trembling as the scene ended with a kiss which, in this rehearsal, was acted only in the two players' minds.

She could not look at him, nor did she reply when Seton jumped up, hurriedly brushed a tear away with a knuckle, and took the script from Sir Nicholas. 'Thanks,' he croaked. 'Amazing. I'll go and find Master Burbage. He's Benedict. He'll have to learn the new ending. Thanks.' His footsteps padded on the soft grass, his dark suit melted into the wall.

Like so many other things, this was not what Adorna had intended. She stood up. 'Excuse me, I must go, too. I'm sure you must be especially busy today.'

'Well read, Beatrice. Now we both know how it ends, even if the getting there may vary in detail.' Sir Nicholas stood with her, escorting her along the terrace to where the steps led downwards. A gardener and two ladies with a dog had entered the lower pathways to walk waist-high in lavender and St. John's wort, their voices hardly audible, only the gardener's hoe clinking on the soil. 'You are unusually subdued, mistress. Were you convinced by it, or are you musing on the bit we missed out?'

She accepted his hand down the slippery steps and then removed it quickly. 'Missed out? I don't recall missing anything. Does Seton know of it?'

'Oh, most certainly. Bear with me. I'll tell you by the gate. I'd not want to be overheard and have the plot spoiled.'

She had lived with the sensation of being close to him, yet nothing she remembered could compare with

the reality of his presence, of vibrating to the warmth
of his hand as it deliberately claimed hers again. For
the benefit of the curious women, she thought, cyni-
cally. She left it there, feeling his grip tighten as they
reached the gate in the high wall. The touch of her
arm on his sent a thud of excitement into her chest
and, struggling to keep her voice level, she glanced
down at the script in her hand. 'Which bit did Seton
miss out?' she said.

'Not Seton. Us.' He pulled her to one side where
the eastern sun caught the pink brickwork full on, facing her into its rays so that he became, for that moment, a dark silhouette. By which time it was too late
to evade his arms, and she was bent into him with her
head pressed into his shoulder, his lips already taking
hers with a fierce urgency that belonged as much to
her as it did to him.

She had nursed her fears and resentment for well
over a week since their last eventful meeting, during
which time she had schooled herself to adopt a façade
of unconcern. But at this first physical contact the façade was flattened; it was as if he had reached behind
it to drag forward the response he wanted. Helpless to
keep up the pretence, she was angry that he had not
been fooled by it, and shamed to have her needs exposed as if they were as accessible as he chose to make
them. A storm of hunger shook her like an earth
tremor, and she responded, blind and unthinking, ravenous for the hard pressure of his body, warm and
overpowering. A memory stirred and then faded.

His mouth opened and she felt him shudder, sending

a soft gust of air like a sigh through her lips. 'That,' he said hoarsely, 'is what we missed. Both of us. And that's what you'll have to imagine when you watch the play. As I shall.' His voice was harsh and angry. 'And I've told you before, woman, that if you try to evade me, I shall find you. Run as fast as you like; it will make no difference.'

Her breath was exhaled in a sob before she could stop it. 'Then ride your fleetest horse, Sir Nicholas,' she panted, 'for I shall never wait for a man. Not for you, not for anyone. I waited once, but never again. Never.'

'You will, woman,' he said roughly. 'You'll come to me within days.'

'Never!'

'We'll see, shall we?' His release of her was so sudden that she fell back against the wall while he clicked open the gate and disappeared, leaving it ajar for her to follow at her own pace. The two women stood by the fountain, staring at her instead of at the water and ignoring the dog's constant yapping.

Her eyes welled with sudden tears as she turned her back on them to avoid their pitying eyes, silently cursing herself for allowing him to see, yet again, how she melted at his touch. Just like all the others. Fool. *Fool.* Now she would have to begin again, to work even harder to rebuild the façade, to stem the inevitable gossip already being generated behind her.

Straightening the crumpled sheaf of papers, she waited and then slipped through the gate. But what had he meant by 'I've told you before'? What had he said? When?

Hester's chamber door opened as she passed. 'Come in,' Hester called. 'Come and tell me how this looks.' She twirled, half-dressed and pinned into the skirt of a mulberry silk over a pale grey petticoat. 'Ellie says this one will suit me best. Do you agree, Adorna?'

'Yes, as it happens, I do,' Adorna said.

The twirling stopped suddenly, but Adorna had already moved upwards to her own chamber where Maybelle was clearly indignant. 'Someone's going to have to tell that Ellie,' the maid hissed, pointing to the floor. 'She's chosen that—'

'Yes, I know,' Adorna said. 'I never wanted it anyway. She's welcome.'

'But you're angry. I can see.'

'It's nothing. Come, find that lovely cream silk with the embroidered flowers. And jewels. And feathers. And a saucy hat. The Queen will be here by mid-day and I have some serious flirting to do by then.'

Maybelle smiled her broadest smile. 'Cream silk it is, then. With feathers.'

For all her determination to prove how wrong his prediction was, Adorna was not only shaken by his kiss but by his noticeable anger, too. That had been something unexpected; exasperation, perhaps, or a gentle reprimand such as that given by thwarted young men like Peter, but not anger, not the rough handling Sir Nicholas had meted out. And why the talk of avoiding him, which he had patently noticed, when he had not known she would be here in the first place?

Or had he? As for coming to him in days, he for one would be far too occupied to notice her coming or going, once the Queen's party arrived.

In fact, it was almost evening when the Earl of Leicester escorted Elizabeth and her train across the high causeway with water on each side that reflected the columns decorated with fruit, birds in cages, fish, armour and musical instruments. A cannon salute boomed from the castle, the clock on the tower was stopped at the time of her arrival, and the glittering cavalcade entered the castle bailey like a tidal surge of jewels and lace, silver and gold, faces almost lost in a sea of priceless fabrics, tinkling harnesses, hands lifting and voices laughing in extravagant greeting.

Surrounded by admirers and friends, Adorna stayed well within Peter's range, but was unable to stop herself searching at regular intervals for the Queen's Deputy Master of Horse, lavishly attired in cloth of silver with gold embellishments, and an ostrich-plumed and tasselled cap. His grey stallion was hardly less magnificent.

That evening, wearing the exquisite cream silk gown with an open ruff that enhanced her long neck and lovely bosom, she danced and laughed and flirted as heartily as she had always done, though few could have guessed where her thoughts lay, or how irksome it was for her to see Sir Nicholas apparently so popular with the ladies of the Court, many of whose bosoms were shockingly exposed to view. After the fiasco at the masque, that was something against which she had no intention of competing, the men's leers being with her still.

The earl had invited about thirty other guests, including his sister and her husband and son, and the countess of Essex, whose husband was away on service in Ireland. With all their servants and attendants, it still surprised Adorna that she and Hester had been made so comfortable when many others were being squashed together like rabbits in a burrow. Diplomatically, she did not broadcast her good fortune, though she was unable to prevent Hester from doing so.

'Does Mistress Hester need rescuing, d'ye think?' Peter said to Adorna after the supper had been served. 'She's hardly used to this kind of thing, is she?'

Hester was by now quite out of her depth, her attempts at indiscriminate flirting having given false hopes to a clique of confused and bickering young men, none of whom interested Hester in the slightest. The situation was about to become heated as she was being invited to dance by two equally determined admirers.

'Yes, Peter. Go and calm things down, or there'll be a riot.'

Hester looked relieved as Peter approached, holding out his hand to her. But Sir Nicholas had also noticed and, despite Peter's approach, he too had gone to her rescue, both men now adding to Hester's choices, though with more success. She accepted both their hands, smiled wistfully, and allowed herself to be led away from the disgruntled group without knowing what she had done to cause their discontent.

The musicians, playing the introduction to an allemande, prompted Peter to go one step further and ask Hester to partner him before Sir Nicholas did. Sir Nicholas bowed and stepped back while Adorna, sure that he would continue to leave her to her own devices as he had done all day, prepared to turn back to her friends. Instead, she found her hand being lifted into his and firmly held, not so much requesting as expecting her to join him. The surprise must have shown in her face, though he said not a word to persuade her while waiting for any one of a variety of responses, disdain, scorn or refusal.

She might have taken this chance to snub him in retaliation for his overbearing behaviour that morning, but he had partnered no one else that evening until now, and the thought of allowing the chance to slip past her was more than she could bear, for he was the most exciting partner she had ever danced with. So, with only two reasons to accept and at least a dozen not to, she moved slowly forward with him into the stately beat of the allemande, their eyes having not once unlocked in this duel of wills.

Changing couples moved gracefully forward and backward, meeting and parting, sweeping past, eyes reuniting with hands, bodies swaying and responding, while onlookers stilled to watch the couple who might as well have been alone for all the notice they took of anyone else. The rhythm altered and the pace quickened. As at the masque, they excelled all others in their grace, she in her cream-flowered silk with a shadow of pale violet, he in tones of violet and silver that made it appear as though they had consulted each other beforehand. Once again, they danced for themselves and for each other, their harmony of mind and body temporarily negating previous conflicts as if, for those rare and precious moments, the music was holding them in another world. Neither of them spoke, for there was no need, yet their bodies, hands and eyes said far more than words until, at some time in the distant future, one of them would be prepared to concede.

'Lavolta!' someone called as the music changed again to a determined beat in the Italian style. 'Remove cloaks and rapiers, gentlemen!'

Partnered by an earl stripped down to his doublet, the Queen took the centre of the floor while those about her watched entranced as the two, perfectly matched, executed the complicated movements and astonishingly intimate lifts of this most daring of dances. Then came the signal for others to take over, though there were relatively few who knew it well enough or who had the energy for it. Except Sir Nicholas, who had kept hold of his partner's hand till now, who unbuckled his sword-belt and threw aside his short cloak and drew Adorna straight into the movements without hesitation, appearing to appreciate her ability with a wholeheartedness that quickened every one of her responses.

His lifts threw her high into the air as if she were a child while women yelped with excitement and men stood silent with admiration. And when he lowered her with infinitely slow control down the length of his body, there was nowhere for her to place her hands except round his neck. She had seen it performed before at Richmond, but this was the first time she had danced it, her dancing-master having drawn the line at the capriole. She was breathless with exhilaration, yet not unaware of the fact that it was her partner's expert direction that reminded her of each move; she had only to watch his eyes, feel the pressure of his fingers, the swing of his shoulders.

Sir Nicholas was not the only one to recognise that here was another common ground on which they could be, at least for a time, at peace and in unison. While he held her mind and body in the rhythm of the dance, she was obedient, willing and sweet-tempered, giving in to his control without those recurring doubts and defiances with which she was otherwise besieged. But if this was the key to his success, then it was a fragile one, for who could dance their way through a court-ship?

The others to see the connection were her father and the Earl of Leicester, who stood together as the last beats faded to the dancers' flamboyant courtesies.

'Well, Sir Thomas,' said the earl, watching his deputy lead Adorna towards them. 'As long as you can keep your musicians playing dances you have a chance of keeping your daughter within reach of her partner, it seems. Ah, here they come. Isn't it time we were formally introduced? The last time I saw the lady, she was less than happy with her lot.'

Hearing the earl's last comment, Adorna easily re-called their last meeting when introductions would have been difficult, if not impossible. She sank into a graceful curtsy before him as her father smilingly went through the ritual words, still chuckling from some-thing the earl had said.

'My Lord,' she murmured.

No one could have been surprised by the Queen's long-lasting infatuation with this man whose excep-tional good looks and manly figure were paired with an equally exceptional intelligence and good nature, though they were not by any means his only attributes. His heavy-lidded scrutiny missed nothing as Adorna took his offered hand. 'Mistress Pickering,' he said in a melodious voice that women swooned over, 'wel-come to my humble home. We look forward to enjoy-ing your brother's performance as much as we have enjoyed yours just now with my deputy here. He and I will be offering a performance of our own to Her Majesty tomorrow morning. I shall see that you and Sir Thomas, your brother and cousin are given a good view. I think you'll be impressed.'

'You are most kind, my lord, I thank you.'

'And your quarters? They are comfortable?'

'Indeed they are, my lord,' she smiled. 'We are hon-oured.'

'A small thing to do for one I value so highly, mis-tress.' He glanced at Sir Nicholas and back to her so quickly that, if she had not been watching carefully, she might have missed it. In that moment, her earlier suspicion grew apace. 'I'm relieved to see that it appears to be working, eh, Sir Thomas? You, too?' Bowing to them both, he released her hand and moved away, bending towards Sir Nicholas as he passed. 'Got the Palomino in your stable at last then, man? Well done.'

It was too late for Sir Nicholas to make any reply, the earl already having begun a greeting to others.

Frostily, Adorna took Sir Thomas's arm, pretending not to have overheard. 'Come, Father, it looks as if Hester may need your help.'

'Again?'

They turned together, but Sir Nicholas was already on his way, and Adorna had the dubious pleasure of seeing her cousin's face light up at his approach, her ready acceptance of his hand towards the banquet table. She watched just long enough to see Hester accept a glass of red wine, but not even at the amazing show of fireworks later on did Adorna look again to see where he and her cousin were, though she knew that Peter did, more than once.

Next morning, she discovered from Maybelle that Hester had returned some time later than herself, though it was too dark to see who her escort had been.

Trying hard to play down the impression that Sir Nicholas's attitude towards her appeared to be alternating between the courteous and the severe, Adorna began to waver in her plan to ignore him completely, especially after his warning that any evasion of him would fail. Formerly, this would have made her even more adamant, but his firmness with her had begun to add a new dimension to the affair that filled her with unease, shaking her certainty that she would be able to handle it in her usual way. Clearly, there was nothing usual about it, for never before had any man treated her with such arrogance or left her so unsure about what to expect from him next.

Another awful thought that recurred with sickening force was that her original plan to avert his attentions by throwing Cousin Hester in his path was now also going askew, for Hester seemed to be quite capable of throwing herself in his path without any assistance from Adorna, if her face last night was anything to go by. And that was not supposed to happen except in controlled circumstances. The dancing was all very well, but it had been Cousin Hester he had stayed with after that.

The Earl of Leicester's display of horsemanship before the Queen and her Court was yet another example of Cousin Hester's admiration for Sir Nicholas, for she had been there when he and her uncle had practised together at Bishops Standing. Like the earl, Uncle Samuel had brought over an Italian horseman to teach him the higher arts of equestrianism, the complicated manoeuvres which were now all the rage both here and in France and, like the earl, they had used Grisone's manual of 1550 to teach them how to school their best horses.

Not surprisingly, it was Hester who whispered to Adorna what to watch for as the horses and riders performed on the sand-covered tournament ground, though it was Adorna who was best able to compare

his skills on dancing horses with those she had encountered last night. She also understood the signifi-
cance of the earl's remark when he assured her that
she would be impressed, for he was obviously thinking
of the similarity between the two forms of exercise,
the mutual harmony of two creatures, one of them controlling, one obedient, responsive and supple. The
horses and riders, in perfect accord, turned, pirouetted
and circled, changing direction, every movement
named for them by Hester.

'The levade,' she whispered, as Sir Nicholas's horse
squatted on to its haunches and lifted its front legs
clear of the ground, staying powerfully motionless until he let it down. 'Takes years to teach that,' she said.
'This one's called the piaff, like a trot on one spot.'

'Why doesn't the horse go forward?'

'Because they train it facing a wall so it can't. Sir
Nicholas is so good at this.' The horses were galloped
and pulled up on the spot, wheeling round on their
hocks. Sir Nicholas, according to Hester, was brilliant
at that, too. They changed legs, leapt and cavorted.
'Uncle Samuel would be so proud of him,' she said,
applauding, flushed with pleasure and more animated
than Adorna had ever seen her.

In the privacy of the tower chamber, Maybelle regarded a white lawn chemise with blackwork round
the neckline. 'Plans not working?' she said.

Adorna sighed and glanced at Seton's script that lay
on the window-seat. She had been learning his lines
to keep her mind off other matters. 'Not yet,' she ad-

mitted. 'He doesn't accept the cold-shoulder like others do. He seems to think he's in control.'

The maid searched amongst a pile of clothes on the bed, flinging aside smocks and stockings in annoyance. 'Don't tell me that girl has helped herself to your—' she hauled out a bodice in two parts, stiffened with whalebone '—your pair of bodies,' she said. 'Do you know, I saw her give Mistress Hester a note yesterday that she read and tucked down the front of her bodies. Looked mighty pleased with it, too, she did.'

'Who from?' Adorna said, squirming inside the contraption.

'Now that, mistress, I cannot say. She's not lacking in admirers though, is she?'

'With all that wealth, no one would.' That was uncharitable, and she regretted it, instantly. 'No, well, she's begun to look pretty, too. Prettier clothes, no problem with listening. Men admire that. But I wonder who's sending her notes, Belle.'

'Could be anyone.'

Adorna did not agree, but for want of a better strategy, accepted Maybelle's opinion that her own avoidance tactics had not had much effect so far because she had been too half-hearted about them. With all these daily activities, Belle said, it ought to be possible for any woman to make herself inaccessible. 'If she really wants to, that is.'

'Oh, Belle. I don't know what I want.'

'I think you probably do,' Belle said, pulling at the laces. 'But unfortunately you can't have your freedom,' she grunted, 'and his controlling arms…ugh…

at the same time…ugh…can you? There now. Are you still breathing?'

'Well, that's what *he* seems to want!' Adorna said, testily. 'Having me in his sights doesn't seem to stop him having a good time with whoever he pleases. I wonder how many women he's bedded since he's been here. Too many to count, I expect.'

'Or perhaps none at all. What have you been hearing?'

'Nothing, but I've seen how they swarm around him.'

'Bees swarm,' said Belle, dropping a cloud of underskirt over Adorna's head.

'Flock, then. Silly sheep flock.'

Regardless of her misgivings about the effectiveness of trying to stay out of his way, the programme of events at Kenilworth was so full, as Maybelle had pointed out, that she seemed at last to be managing it. At night, she was reminded of his kisses as well as of his warnings, and tried to recall how far things had gone on the night of the masque, partly to bathe in the bliss of his lovemaking and partly to haunt herself with the folly of it. His dancing whirled her into sleep. His performance with the horses pervaded her dreams except that, here and there, things became confused and she woke to find that the restraint against which she fought was Maybelle's arm across her neck.

The sparkling days of the Queen's visit were indeed packed with a constant round of entertainments of the most extravagant sort where boating on the lake became a sea-symphony of mermaids, dolphins and musicians, and where archery, tennis and jousting became picnics and pageants rolled into one great festival. The feasts sparkled with the earl's best gold and silverware, glass and jewels, ivory and damask, the foods concocted into masterpieces of ingenuity that had taken a fleet of cooks weeks to prepare. When the Queen mentioned that she could not see the knotgarden from her south-facing window, the earl hired men to work in silence throughout the night to construct one on the flat ground below her apartments. By morning, the Queen's new garden was complete.

They hunted, attended masques and a country wedding at which the poor bridegroom hobbled on a broken leg, injured at a game of football. There were more fireworks, bear-baiting, acrobatics and wrestling, water-games and music parties and plays put on by local people who were allowed to attend wherever there was enough space. Even at church, Adorna surrounded herself by a tight company of friends, thereby keeping herself bodily apart from Sir Nicholas, though her father remonstrated, gently. 'You didn't even allow him to help you dismount,' he said.

'Peter was there first.'

'And even at the picnic by the lake…'

'The mare doesn't care for water, Father. I stayed well away from it. It's the ducks, I think.'

'He was waiting to take the mare back to the stables.'

'Well, I sent it with Hester's mount. I'd promised to learn the tennis game.'

'That's not for ladies, Adorna.'

'No, I discovered that, soon enough. Good fun, though. The men beat me.'

'All the same, I believe he's serious about you, if only—'

'Father!' Adorna scoffed, laughing. 'Men like that are not serious for more than a week or so. You know that as well as I do.'

'Then you'd better start reckoning backwards, my lass!' he scolded, watching her swing away. 'If you have a spare moment!' His sarcasm was lost in her laugh.

From the Swan Tower, Adorna's view of the beautiful knot-garden was probably better than the Queen's new one, for this one had the octagonal fountain, the gilded aviary, and the colourful gowns of guests that floated knee-high through hummocks of flowering herbs. An arbour at one end made a tunnel of roses where ladies and gentlemen strolled in the perfumed shade, though by evening they were coupled with the shadows of their lovers, their chatter and laughter muted to whispers, like the fountain. Some of the courtiers called it the paradise like the one at Richmond, though for Adorna it did not have the same connotations until, that night, its scented magic drew her to the window to breathe in the warm air and to search the blue-grey patterns.

Her heart thudded as she recognised the shape of a tall man standing alone on the grassy pathway, his back to the moonlit fountain. He faced the window from which she leaned, his posture telling her that, this time, he was waiting for her and no one else. Across the dark plots of foliage, their eyes met as a silent entreaty was sent again and again, and was rejected. Too afraid of what might happen, or of relinquishing her hard-earned successes, she drew back and closed the shutters. And when she looked out again, much later, he had disappeared. Then she began to reckon backwards.

Chapter Eight

A light shower of rain held the company indoors for most of the morning, giving the Queen a chance to attend to state business and then to rest. It gave Adorna a chance to ride to the sign of the Laurels in Kenilworth to help her father sort out some of the robes; they were getting into a mess, he said.

In an adjoining room of the rambling inn, Seton was nervously biting his nails, already in a lather about his first performance that evening, his voice more unstable than ever.

'Hardly eaten a thing,' Sir Thomas said, busily sorting through piles of used liveries. 'Those are finished with.' He handed Adorna a pile of velvet hats. 'They go in that basket over there. They'll need cleaning up. Poor Seton. I've never known him so nervous. I thought he enjoyed it.'

'I'll go and have a word with him,' said Adorna.

She sat with her brother on his bed where he stared gloomily at the window, his eyes like grey saucers.

'Want me to go through it again, love?' she said. 'It might help.'

'I can't do it,' he croaked, miserably. 'I can't, Dorna. Honest.'

'Oh, come on, love. Of course you...'

'I can't! Not before Her Majesty when my voice is cracking up. I'm a writer, not an actor, and I'm not a woman, either. I have to kiss Master Burbage, Dorna,' he almost squealed in disgust. 'Can you imagine *kissing* Master Burbage at the end?' He stared at her, panic-stricken.

Adorna could not. 'Well, you don't actually...kiss, do you?'

'Yes,' he squawked. 'He insists on being convincing. I can't do it. I shall be sick.'

'Oh, dear,' she whispered. 'There has to be a way round this.' They both knew, at that same moment, where the answer lay, though neither of them wanted to be the one to suggest it. It was unthinkable. Women did not make exhibitions of themselves in public. A woman performer would get the earl and his company—Leicester's Men—into serious trouble with the Revels Office of which their father was the head. Seton would never be employed again, Sir Thomas would lose his office, and she would be talked about for the rest of her life as the woman who acted before a public audience. Personifying a Water Maiden for the Queen's private masque in music and dance was not the same at all. None of the family would live it down if it became known, but nor would the earl gain any favour with the Queen if the leading female role,

Seton, made a mess of the production. Even so, Adorna's involvement was quite out of the question.

'No one need know,' Seton said in a low voice. 'Just this once. You and I are so alike, not even Burbage would know if you wore my wig.'

Adorna stood up, shaking her head. 'It's a nonstarter, love,' she said. 'I'm supposed to be in the audience with Hester. Are *you* prepared to be *me* for the rest of the evening? Don't be absurd. You *have* to go through with it.'

'You know the lines,' he said, bleakly. 'You told me you'd learnt my part.'

'That's nothing to do with it. Now come on, buck up.' She left the room, closing the door with a sigh, knowing she had failed him when he needed her most. 'He'll be all right,' she said to her father. 'He'll have to be, won't he?'

The Queen hunted that afternoon in the forests around Kenilworth, followed by the whole Court who were used to its lengthy rituals, its standing about, its distant removal from the real thing. On occasions such as this, the ladies were not expected to chase after the deer as the men did, but to station themselves with the Queen inside a carefully constructed bower ready to shoot at them as they were driven past. It went without saying that the bolts from Her Majesty's crossbow never missed their mark.

There were some women, however, who chose to join in the chase, people like Adorna and Hester for whom the fun was missing if there was no riding. They were well surrounded, and there appeared to be no obvious reason why any of them should be in danger except, perhaps, from the effects of the recent rain. Yet they had not been galloping long when Adorna discovered that Hester was not amongst the group and that Peter had already pulled up and was heading back towards the woodland. She waited a while and then followed, eventually spotting Hester in her emerald green hunting-dress lying on the wet ground with Peter bending over her.

'She's hurt?' Adorna cried. 'Oh, Peter! What's happened?' She leapt down from the saddle, fearing the worst.

'Don't know. Her mare didn't fall. Must have refused that log. She's had a nasty tumble, poor lady. Looks to be in a bad way.' His face was a picture of concern.

'Careful, she may have broken something.'

Hester was not unconscious, nor did she have any visible signs of injury, only a badly muddied gown, much loosened hair, and a face contorted with pain. 'Oh, dear,' she moaned. 'Oh, dear. Is that you, Adorna?'

'Yes, dear. Me and Master Fowler. Lie still. Let him lift you.'

Peter was strong and Hester was not particularly heavy. Between them, they managed to lift her on to his saddle where he held her before him all the way back to the castle, Adorna following with the chestnut mare. This was a worrying development. Her father would say that they should have stayed with the Queen and her other guests. Poor Hester. It was unlike her to part company with the saddle, for her horsemanship was one of her stronger attributes.

They took her back to the Swan Tower where Ellie, full of sympathy for her poor mistress, helped to undress her and put her to bed, though neither Adorna nor Maybelle could find the slightest sign of bruising. 'It's my head,' Hester moaned. 'My head hurts so badly. I think I must have hit it when I fell. Oh, dear!'

'Rest,' Adorna said. 'Ellie will bring you a warm posset from the kitchens and we'll stay here. Thank goodness Peter found you. It's not like you to take a fall, is it? Was the ground slippery, or was it the mare?'

'Treacherous,' said Hester, holding her forehead.

'I think I may seek the advice of her Majesty's physician,' said Adorna. 'You may have done more damage than we can tell. You're obviously in great pain.'

'No…oh, no! Don't do that. I shall be well enough with some rest. Really. Just rest and quiet. That's all I need. I'm not used to all this activity, you know. Maybe it's all been a little too much for me after such a journey.'

'Poor Hester. You'll miss tonight's entertainment.'

'Yes, I shall not feel like attending yet another event. It's too much.' She turned her head on the pillow and closed her eyes, snuggling into the soft coolness with a sigh.

Leaving Ellie in command, they left Hester to sleep in peace, though Adorna's prime thoughts were for some professional attention for the patient. Her secondary ones were for the evening's activities, the play being scheduled for after supper. For Seton's sake, she must help him to prepare; that was the least she could do.

She told her father about Hester's accident later that afternoon as he came to escort her to supper, though she felt that his reaction to her cousin's distress was a little hard-hearted.

'She'll be all right,' he said, outside the door. 'I expect she's fallen off a horse plenty of times before, though I doubt she's received anything like the attention she's getting now. If you were to ask me, what she needs most is a bit of fuss. Let her stay there.'

'But what about her head, Father?'

'If it's anything like her father's it'll be a damn sight harder than yours. Nothing much wrong there or there'd be other symptoms. Take a look at her urine in the morning. Now then, come on, I'm starving.'

'Should I stay with her this evening?'

'What, and miss Seton? No!'

Seton did not appear at supper, and by that time Adorna's concern for him had done little for her own appetite. She made her excuses as soon as the Queen had left the hall and went to search the small chambers set aside for the actors' dressing-rooms. It took some time to find him amongst the orderly chaos of costumes and props, assistants and actors, every cramped space piled with baskets of weapons, wigs, wine-jars and shoes, but when she did, her worst fears were confirmed. In a small chamber lit by a pair of candles he sat alone with his head in his hands, shaking with fear and as white as a sheet.

'Heavens above!' Adorna said, closing the door quietly behind her. 'Where's your dresser? Don't you have one?'

'Dressing Master Burbage,' Seton whispered. Beads of sweat sprinkled his forehead like dew. 'I've told him I can manage. I thought you might come.'

'Well, we can make a start, can't we? Oh, dear, love, you *must* try.'

The effort of speaking made him double up over a basin, his stomach cramping with another spasm of pain. 'Dorna,' he gasped. 'Help me!'

The dead weight of fear grew at the bottom of her lungs. 'Don't you have an understudy?' she said, mopping the dark points of hair at the back of his neck. 'There must be somebody else, surely?'

'No,' he said, miserably. 'Nobody.'

She had always been stronger than Seton, and the thought of seeing him fail in front of so prestigious an audience tore at her heart. She could not let him do it. Moreover, the situation had changed since morning and now her absence from the audience would be taken as an indication that she was with Cousin Hester. 'I don't know the stage directions,' she said, flatly, eyeing the large wig of brown hair. 'I've no idea what to do.'

'It won't matter,' said Seton. 'You'll pick it up from the script, and the others will help you like they do with me.'

'This is ridiculous,' she snapped, gently.

'Please,' he whispered.

'Tch! Put a chair against the door. Where does Master Burbage dress?'

'Next door. I can hide in here while you're on. No one will come.'

'I hope you're right. Show me what I'm supposed to wear and tell me what I'm supposed to know, or my performance will be worse than yours.'

Even to Seton himself, the transformation was truly remarkable. Having no need of padding, Adorna used the extra time to fit the bulky wig over her own hair, a problem that Seton with his trimmed fair locks did not share. Their features were so alike that it required only the stage rouge, lip-carmine, soot-darkened eye-lashes and brows to change her into Seton's Beatrice, and by the time they had found a large clothes basket for Seton to hide in, she was primed about what to do in the first act. The second and third would have to wait. The call came almost immediately. She took a deep breath.

Master Burbage peered at her in the dim passage-way. 'You all right, lad?' he said. 'Let's have a look at you.' He moved her towards the nearest flickering torch on the wall and looked pointedly at her bosom. 'Hm! You seem to have got that lot in the right place for a change instead of stuck under your chin. Now don't let your voice squeak, lad, eh? And keep your head up. That's it. Right, let's get on with it, then.'

'Yes, sir,' Adorna said, following him.

Until that first public performance, she had sus-pected nothing of the inner excitement, the power, or the extra level of experience that acting could bring. She forgot Seton, Sir Nicholas, the Queen and the earl, her father, the audience, even Master Burbage, the principal and most experienced actor. He was Benedict and she was Beatrice and, while she was separated from everyone else in that large hall by a footlight of glowing torches, another life enveloped her.

The story took her into an experience similar in many ways to the one she shared with Sir Nicholas, disliking and being a little afraid of a man, yet being totally bewildered by an overpowering attraction that could not move beyond a battle of two minds, both of them so determined not to yield an inch that their fragile relationship seemed doomed to failure. Consequently, she brought to the part an authenticity that Seton could not, and an innate love of performing that not even she had realised until then. She knew the lines as if they were hers; the stage directions she either picked up through some extra sense or made them up as she went along, the other players following her rather than the other way round. James Burbage was a good actor, yet he too was surprised to see his Beatrice take on a new realism that he could never have foreseen. The audience were enthralled, greeting each scene with ecstatic applause, carrying her, lifting her confidence.

She hurried back to Seton at the end of each act but found him fast asleep in the basket. Placing a coat beneath his head, she left him there and went on with the deception, floating on her success into the next two acts. It was as if she knew not only the words but the feelings behind them, the pretences and heartaches, the self-deception and the love she dared not admit, adding a new layer of meaning to Beatrice's simplest lines by her expressions and gestures. When the two lovers came to Beatrice's last heart-stopping admission that she could no longer maintain her coldness, the one she had read to Sir Nicholas in the garden, James Burbage responded with the most moving speech of his life, which had been written by Sir Nicholas himself. The kiss that Seton had dreaded followed so naturally from their reconciliation that Adorna felt no sense of strangeness, for they were still in a private world of their own. Apparently Mr Burbage suspected nothing, nor did he have any reservations; he was, as Seton had said, all for a convincing act.

At the end, the audience went wild, laughing and crying, rising to their feet, utterly won over by the magic of it all. It was many minutes before the actors were allowed to leave, by which time Adorna's scrutiny of the audience had shown her that Sir Nicholas was not amongst them.

Behind the scenery, Master Burbage and the other actors poured out their congratulations. 'Well done, lad,' the great actor said. 'That was some performance you gave. I knew you had it in you. Well done. Now, go and get cleaned up before we go and see Her Majesty.'

'Yes, sir, thank you. Shall you go on? I'll see you there in a little while. I need a rest first.'

'A rest? Oh, yes, of course.' He studied her closely,

but his eyes showed nothing unusual. 'But you'll come, won't you? His lordship expects us.'

Trembling with relief and elation, she was swept along the passageway, just managing to open the chamber door and close it again before anyone could follow her. What she saw brought her down to earth with a crash. 'Oh…God…no!' she whispered.

'Beatrice?' said Sir Nicholas. He had been sitting on a stool opposite the open basket where Seton still slept like a child, but now he rose to meet her, taking her hand and drawing her away from the door. 'He doesn't look at all well,' he said, following her eyes.

'He's not,' Adorna snapped. 'But look…this is not his fault. And why do *you* have to be here? If you suspected something, couldn't you have kept it to yourself for a while? There's no harm done. No one else has noticed, not even Master Burbage.' She kept her voice low but there was no hiding her fury. Still tightly wound-up from her performance, she was still Beatrice being brought too suddenly back to reality. 'Couldn't you have let it go?'

She sat on the stool he had just vacated, shaking with exhaustion and a return of the earlier fear that the worst had actually happened, despite the success of the play. Seton's play. Her eyes skimmed over his elegant Court dress, pale grey velvet and white satin, cloth of silver spangled with gold and, instead of a ruff, the collar of his shirt was a falling-band of fine lace that framed his square jaw. He was not smiling, but there was an admiration in his dark eyes that made her blush beneath the rouge. She pulled her hand out of his, feeling suddenly ridiculous in the brown wig and Beatrice's strangely gaudy clothes. 'Well, I expect you can't wait to go and break the news to everyone. Don't let me detain you, sir.'

Sir Nicholas poured a beaker of ale and handed it to her. 'We can discuss the implications later, if you wish,' he said, calmly watching her drink. 'But now we have to get you out of those things quickly and get Master Seton back on his feet. He'll be expected to join Master Burbage before long. Come on, my lass, this next bit of acting will have to be every bit as good as the last. Now, where do we start? With that dreadful wig?'

'I need Maybelle,' she said, bleakly. 'It's Seton who needs your help, not me.'

'Then I'll get her. Leave it to me.'

Outside the door, he took hold of a passing lad by the scruff of his neck. 'Hey, lad! What's your name?'

The lad flattened himself against the panelling. He was young, stage-struck, and not supposed to be back-stage at all. 'It's Will, sir. Please, sir, I'm not thieving, sir, honest. Let me go back, sir. Please.'

'You were in the audience just now?'

'Yes, sir. With my father. It was brilliant.'

'Then run as fast as your legs can carry you to the Swan Tower and ask for the young lady called Mistress Maybelle. Say Sir Nicholas has sent you. Escort her back here. Fast, boy!'

In less than ten minutes Maybelle was with Adorna, her fingers rebraiding the pale blonde hair and coiling pearls into the strands as it had been before. Then, with the stage-paint removed, the true beauty took shape once more, the oyster and cream silk petticoats and bodice, the tiny lace ruff, the ropes of pearls and the earrings, the stockings and slippers. Maybelle missed no detail. 'Is Master Seton going to be all right?' she whispered.

Adorna glanced across to the corner where Sir Nicholas was holding a wet cooling rag to her brother's forehead. 'He will be,' she said, 'but he needs some of that black stuff on his lashes. That's the worst part to remove.'

As Maybelle obliged in the deception, Adorna's fears grew, for now two people knew of the offence. 'That messenger you sent,' she said to Sir Nicholas. 'Does he know, too, d'ye think?'

'Not a chance.'

'Is he one of the company?'

'No, he's a little eleven-year-old lad from Stratford-upon-Avon, about three hours' walk away. He came to see the festivities with his father, a glove-maker. Will, his name is. Will Shakespeare. I gave him two pennies and he thinks Master Seton is the Archangel Gabriel. Stop worrying. It's time we were out of here. Are you ready to go?'

'I'm ready. But…Sir Nicholas…are you going to…?'

He took her by the shoulders and spoke so that only she could hear. 'You think I'm going to shout about this from the rooftops? Think again, woman.'

'I see. So there'll be a price to pay, will there? I should have known.'

'I think,' he replied, 'that this is neither the time nor the place to be discussing terms. Later on, perhaps. Come, you are now Mistress Adorna Pickering who has come with her maid to attend her brother after his performance. You, of course, didn't see it, but you heard from me that he was quite sensational. And you will, naturally, stay close by my side at all times.'

'Of course,' she said. 'How could I think otherwise?'

Seton, pale but steady, had been perspiring and shivering and, now that his lashes had been darkened, had the look of an exhausted actor more convincingly than his sister did. Although the stomach-cramps and sickness had abated, he was still far from recovered. 'It'll pass,' he whispered. Then, like a child, he threw his arms around Adorna and hugged her. 'Thank you, love. Sir Nicholas has told me you were amazing. The best ever, he said.'

'Must have been the rehearsal we had,' she said. 'But Seton, you'll have to pretend now, just the same. It was *you*, remember.'

'Yes, love. I know. I'll do it. You go and enjoy the rest of the evening.'

Over Seton's shoulder, her eyes met Sir Nicholas's and now, as well as admiration, there was something in them she found difficult to read but which might conceivably have been triumph.

The dramatic change from Beatrice's brunette to Adorna's startling fairness no doubt helped to make any comparison more difficult, especially when she rejoined the company with her brother at her side, whose boyish good looks were what everyone expected to see. While he was instantly surrounded by applauding people, Adorna and Sir Nicholas went without delay into a stately pavane that had begun to form to the musicians' first notes, the concentration needed for its measured steps being exactly what was required to draw her mind into some kind of order. Its four-four-time beat a way into her heart, pacing it, slowing it, moderating it to accept what had happened and what was about to happen, events no longer under her control.

She had read his face correctly. He was triumphant about the outcome of her grave offence, about his prediction and about reminding Master Seton of his sister's talents. As he had suspected, it was not only acute stage-fright from which the lad was suffering but also a stomach infection so common on visits to different parts of the country where food was handled by all and sundry. Somebody always caught it. But Seton's loss had been his gain, the lady's mind already seeking a bargain for his silence, a development he had no intention of refusing if it was offered. He would never have told a soul what had happened that evening. He loved the courage she had shown by saving her brother from humiliation. But although she obviously believed he, Nicholas, intended some kind of blackmail, he would not be surprised if she used the situation, unconsciously of course, to do what she could not otherwise do without appearing to change her mind. Like

Beatrice, she was a proud woman, not used to backing down without a very good reason. This, for her, would be the best of all possible reasons. It would salve her conscience.

The pavane finished and her second ordeal began with a volley of comments about Master Seton's amazing performance. She handled it well, as he had expected her to do, and when he thought she had had enough, he took her elbow and led her away, to her relief, he thought.

Her father could not be kept at arm's length. 'Adorna! Ah, there you are. What a pity you missed Seton, m'dear. You were right about him, you know. He *was* all right. You should have heard that last scene, though. Not quite as I remember reading it, but absolutely marvellous writing and acting.'

'He's not too well though, Father.'

'Rubbish! He's as fit as a fiddle when he has to be, our Seton. I saw him. How's Hester?' Maybelle had told Adorna how Hester was sleeping, but Sir Thomas's enquiry held no real interest, for he was already looking elsewhere. Again, she responded quickly to the gentle tug on her hand.

'Come,' Sir Nicholas murmured. 'You need something to eat.' Normally, she would have argued, but not this time. He found a quiet corner where they could speak in low tones while a troupe of acrobats performed spine-bending contortions. He brought her a platter heaped with tiny pastries, gilded marchpanes and biscuits, a goblet of watered wine.

She drank it without comment but could not wait

for her mouth to empty before launching into the subject uppermost on her mind. 'Well?' she said. 'What's the price to be, sir? Is this to be the start of it?'

Sir Nicholas took a gold star-shaped biscuit and scratched the foil off at one corner to reveal the brown underneath. He looked at it hard and then ate it. 'This?' he said. 'Meaning what?'

'You know what I mean. My company for your silence.'

'Is that what you are offering me? Your company?'

'Isn't that enough?'

He sat up and turned to her, helping himself to another biscuit. 'I think, mistress, that you had better let me ask the questions while you supply some answers. Yes?' He picked a crumb off her chin and ate it. 'Now, it makes more sense if you tell me what my silence is worth to you. Have you thought—?'

'Well, of *course* I've thought, Sir Nicholas!' she snapped, taking the pastry from him on its way to his mouth. 'I've done nothing *but* think. This is as serious for Master Burbage and the company as it is for our family, yet it would have been equally serious for his lordship if Seton had performed tonight.'

'Shh! Keep your voice down.'

'But if you are quite determined to make some capital out of it, I can't prevent you.'

'Yes, you can.'

'Well, that's arguable. You know how it is when people make demands. They keep on making greater ones.'

'So I believe. Just as well then that I haven't made any, isn't it?'

'You've been careful, I grant you that. Still, the implication is there.'

'It is?'

'And you know how opposed I am to what you have in mind.'

'What do I have in mind? Remind me.'

'I will. You said I would come to you within days. You planned this days ago, didn't you? You must have.'

'If you mean, my lovely Adorna, that I knew Seton would be unwell tonight of all nights, then you must think I've been blessed with second sight. If you mean that I had a hunch he'd try to persuade you into it then, yes, I did. But as for planning anything, well, that would hardly have been possible, even for me. However, you *have* come to me, and so far so good. Now it remains for you to decide, as I said before, exactly what my silence is worth to you.'

'You mean…how far…?'

'I mean,' he said, helping her out, 'that the time has come for us to be seen as a pair, for me to have prior claim to you at all times, and for you to make yourself more accessible to me.'

'In other words, to add me to your list.'

'Ah,' he sighed, 'the list again. No, I'll scrap the list and start a new one, if you like, with your name on it alone. Will that do?'

'For how long? Are we speaking of days? Weeks? Months?'

'I shall let you decide, but I had years in mind.'

'Now I *know* you can't be serious.' Her hands twisted the rope of pearls that hung down to her waist. 'You realise, don't you, that this kind of bargain goes against all my intentions? I would rather you had demanded money.'

'I have money, thank you. And I haven't demanded anything. I asked you to make me an offer and you have done.'

'Same thing.' She did not contradict his statement, though she could have done.

'If you say so. Nevertheless, it had better be understood that you have accepted me as a suitor and that, to all intents and purposes, you are mine. My lady, my woman, call her what you will. There will be no more evasions or refusals.'

If that pronouncement had come a mite faster than she expected, it must have showed on her face, for her eyes filled with deep concern. 'We're not talking about...you know...are we?' Her voice was breathless, almost lost beneath the peals of raucous laughter that filled the hall.

He put out a forefinger and tenderly smoothed away the folds between her eyes that had puckered with her words. 'Easy...easy,' he whispered. 'One step at a time, eh? I'll not go too fast for you.'

'You did before, I think.' Her voice found an accusing ring.

He had by now turned himself to her so closely that their faces lay openly exposed to every nuance of expression, and although Adorna had proved her ability to act, there was neither script nor make-up nor scenery to help her here. Her concerns were never more genuine than those he saw in her eyes at this moment, for she had backed herself into a corner and was already fighting at shadows. Metaphors, he thought, could be so apt at times like this.

'Yes,' he said. 'I did, didn't I? There was a challenge, I seem to remember. Irresistible, in the circumstances, but no harm done.' He saw her eyes flash, angrily. 'Maybe I should start at the beginning again, d'ye think?' But her thoughts on the matter were hidden as he watched her eyelids close over them, the softness of her lips being the only reply he needed. He felt the intake of her breath as his mouth claimed hers, and he knew a pang of pity for the conflict that raged within her, like Beatrice, wanting yet furiously denying, and angry with herself for this blatant self-deception. For her sake, he would pretend she had no choice, yet the one question she could, and should, have asked was the one she had studiously avoided. *Did he intend to expose the two actors?*

The kiss ended. Her eyes opened and shifted, nervously. 'In public?' she whispered.

'It's allowed, between lovers.'

'My father…!' She placed her hands against his chest.

'He approves of me.'

'How d'ye know?'

'He told me so.'

Her lips tightened. 'I thought as much. But what about Hester?'

'She does, too.'

The fine brows squirmed. 'That's not what I meant.'

'Then what did you mean?'

'You know…'

'No, I don't. Hester and I are friends of long standing, that's all.'

'That's not what Hester would like to believe.'

Their eyes, inches apart, searched for more information until Sir Nicholas asked with a frown. 'Exactly what would Hester like to believe?'

Adorna looked beyond his ear to the dark silhouettes of figures and the occasional face that turned in their direction. 'She's very fond of you. She speaks of you, often.'

The facetiousness returned. 'Hester speaking often. That's new. Then I shall keep her on the old list. There, how will that do?' When she made no reply, he moved away carefully and stood up, taking her hands and pulling her upright. 'Come on,' he said. 'As soon as Her Majesty leaves, I'll take you back. And listen…' he pulled her even closer until she was within his arms, ignoring the open stares and smiles '…I'm going to suggest to your father that your brother stays here in the castle with me. I have a man who'll tend him. He needs rest and time to prepare for the next play. Have you seen the script yet?'

'I have a copy, yes. I've read it.'

'Good. Let's hope he's well by then.'

The next play was to be in three days and Sir Nicholas did not believe that Seton's problems would be gone in that time. Rather the opposite. Sir Thomas

Pickering, however, would be hard to convince that the problem existed at all. He would insist that Seton pull himself together: Seton would be a disaster: questions would be asked about how he could be so bad after being so good: the truth would be sought and Seton would admit the deceit. It was essential that Adorna should prepare, and that Seton should be kept calm until then. The play could be cancelled, of course, but the earl needed all the credit he could accrue and disappointments would not help.

'Sir Nicholas,' Adorna said, pushing gently at his chest, 'people are looking, and I'm not used to being seen like this.'

He was unmoved. 'Gets easier with practice,' he said.

Half-an-hour later, Adorna was beginning to understand something of what it meant to be seen as Sir Nicholas's new lady, a kind of emotional captivity she had sworn to run from until she grew too old, docile or broody to run any more. Which she had hoped would be light years away, God willing. With the full force of her antagonism brought back by the chill of the dark summer night, she rebelled against the decision she herself had taken only an hour ago. 'I suppose the Swan Tower was your doing, too,' she panted, trying to free herself from his grasp as he held her back against the wall. 'Which is why you were...let me go!'

'Not surprised to see you? Of course, woman. Yes, I had you invited to Kenilworth; what use is it having

the earl as patron if one doesn't make use of the connection, once in a while? I knew you'd come.' He held
her hands together in a cruel grasp. 'At least you're
comfortable here.'

'I should never have come. It was a mistake.'

'You couldn't stay away, could you? You knew
what would happen.'

'No, that's not—'

His mouth closed over hers, stopping the last futile
protest, his body attuned to her every move, sensing
the exact moment of her surrender. To reinforce his
victory, he made it last.

There were to be no more words that night, she
having digested as many in one short time-span as she
had in a whole week, and he having achieved his aim
by different methods. He took her to the door of her
room and delivered her to Maybelle. 'She's had
enough for one day,' he told the maid. 'Straight to
bed.'

Maybelle recognised the new development immediately; no man except her father had ever told her
mistress to go to bed, that she had had enough. 'Yes,
sir,' she said, marvelling at Adorna's compliance.

The damage had been done and there was now little
or nothing she could do to undo it, however much she
vacillated over the solution that had all too readily
been accepted. She had wept before falling asleep and,
understanding her mistress as well as she did, Maybelle had rocked her to sleep in her arms without ven-
turing any opinion one way or the other. The confusion was great enough to be left alone.

* * *

In the morning, some of the old opposition surfaced alongside premonitions of disaster. 'What am I to tell Peter?' she said to Maybelle, holding her foot out for a soft blue kid slipper. 'He'll think I've gone mad after all he's been helping me to do to avoid Sir Nicholas.'

'If Master Fowler isn't used to your ways by now,' Maybelle said, straightening the blue silk skirts, 'then he never will be. I shouldn't waste too much pity there, if I were you. Besides, he'll have to move on to the next venue soon, won't he?'

'Mmm, Staffordshire. But what about Hester? She's going to be a bit put out, to say the least. She was entertaining some hopes, Belle.'

'Mistress Hester's not going to be entertaining anything for a day or two, and then she'll have to accept that she doesn't stand a chance. Well, not for a while, anyway,' she added with unfortunate candour.

'No, not until he returns to the original contenders.'

The cynicism was not lost upon the maid. It was time for some plain speaking. 'Look,' she said, sitting on the chest opposite Adorna, 'things have moved on. *You*'ve moved on. And if Sir Nicholas has got Sir Thomas's approval, as you say he has, then he'll have to be careful what he gets up to, won't he? If you stop to think about it, he was actually helpful last night after the performance, and he's going to look after Master Seton, which is more than most men would do. And anyway, you'll probably tire of him by the time he's tired of you, then you can both go your own ways again.' Her barb found its target.

'The whole point, Belle,' Adorna scolded, 'is that

he *will* find someone else who takes his fancy *long*
before I do, and that is *precisely* why I didn't want
anything to do with him in the *first* place. I'd rather
not be one of his old flames if I can't be...' She put
up her hands to cover her face.

'Can't be what? The last love of his life?'

'I thought you knew that,' she said, hoarsely.

I did know that, Maybelle said to herself. *How could
I not know?*

Later that morning Adorna found that her father had
already been approached about allowing Seton to stay
in Sir Nicholas's quarters and had given his immediate
consent. She suspected that he welcomed the move by
Sir Nicholas to involve himself with the Pickering
family, but she made no mention of it even when Sir
Thomas teased her about Peter's reaction to her apparent change of heart. 'Spent the evening looking like
a dog that's lost its best bone.' He laughed. 'Didn't
you see him glowering?'

'No, Father. I didn't.'

'Not surprised. You were otherwise engaged,
weren't you? Still, I'm pleased to see you and Sir
Nicholas on better terms. He'll look after you.'

It was not long before Master Fowler found his way
to Sir Thomas's side with a similar custodial request
that had nothing to do with Adorna or Seton. His concern was for Mistress Hester. 'She's quite unwell, sir,
so I'm led to believe,' he said as they walked together
over the moat-bridge to the castle. 'She has quite a

delicate constitution. I wondered if I should escort her back to Richmond.'

'No!' Sir Thomas said, with a usual lack of sympathy. 'The Pickerings are not as delicate as all that, lad. She'll be fine after a day's rest.'

'But the conditions in the Swan Tower are not spacious, and—'

'And she'll be as bored as hell at Richmond. She's created quite a stir here amongst the young men, our heiress. No, she'll be fine. Leave her where she is.'

Aware of the Pickering obstinacy, Peter knew better than to press the point, for it could be argued that a journey was not the best cure for a sore head.

There was a tournament in the Queen's honour that day. Sir Nicholas was splendidly equipped in a suite of shining jousting armour, his helm topped by a tall crest of dyed ostrich feathers that echoed those set between his horse's ears, while embroidered on his horse's caparison were his family coat of arms like those on his shield. Round his upper arm he wore a streamer of cream satin ribbons which Adorna had removed from her own girdle to tie there in full view of the spectators, which had seemed to both of them to be some kind of turning point in their new relationship. The spectators, seated on stands draped with costly silks, had applauded, and although Sir Nicholas was well known for his skills at jousting, she had whispered private prayers for his safety throughout the contests. The action was brutal and fierce, despite the blunted lances; a fall in full armour from a careering horse injured many a knight that afternoon.

Adorna hid her concern from the friends with whom she sat to watch, just as she secretly hoped he would do nothing more to demonstrate his new hold over her. But he did better than that, sending a message to request her presence in his arming-tent, an invitation she was strongly urged by some of the young men to ignore. The young women laughed enviously, chiding her on her fickleness, knowing her teasing games and wondering if, this time, she was about to get her come-uppance from the accomplished knight.

She was not inclined to risk the consequences of a refusal. She was led to his blue-and-white chequered pavilion by his squire, a young man of impeccable manners and lineage whose face gave no sign that he might have performed the same kind of errand dozens of times before. He held the tent-flap open for her, bowed, and left her to face Sir Nicholas alone inside the shady canvas.

He had not finished dressing, but was tucking his white linen shirt into his breeches as she entered, the fabric sticking to his body as if he had not had time to dry, and showing a wide V of chest thickly forested with dark hair. His hair, still wet from his bath, fell onto his forehead in a tumble of spiked curls, and on one cheek was a red bruise where his helm had buffeted him. Adorna had seen her two brothers and her father in similar stages of undress more than once, but no domestic scene at home could have prepared her for this encounter. Her first reaction was to make a quick exit.

He caught her in one long-legged bound that startled her with its speed, drawing her into the tent with the kind of soft sound he would use to a startled filly. 'Whoa...whoa...lass!' he laughed. 'Shh! I'm dressing, not undressing. Sit ye down here, see.' He led her firmly to his arming-chest, slammed the lid shut and eased her down on to it, standing between her and the exit to prevent a departure.

There were two angry spots of red on her cheeks. 'There is no need for this, Sir Nicholas,' she said, refusing to look at him. 'I know what a man looks like.'

He squatted on his haunches before her, his knees enclosing her full skirt. 'Then why did you think of bolting?' he whispered, touching her cheek with one finger. It meandered gently downwards over her bare neck while she held her breath and let it out slowly, finding it impossible to answer him, his touch drawing all her senses towards a delicious peak of delight. He held her eyes with his own as he traced a path over the swell of her breasts and lingered, caressing the softness above the hard edge of her bodice. She knew, at the back of her mind, that he had been further than that and that he remembered it better than she. His eyes were telling her so.

The caress continued. 'Well, lady?' he said. 'Did you pray for me to win? Do I deserve your approval?'

'Yes,' she whispered. 'I did. You do.'

'And you are going to reward me?'

'Isn't this…this your reward?' she gulped, trying to take hold of his wrist.

His hand twisted and caught hers instead. 'No, it's yours.'

'Then…?'

'This,' he said. He guided her hand to his own throat and left it there. 'Come on,' he whispered.

She hesitated, not knowing that the caress could be almost as exciting for her as it would be for him. Then she found, as she explored, that the hair on his chest was soft, not harsh, and that as she slipped her hand beneath his damp shirt, the warm vibrancy of his skin was like no other sensation she had ever encountered, the contours being quite different, the softness only skin-deep over iron-hard muscles.

Suddenly aware that she was enjoying it against her will, her hand changed course, slipping upwards to his cheek where her fingers came to rest against the raw bruise. She caught the approval in his eyes, his maddening controlled approval. This had, of course, been a lesson. She snatched her hand away. 'So controlled, Sir Nicholas,' she said, turning her head. 'Always so very controlled.'

He brought her back to face him with his fingers beneath her chin. 'And that's something else you're not used to, isn't it, my lass? But you will. You're learning to come to me.' He stood upright, pulling her to her feet. 'And that's a good start.' She would have loved to prove him wrong, but he seemed to read her mind. 'No, we'll go together,' he said. His kiss was sudden and hard like his grip upon her arms, and she was left with tears burning her eyelids and no words to wound him as she would have liked.

They did leave the tournament ground together, she riding pillion on a cushion behind him with one arm about his waist from where she could see the expressions on the faces of those who had witnessed her earlier attempts at avoidance. She saw nothing in them to offer her any comfort, only various renderings of 'I told you so.' Nor could she escape the foreboding that she must now be prepared for similar public displays of his victory in the days ahead. That was a development she had not anticipated, though it would have made little difference if she had. Nor did it seem that she would be allowed to balk, his hands on the reins having noticeably tightened, so to speak.

She was relieved to find that Peter's attitude to his loss was more philosophical than the sulk her father had described. 'I saw it coming,' Peter said. 'We can still be friends?'

'Of course we can,' Adorna said. 'I don't intend to lose friendships this way. It'll not last. Give it a few weeks. Months, at the most. You'll see.'

'Are you talking about you, or him?' said Peter, though he neither expected nor received a reply.

Slightly more disturbing was the nagging problem of Seton, whose continuing and acute nervousness threatened to call a halt to his association with Leicester's Men. After the brilliant performance before the Queen, Master Burbage said, he was not prepared to coach one of the other young men in the part if there was the slightest chance that Master Seton would by then have overcome his tiredness and stomach upset, which were the reasons given for Seton being unavailable to rehearse. He was therefore in complete agreement with Sir Nicholas that Seton should be given total peace in which to study. There was still, however, the problem of rehearsals.

'He was rather under-rehearsed on that last one,' James Burbage told Sir Nicholas, meaningfully. 'Superb, I grant you, but it would have helped if he'd let us know in advance what he was about to do. If you see what I mean, sir?' He stroked his neat beard and waited for the younger man to suggest a solution.

'Then I think the answer, Mr Burbage, is that you and Seton should rehearse in my room, in private. In that way you could discuss stage-directions without tiring him too much before the performance.'

'An excellent notion, sir. And Mistress Adorna? Perhaps she would like to attend the…er… discussions? Just to give her brother some support?'

'I shall see that she is there on each occasion, Master Burbage.'

'Good, good. That's understood, then. Quite a relief!'

Sir Nicholas told Adorna of this arrangement at the masque that evening, after which she became quite certain that Benedict's convincing stage-kiss had not been intended for Seton at all, neither by Sir Nicholas nor Master Burbage.

There was better news about Hester's condition,

though Adorna could not help wondering exactly what the connection could be between her rapid recovery and a letter that she hurriedly pushed under her pillow as Adorna walked into the tower chamber. Not being of a particularly suspicious turn of mind, Adorna put this act of secrecy down to the admirers who had constantly asked about Hester's health, though she wondered why, if it was so innocent, Hester could not have shown it to her. Still, she was relieved to know that Hester did not feel quite well enough to attend the masque, for Adorna wished to delay for as long as possible the news that she herself was now being widely regarded as Sir Nicholas's woman. That, she believed, would do Hester's head no good at all.

Chapter Nine

From the very first of these private rehearsals to which she had been invited ostensibly as an onlooker, Adorna realised that she was in fact the one for whom they had been arranged. Nothing was said to this effect by any of the three men, not a word, nor did Master Burbage consult her except via Seton, while she made her own tentative suggestions as if they were for Seton's consumption rather than for hers. It was all rather bizarre, and although they had to be careful, it appeared to give back to Seton some of the confidence he had lost as a playwright and to restore Master Burbage's stability as principal actor.

What it did for Adorna was less easy to define, except to highlight the way that things had slipped well beyond her control since coming to Kenilworth and how, by the same token, her love for Sir Nicholas verged on hate, so intensely painful was it for her to see him even speak to another woman.

She supposed, in her more rational moments, that her own semi-romantic experiences would have cushioned her from such fears and given her enough self-confidence to deal with love's waywardness. But it was not so. Her dealings had been with boys, youths seeking experience, and widowers looking for second wives, not men like Sir Nicholas who challenged rather than adored. She had heard of jealousy, but had never encountered its terrible madness until this.

'Why are you doing this?' she asked him as they walked through the stable after a meeting. 'One performance was bad enough, but another one makes it even worse. What if I'm found out? Has it crossed your mind that I'll be ruined? And Seton? And the rest of us? Except you, of course.'

They turned into the palomino's stall and stood in the warm space at the mare's side, Sir Nicholas with his arm across the silken coat. 'Well, of course it's crossed my mind,' he said, taking Adorna's hand. At such times he was tender and exceptionally patient. 'But what good would it do your brother to abandon him at this stage, to tell him he must perform as best he can? How would it look now if he had to become Queen Titania of the Fairies? Could you let him do it, sweetheart?'

Her knees quivered at his use of the endearment. 'No,' she whispered, crossly. 'But if he knew how unsuitable he would be for the part, then why did he write it? He dreads this part even more than the other.'

'Well, a playwright doesn't simply write parts that he wants, he writes whatever is appropriate for the occasion. Perhaps Master Burbage suggested the fairy queen theme to him. Who knows?' His hand slipped around her back, easing her into his arms. 'And I can see no other woman who more closely resembles the Queen of the Fairies than the one who'll be playing her. Beautiful, talented, tender-hearted, fierce and womanly, yet still an innocent in so many ways.'

'Then you haven't read Seton's play all through, sir. She's also a flirt and a tease who's not willing to be ruled by a man. She's more vindictive and strong-willed than Oberon thought when he married her.'

'Then if I were Oberon,' he said, touching her cheeks and mouth lightly with his lips, 'I would teach her how to accept him as master. She'd not find it too uncomfortable.'

Adorna eased herself away. 'Then I'm glad you are not, sir. Seton's Oberon is made to prove his constancy. I much prefer that version.'

In retrospect, that was one of the few occasions on which she was allowed to have the last word on a subject so close to both their interests. Maybe, Adorna thought later, it was because he was anxious not to disturb her any more than she was already before the play. Maybe that was why his lovemaking was suspended altogether for those few days, and why she was required only to be seen at his side during the *al fresco* meals in the grounds, the hunting, the water pageants and the dancing, which was, in a way, as close to lovemaking as one could come in public. It suited her well enough, though she did not suppose the situation would continue in that way, judging by his sometimes transparent expressions.

Convinced that Cousin Hester's affections were still

directed more towards Sir Nicholas than anyone else, despite the competition of others, Adorna made every effort to include her in their party so as not to hurt her feelings by any display of fondness. She had no wish to antagonise Hester, being equally sure that, once he got what he wanted, Sir Nicholas's attentions would probably be diverted once more. If Hester was, as he had implied, on his old list, her total innocence in such matters would hardly prepare her for the ebb and flow of inconstant dispositions. Such were the effects of jealousy that coloured Adorna's view of things and showed her the contortions of her own mind rather than what was actually there.

If it had been jealousy alone that caused her to re-main adamantly opposed to being Sir Nicholas's woman, her brother Seton might have been able to make her more aware of it. But there was more to it than that. After one of the discussions in Sir Nicho-las's quarters, Seton stood lethargically by the window watching the door close behind Master Burbage. 'You're in love, aren't you?' he said, quietly.

They had just been over one of the quarrelsome scenes and Adorna's eyes had begun to fill. It was too much for her. She pressed a hand over her bodice. 'Am I?' she said. 'Is that what it is? It hurts.'

'Haven't you told him?' Seton's voice sounded re-assuringly low and manly.

She shook her head. 'He's so…so sure of himself. So confident that I'll give in, as if nobody could resist him. I'm not ready to give in, and when I do it will be to somebody who knows how to hold my heart for life, not just play around with it for a while and then drop it.'

'And what have *you* been doing since you were fourteen?'

'That's different. You know it is. That was just... oh, flirting. Nothing serious.'

'You mean *he* takes women further?'

'Much further.'

'Yet you've allowed yourself to be caught, Dorna.'

'*Allowed* myself?' It was all she could do to keep silent after that, for she could never tell him that it was by helping him out of his dilemma that she had put herself in this position. It had been for him. Or had it? 'Yes, love. I suppose I have, haven't I?' she said at last.

Seton was not the only one that day to remark on Adorna's capitulation, for while the Queen took a ride on the palomino mare that had attracted her attention on several occasions, Adorna was left on one side of the Queen's Irish grey where, unseen by two of the royal courtiers, she became the subject of their speculation.

'So, the Palomino is well and truly stabled then, is she?' one of them said.

'Looks like it, certainly. She took a bit of catching, mind you,' said the other.

'We'll see how long the schooling takes. What'll you wager—weeks or months?'

Then their horses were turned and she caught the word 'mare' and no more. Promptly, she walked the Queen's grey across to Sir Nicholas in full view of the two riders, determined to retaliate. 'Sir Nicholas!' she called. 'We're the subject of a wager, I believe.'

He came riding towards her, smiling, and took from her the grey's bridle. 'Are we really? Tell me, fair lady.'

'There are some here who need to know how long it will take me to school you. Will it be weeks, or months? Are you a difficult colt, sir?'

He understood immediately what had taken place, and his reply was suitably loud enough to reach the ears of the two embarrassed courtiers. 'No!' He laughed. 'Weeks? Never! I'll be eating out of your hand within the hour, sweetheart. Come up, my lass!' He leaned down and extended a hand to her, knowing exactly how to stem the gossip.

Placing one foot on top of his, she grasped his elbow and sprang up behind him, settling herself like a cloak across his back and hugging his waist, relieved by the speed of his response, by his protection, and by his contempt for their critics. For the rest of the ride she clung like a limpet behind him, partly to confound their calculations and partly because it seemed like a wonderful place to be.

For his part, Sir Nicholas wished she would encounter comment like that a bit oftener, if this was to be the result, and made sure that their kiss at the castle stables was seen by the gossips. Nevertheless, Adorna experienced some anger and bewilderment as a result of the men's jest, and wondered how much further things would go before she could find a way out of her plight.

*   *   *

By the time the performance day had arrived, it was scarcely necessary for Seton to plead his case a second time, so sound had been his sister's preparation and so subtle that not even by a gesture had Master Burbage acknowledged that his leading lady might not be Master Seton himself. The company prepared as usual, and Master Seton went to his dressing-room with his sister and her maid to help him dress, while Sir Nicholas kept a careful guard outside the door, having put it about that Mistress Adorna would be staying backstage, the costumes being excessively complicated.

Adorna had tried, that same day, to take some control of her immediate future by asking her father to take her with him the next day when he returned to Richmond with Seton. They were to set out from the inn at dawn. She could meet him there: she longed to be back home, she told him. He refused, as she had half-expected, saying that she was to go on up to Staffordshire with the Queen's entourage. Sir Nicholas would take good care of her and Cousin Hester. He was glad she and Sir Nicholas were getting on so well together. He would tell her mother the good news. If only he knew, Adorna thought.

After all the preparations, the performance itself was an outstanding success, not only because Adorna's disguise was totally believable once more but because her portrayal was consistent with her previous one. Backstage, the presence of Sir Nicholas ensured that no one disturbed her, that Seton remained well hidden, and that it was only Master Burbage who came to give a final check to her appearance. Then, Sir Nicholas es-

caped to the audience. At the end, it was Master Burbage who clapped her on the back with, 'Well done
again, Master Seton! Another great success, my boy!'
in the hearing of the company. 'Now, let this young
man get back to his dressing-room, you lot, and leave
him in peace till later. Eh, young master?'

A stage-hand grabbed him by the arm. 'Master Burbage, sir! Her Majesty wishes to meet the cast. You're
to bring them back, sir!'

Adorna's arms prickled with fright. 'No, Master
Burbage,' she said. 'I cannot do that. You must see...I
cannot!'

He took her to one side, his face still strangely unfamiliar as the grotesque fairy king, his wings lending
another element of unreality to the scene. 'You *can*,
Master Seton,' he whispered. 'Everyone is deceived,
even me. Keep it up. And keep your voice down now,'
he added.

'Down, sir?'

'Yes, down. Master Seton's voice has gone this last
week. Hadn't you noticed?'

Of course. The drop from soprano to baritone was
now complete and it was true that she had hardly been
aware of it. Now she must try to do the same. Her
head reeled, dizzily.

Fanning herself with a massive cluster of coloured
feathers, the Queen scrutinised the actors who dropped
to their knees before her, not knowing how the fairy
queen quaked before the dozens of eyes that examined
her in minutest detail from head to toe. It was the
Queen's questioning, however, that was almost

Adorna's undoing, and had it not been for Master Burbage's quick thinking, she might have given the game away.

As always, Her Majesty was gracious. 'I hear that your brother is a keen actor, too,' she said to Adorna. 'We must try to persuade him to perform with the company to see how he does. Is he presently at Richmond?'

Adorna's efforts to reproduce Seton's new voice were thrown off-track by talk of a brother. 'Er...no, Your Majesty, he's in the...' she squeaked and growled alternately, completely at a loss. Where was he?

Master Burbage stepped in quickly. 'Master Adrian stayed at Richmond, Your Majesty. He wishes to perform with us like Master Seton here, but he is still young. They make a talented pair, the two Pickering brothers.'

'Indeed. A talented family, Master Burbage,' said the Queen. 'I knew their uncle, Sir William, quite well. He and my lord were rivals for my hand once, eh, Robert?' She turned to the Earl of Leicester, and the discussion swung quite naturally to embrace her doings rather than the players, allowing them to retire at last.

But Adorna was visibly shaken and close to tears at the way, after all their efforts, her over-excited wits had refused to cope with both Seton's newest voice and with her triple-identity before an assembly of eagle eyes, all keen, she was sure, to find fault with her disguise. She sobbed as Maybelle removed the outlandish make-up and restored her looks through the tears, refusing to be comforted by Seton or by the appearance of Sir Nicholas.

But once Seton had left to join the Queen's company, Sir Nicholas took matters into his own hands and, waiting until fewer people were about, he escorted Adorna back to the Swan Tower, though the summer night was still streaked with light in the west.

She was still overwrought. 'No more,' she croaked. 'Never again. I'm done with this charade. My head doesn't work in three directions at once.'

'I'm relieved to hear it,' Sir Nicholas murmured, opening the door of her chamber, 'though I have my doubts on both points.'

'And you shouldn't be up here at this time of night, sir.'

The distant thudding of tabors reached them through the open window, the high whine of viols and pipes, a man's shout and a woman's excited laugh. 'Since you have now rejected all pretence, sweetheart, this seems to be the best place for me to be. There now, it's all over…shh!' He took her gently into his arms as a late sob sent tremors through her body. 'Shh! You were superb, my lovely woman. They'll never have another leading lady like that. Never. But now you can forget the whole thing. Seton and your father and the players leave in the morning, and I can replace Burbage's kisses, can't I? Yes?' He gathered her up and laid her on the bed, slipping her fine kid pumps off her feet and straightening her skirts. 'What you need now is some rest. I'll leave you to Maybelle when she arrives.'

'Oh,' she said.

He smiled and sat beside her, bridging her body with his arm. 'Was that an ''oh'' of relief, or disappointment?'

Unwilling to commit herself to either, she remained silent, but her eyes could not hide the needs of her body now that the last few hours of deception were over. They roamed over his face, lingering on his lips and watching as they came closer. Her eyes closed and her arms lifted to feel the warm bulk of his body pressing her into the coverlet, releasing her into the need that had plagued her for what seemed like years. Eagerly, she took her reward with hardly a pause for breath, surprising him, delighting him.

The door opened without warning, breaking them dreamily apart. Maybelle had returned. But no, it was not Maybelle, it was someone who stood on the threshold for long enough to see what was happening, then closed it again.

Adorna pushed him away. '*Hester!* Oh, no! I don't believe it!'

Sir Nicholas sat up and eyed the door. 'I can't see that it matters,' he said. 'She must know by now, surely?'

'She mustn't!' Adorna said, sitting up. 'Now she'll think…'

'What?' He eased her backwards again and held her there with one hand. 'That we're lovers? Well, if she hadn't guessed before, she'll discover soon enough, won't she? Let her deal with it in her own way, sweetheart, there's nothing you can do about it, and she'll recover from the surprise, take my word for it.'

'It's not me she'll be bothered about, but *you*!'

'Why should she be? Because you think…? Oh, that's lunacy. I told you, we're friends, that's all. It's not my problem or yours if she wants to think otherwise. She'll soon get the idea. Now, you stay there and let Maybelle tend to you.' He turned as the maid entered carrying a bundle of clothes from the Wardrobe. 'Good timing, Belle. I have to go.'

'Where to?' Adorna said, already dreading what he would say.

He showed no sign of impatience at her wariness, but sat down again on the bed and took her hand. 'I am going,' he said deliberately, 'to prepare my lord's horses, coaches and furnishings for tomorrow's events. We'll all be going up to Staffordshire the next day and preparations must be in place by then. I doubt if I shall be in bed much before dawn.' His thumb brushed tenderly across her lips. 'Sober, manly occupation.'

'You had no need to explain,' she said, ashamed.

'No, of course I didn't. Sleep well. It's all over now.' He kissed her fingers and laid the hand on her bodice. 'I bid you both a goodnight.'

Dumping the clothes on the chest, Maybelle closed the door behind him and came to sit on the end of the bed. 'Who'll soon get the idea?' she said. 'Was that Mistress Hester he was talking about?'

Adorna pulled herself upright, swinging her legs over the edge. 'Yes it was. Did you see her?'

'Did I *see* her! She nearly knocked me flying as I came in at the lower door. She went haring across towards the garden as if the hounds were after her. What's wrong?'

Adorna's sigh became a groan. 'Oh, Belle. She saw us, here on the bed. Tch! I'd better go and find her and explain that it's…oh, where are my pumps?'

They were, at that moment, being slowly kicked under the bed by Maybelle's toe. 'Never mind Mistress Hester,' Maybelle said, soothing with her voice. 'Come on, love. You're shattered. It'll do tomorrow. Time enough to explain then if you still think you must, though for the life of me I can't see that it matters. You've got enough on your plate without bothering about Mistress Hester's heart-strings. It's time you were out of this bodice, for a start. Turn round.'

Overpowered by exhaustion and the forces of common sense, Adorna gave in without protest. But the night was a different matter, for then her thoughts refused to leave her in peace.

By daybreak she felt as if she had not slept at all, for she could not agree that Hester's heart-strings were none of her concern, since it was she and Lady Marion who had intended to set them quivering in the first place. She did not believe that Hester had a lover. She believed that the expression on Hester's face had been one of horror and that she would probably not deal with the shock half as well as Sir Nicholas had suggested.

When she found Hester's tower room deserted except for some baskets and a clothes-chest, Adorna assumed at first that she must, after all, have gone with Sir Thomas to Richmond, although this had not been planned. She sent a young page to the inn at Kenilworth to find out, but the reply was negative and her father's party had already left. Nor had Hester's horses been taken from the stable. Adorna's concern grew as she sent two pages to scour the castle in case she had changed her accommodation, but there was still no sign of her or the maid Ellie. Meanwhile, Maybelle asked at the gatehouse that led towards the Warwick road. A lady with her maid and two packhorses had passed through at dawn, refusing to tell the gatekeeper where they were going, though it was obvious to Maybelle they were not intending to meet Sir Thomas, whose exit from Kenilworth was from a different direction.

'You see?' Adorna said. 'She must have packed up last night after seeing Sir Nicholas with me. She's gone, and it's my fault. All my fault. I shall have to get her back, Belle. She's never travelled alone before and she'll not know what to do. I doubt she'll even know which direction home is. She must be very distressed.'

'If she wanted to go home to Richmond she'd have gone with Sir Thomas and Master Seton, wouldn't she?' Maybelle said with disarming common sense.

Leaning on the wide stone window-ledge that overlooked the garden and the keep at the north side of the castle, Adorna gazed at the throng of men, horses and waggons that gathered outside the kitchens. They

had already begun to move off round to the south side
of the bailey to begin the day's events when Adorna
shifted back sharply.

'There's Sir Nicholas,' she said, 'getting the Yeo-
men into position. Now look, Belle, if we're quick
about it, we can pack as much as we can carry and go
after her before they all return. She's only had a few
hours start and we may be able to find her before suppertime.'

'Go without an escort?'

'Well, it doesn't look as if *she* has one, and there's
always Peter. He'll go with us, I'm sure of it.'

'Unless he's gone up to Staffordshire to prepare for
tomorrow.'

'Without saying goodbye?'

'Why would he?' Maybelle's cynicism was justi-
fied, for their search revealed that Master Fowler had
indeed left the castle. Making use of the plain and
comfortable linen clothes that Maybelle had 'collected
for repair' from the Wardrobe last night, they dressed
in the manner of ordinary country women who might
normally have been travelling to market on horseback,
with a packhorse behind them bearing, among other
necessities, food from the kitchens.

It was still a risk, lone women being targets for
rogues, vagabonds and thieves on the loose, and had
Adorna not been hopeful of overtaking Hester before
nightfall, she would have hesitated to set off without
a proper escort. Sensibly, she left her own palomino
in the stables in favour of a large gentlemanly bay
gelding which, she hoped, would be less conspicuous

to fellow-travellers. The stable-lad had not thought of asking why, or refusing them the use of a sturdy cob for Maybelle and a packhorse with panniers. He had even helped them to load it, believing it to be a part of the disguisings that took place every day, in one form or another.

Danger, however, seemed remote in the bright morning sunshine, the main concern being Cousin Hester's safety, her vulnerability and the wretchedness she must be suffering It was up to Adorna to put the matter right, to explain that Sir Nicholas's interest was only likely to be temporary. She said as much to Maybelle as they tried, with limited success, to pass through the eastern gatehouse without being recognised.

'And you think that'll reassure her, do you?' said Maybelle, clapping her heels into the cob's chestnut flanks. 'What makes you think Mistress Hester will last longer than you? What makes you think she even has a chance?'

Adorna was empathic. 'She does. She adores him. Talks about him. Everything. It's obvious.'

'No, it's not,' Maybelle argued. 'These things have to be two-sided, you know. And anyway, you and Lady Marion were keen for her to pair up with Sir Nicholas at first. She's very obliging and dutiful. Perhaps she's simply been trying to oblige you.'

'You didn't see her face, Belle. She was shocked.'

'Well, that's not so surprising. How many times will she have seen a man and a woman together on a bed, d'ye think? I doubt Uncle Samuel and Aunt What's-her-name were much of an education.'

'And what about those letters? Why would she hide them?'

'Because she's never had any before, I expect. You did the same with your first love-letters, didn't you? Now, you just laugh and burn them. Anyway, you can't seriously believe they were from Sir Nicholas. It's not his way to send women love-letters.'

They were silent except for a cheery 'good morning' as they passed a cow-herd with two cows and their calves. Eventually, Adorna responded to Maybelle's reproof. 'Is that how I appear, Belle? Hard-hearted? Insensitive?'

Maybelle tugged at the packhorse's leading rein. 'No, love. 'Course not. I didn't mean that. I suppose what I'm saying is that you've had so much more attention than Mistress Hester that you've learned to ignore it, and I suppose that…' She sighed, wondering how to continue.

'That what?'

'That you could go on ignoring without ever finding out that it was the real thing. Sometimes you have to stand back and look at it a bit longer. I know I suggested trying the dropping game, but I've never known a man quite as determined to win you as Sir Nicholas, and I think he deserves more respect than that. Look at the way he's helped you and Master Seton out in the last few days. And at the water. And at the playhouse in London. And the masque.'

'Helped us *out*? Belle, what on earth are you talking

about? Because of him poking his nose in, I'm now in an impossible position that I don't know how on earth I'm going to get out of.'

'Then let him get you out of it. Trust him a bit more.'

'Trust him? Huh!'

'You're not seeing things too clear, are you? People in love see things differently, you know. They see things that are not there and they miss other things that are staring them in the face.'

'What things?'

But Maybelle felt she had said enough. 'Just things,' she said.

With more silence between them than chatter, they reached the town of Warwick well before mid-day without mishap. After a month of riding her skittish mare, Adorna was impressed by the gelding's perfect manners, his ability to anticipate commands, and his obedience at water-crossings. She welcomed the change from the flashy mare whose inclinations were far from predictable. Perhaps, she thought, the mare could have been better trained.

Following the River Avon did not turn out to be as inspired a decision as she had thought at Warwick for, only a few miles further on was a small town which, she told Maybelle, had not been there when they came north ten days ago.

'On the other hand,' Maybelle remarked, 'neither were we.'

They stopped at the sign of the White Lion for refreshment and discovered that they were at Stratford-upon-Avon, which made sense but was not what they wanted to hear.

'We're supposed to be at Banbury.' Adorna sighed.

'Well, how are we supposed to know? Intuition?'

'We've been going south-west instead of south-east. That's the trouble with the sun being overhead. It's no help at all.'

'So remind me, why are we heading for Banbury when for all we know Mistress Hester might be going anywhere?'

'Because,' Adorna replied sharply while preparing to mount, 'I don't have any of that intuition, either. It's the only place I can think of that she might be going, since it's south and so is Richmond.'

'But she might be—'

'Look, get on your horse, Belle, and stop arguing. We've lost valuable time.'

It was, however, further to Banbury than they thought, travelling at the pace of the loaded packhorse. As exhaustion slowed it down, the light began to fade and, as if to protest even further, the creature cast a shoe and began to limp. To be out in the middle of the countryside, alone, was no place for ladies.

With the greatest good fortune, they came to the beautiful pink-brick house of Compton Wynyates set in a deep hollow of green hills and surrounded by a glassy moat that shone pink and purple with the last of the evening light. The glowing serenity of the picture lured them on across the moat bridge where they were welcomed by Lord Henry Compton and his lady who knew Sir Thomas and Lady Marion Pickering and whose connections with the Royal Court stretched back many years. They had often entertained the Queen here and given hospitality to her officers on their progresses. Like kindly relatives, they welcomed the travellers and accepted their modified explanation as praiseworthy, if a little risky. Two extra mouths to feed at the high table were nothing at all in a household of over seventy.

At dawn, they were away on the road to Banbury with a fresh packhorse and the warm sun in their eyes, though now the possibility of finding Hester had grown more remote than ever. It was a ride of less than eight miles, yet they could not have known, as they approached the first of the whitewashed cottages from the west, that Sir Thomas Pickering's slow and cumbersome cavalcade of waggons was leaving Banbury from the south towards Oxford, which they hoped to reach by nightfall. After enquiring at all the most likely-looking inns, the two women found no indication that Hester had been there, and Adorna was then forced to agree that her cousin must have taken a different direction for reasons best known to herself.

As they rested outside an inn where the sign of the Swan hung above the doorway, something else was responsible for delaying them, a feeling that had been growing ever since dawn when they had broached the new day with only hours of peaceful riding ahead of them. Rather than having their time directed, manipulated and planned to fit each minute around the

Queen's entertainment, they now had no plans except to find Hester, few clothes to change into or out of, no noisy formal meals, meetings or evasions, no worries about Seton. They were free.

'I like it, Belle,' Adorna said, watching the world go by. 'Why don't we stay for a while? The Queen will probably think we've gone back with my father, if she notices at all.'

'Make our own way home? Yes, but what about Sir Nicholas? Is he going to come after you, d'ye think?'

There was the agreement, of course, which she had broken by removing herself from his sphere. He would not be best pleased about that. But, with all the miscreants gone perhaps he would think twice about revealing the deception, especially since he himself had helped in it, at the end. 'He can't,' she said to Maybelle. 'They'll be going on up to Staffordshire today. He has responsibilities. Let's go and pick up the horses; we have a brand new day to spend as we please.'

She was mistaken on one point and only half-right on another. Sir Nicholas's responsibilities could, in an emergency, be delegated. He approached the Master of Horse as soon as they returned to the stables and made some infuriating discoveries about Mistress Adorna Pickering and some of the horses. He had cuffed the stable-boy's ears for the blunder.

'I don't know what's going on, sir,' he said, 'but I think I'd better go and find out. Neither she nor Mistress Hester have gone with Sir Thomas, and her leaving the palomino suggests that she doesn't want to be recognised.'

'Not as well-stabled as you thought then, man. Maybe you should have bolted the door tighter, eh?'

'I intend to, sir, with your leave. Can Paddy and Osbern fill in for me till I get back?'

'Of course they can. They know what's to be done. Take your squire and two men with you for the horses. I wish she'd not taken one of the best high-school bays though, Nicholas. She'd better be taking good care of him. Damn women!'

'Then I'll set off straight away, sir. I can be at Banbury by dusk.'

'Go to it, man. I told you to use a tighter rein.'

'So you did, my lord. I shall attend to it.' He smiled.

'And Nicholas!' the earl called. 'Take your time. Best not to rush it!'

'Thank you, sir.'

A young woman and her maid emerged from the doorway beneath the sign of the Swan just as Adorna and Maybelle turned the corner of the cobbled yard that led to the stables at the rear. They missed each other by a whisker. Two horses, already saddled, were being led up to the stone mounting-block, though it was clear from the weariness on the woman's face that she was tired of riding and was not looking forward to more. 'Do we have everything?' she said to her maid.

'Everything. Shall we…? Why, what is it, my lady?'

'Wait!' The woman shaded her eyes against the sun, frowning a little as a group of three riders pulled up on the cobbles and dismounted, the tallest of them passing his reins to his squire as he looked keenly at her, his handsome face a picture of astonishment.

'Celia!' he whispered. 'No, it cannot be. Can it?'

She held out her kid-gloved hands, shaking her head. 'No, it cannot be *Nicholas*, of all people.' She laughed. 'What in the world are you doing here? You're supposed to be up at Kenilworth, aren't you?'

He took her hands in his as he had done in the paradise garden weeks ago. 'And you're supposed to be in Spain. Aren't you? What happened?' He shook her hands gently, noting the fatigue in her eyes.

Mistress Adorna Pickering and her maid rode round the corner of the inn at that very moment, ready to take to the road and glancing casually at the space they had so recently vacated, now crowded with horses and travellers. Though of a different order, Adorna's shock at seeing these two together was every bit as great as theirs had been, causing her involuntarily to pull the bay gelding to a sudden standstill. Maybelle's cob swerved to one side with a clatter of hooves and a snort of protest.

'Sir!' a young man's voice called.

Sir Nicholas turned sharply to look. 'Damn!' he snapped, softly. By the time he was back in the saddle, Adorna had dug her heels into the responsive bay and was away in one huge bound, leaving Maybelle to hold the packhorse and to exchange bewildered glances with the elegant woman in fashionable but dusty black.

The bay was willing, but its progress was far from straightforward through a narrow street bustling with traders, their carts and baskets, and the firm hand on its bridle soon brought it to a complete standstill.

'Let go, Sir Nicholas! Leave me! Go and tend your lady!' Adorna's voice was not loud, but already an amused audience had gathered to watch. Sir Nicholas was not inclined to give them a show, but instead hauled both horse and rider unceremoniously back to the Swan at a smart trot without a word of explanation. Then, before the astonished group, he pulled Adorna down out of the saddle and marched her boldly into the inn with his hand under arm. The woman in black followed, brimming with curiosity to see at closer quarters the one she had seen only from a distance, interested also to see how Nicholas would handle the situation. She had never seen him react quite so aggressively towards a woman before, and Mistress Pickering was indeed of a direct turn of mind, by the look of things, and very beautiful.

Fuming at this rough and humiliating treatment, Adorna turned on her captor as soon as the door-latch clicked shut. 'You have no right to do this, sir. If you think I want to know what your business is with this lady then you are mistaken. It's no concern of mine and I am no concern of yours. Now, allow me to go on my way, as I was about to do.'

The room was low-beamed and plastered between wooden supports, furnished only with a table and some stools and a sweet aroma of clean rushes on the floor. But in the light from the small-paned window, Adorna was able to see at last the face of Lady Celia Traverson whose name and shadowy form had been the cause of so much heartache, the woman who clearly had bonds with her former lover so acute that she had turned away from marriage for love of him. Well, what other explanation could there be? Her looks were quite remarkable, for she had a strong nose and high cheekbones that gave an impression of being able to make her own decisions. Her dark eyes, straight brows and firm full mouth were handsome rather than lovely. Her figure, Adorna saw at a glance, was superb, her full skirt of finest black velvet and puffed silk sleeves showing her to be a lady of great quality. The white lace ruff was large and quite inappropriate for long-distance journeys, but her rich brown hair was dressed exquisitely in a jewelled bilament that sat around her head and winked in the beams of sunlight. By contrast, the hem of her skirt was stained with dust from the road.

Lady Celia stripped off her kid gloves and laid them on the table before Sir Nicholas could reply. 'Mistress Pickering,' she said, 'please don't leave us without giving at least one of us a chance to explain.'

Still furious, Adorna was not open to suggestion. 'Thank you, Lady Celia, but neither of you owes me an explanation about anything. I'm really not—'

'All the same,' Sir Nicholas said, folding his arms and leaning against the door, 'one of us *is* going to explain and you *are* going to listen.'

Lady Celia was more diplomatic in her approach, seeing Adorna appreciate the sight she was presenting in contrast to her own, not to mention the treatment she alone had had to endure at Sir Nicholas's hands. Not that Mistress Pickering could be anything but lovely, whatever she wore, but her simple country-woman's dress of blue linsey-wolsey and padded doublet, the casually coiled hair in its netted caul, were a far cry from her usual modish appearance. 'Please, Nicholas,' said Lady Celia, 'will you leave us alone for a while? Women's talk? In this, I think we shall do better without you.'

'I'll wait outside,' he said, leaving them to it.

Still defensive and extremely angry, Adorna was determined not to be seen as the loser who must take the bad news with courage. Even so, she felt the sickness inside begin to grow as Lady Celia settled herself upon a stool and invited her to take the other. Seeing them together like that, hand in hand, had enraged Adorna, but she would not allow either of them to see how it hurt. 'Lady Celia,' she said, 'whatever you think, I have no claim whatever on Sir Nicholas and he has none on me. My maid and I were—'

Lady Celia placed a sympathetic hand upon Adorna's arm. 'Your maid and you were doing exactly what my maid and I are doing,' she smiled sadly. 'We are all seeking freedom, I believe, though in a way our freedom is also a refuge, isn't it?' She squeezed on Adorna's arm as she felt an interruption coming on. 'But you are mistaken in thinking that my meeting with Sir Nicholas was planned. On the contrary, it was as accidental as yours and mine. He supposed me to be halfway to Spain by now, but I spent last night here on the way to Stafford where I shall seek refuge with Lord and Lady Gifford. I'm running away, you see, like you, but for vastly different reasons. As I came out of the inn ready to go, Nicholas arrived looking for you, if I'm not mistaken. Well…' she smiled '…I'm *not* mistaken. He's been in love with you since before I left, and there'd be absolutely no point in me trying to reopen our relationship along those lines. None at all. It's been over for some time. Now I have to remove myself as far away from my father as I can, once he gets to know that I didn't sail for Spain as he intended. So you see, Nicholas came to find you, not to meet me.'

The relief almost swamped Adorna, stinging her eyes. 'Lady Celia,' she said, 'I'm so sorry. I misunderstood. Have you really abandoned your marriage to the Spanish duke?'

'Yes, I prefer to make my own choice of husband. I managed to escape at Portsmouth before we boarded, which is why—' she looked down at her dusty skirt '—I'm most unsuitably dressed. Not an easy ride, I can tell you.'

'But how do you know of Sir Nicholas's feelings towards me? He's never spoken of love, though he must have loved dozens of women. How can one take a man with his reputation seriously? You must be as aware of it as I am.'

'Reputations!' Lady Celia scoffed, gently. 'Show me a good-looking man at Her Majesty's Court who does not have a reputation for his friendships with women. They all do. Some deserved, some not. Look at Sir Christopher Hatton, for instance; even he doesn't escape scandal-mongers, though he's one of the most loyal and gentlemanly knights alive. And anyway, what's wrong with a man who knows how to love? Nicholas has never betrayed a woman, nor did he betray me. Nor have I ever known him to chase after a woman as he has done today, especially in the middle of a Queen's progress.' She laughed.

'Probably to recover the horses.'

'No. To recover you. There's a very determined look in his eye.'

'He doesn't like to be defeated, does he?'

'I wouldn't know, Mistress Adorna. But he did tell me that you were singularly unwilling. I see you still are, so I suppose there must be a very good reason.'

'Not one that Sir Nicholas appears to take seriously.'

'Would I understand, do you think? As a woman?'

Adorna could not help admiring this unique young lady in black. What courage she had to defy her parents, disappoint her unseen and unloving future husband and his foreign family, to fly off to seek her freedom over half the length of the country. What spirit. And what compassion, too, to explain to Adorna that she had no cause to misunderstand. 'Yes,' she said, 'you would understand. I think you would understand most things, and I believe that Sir Nicholas will be the poorer for allowing you to go.'

'It was mutual,' Lady Celia whispered. 'Different

religions, too. But what is it that holds you back, mistress? Is it pride, perhaps? You *do* have the distinction of being a sprinter, I believe.' Again her smile softened her words.

'Is that what's said about me?' *Why had it suddenly begun to matter?*

'''Not a stayer'' is how the men put it. Crude, but you know what the men are like. They talk about the whole business as if we were either horses or goddesses. Personally, I prefer the first. It's more realistic, isn't it?'

Adorna felt, in those few moments, as if she was at last changing from a girl into a woman. What common sense this woman spoke. How matter-of-fact and yet sensitive. If she didn't like something, she changed it: if she did, she accepted it. 'Well,' Adorna said, 'I suppose they're probably right, though my reason for not staying the course is that I've not found a man who interests me. When I did, I heard that he was not a stayer, either. To be fair, Sir Nicholas tried to persuade me that that was not a true picture of himself, just as he tried to show me what I've been missing. But unfortunately the circumstances worked against us, and every time I came remotely close to changing my mind, something turned it all sour again. Jealousy, I suppose. And fear. They're both new to me. I don't know how best to deal with them.'

'Trust him, my dear. The best part is to come: the finding-out is something you'll want to lose so that you can find it out all over again. There's nothing in it to fear, not with Nicholas. And jealousy *is* fear, by the way. The two are the same thing. Go with him. You'll be quite safe.'

They stood up together and embraced as spontaneously as if they had been sisters. Adorna took Lady Celia's warm hands to her own. 'I envy you your courage, my lady. I shall think of you and pray for your safety. It must have been fate that brought us both to the Swan at Banbury on the same morning.' The same fate that had brought them so close at Richmond one night.

'Of course it was. Now,' she warned, 'not *too* pliable. Let him think he's still got something to work at, eh?'

They laughed, and were still laughing as they came out on to the inn's forecourt where the sun and Sir Nicholas were waiting for them.

Chapter Ten

Better protected than they had been so far, Lady Celia Traverson and her maid were launched unexpectedly into the last stages of their journey with the added escort of one of Sir Nicholas's men who had orders to deliver her safely to the door of the Giffords' home in Stafford. There, with one of the few remaining Roman Catholic families to be free of serious persecution, she would be able at last to make her own choice of husband.

Still under the influence of Lady Celia's short acquaintance, Adorna already felt that she had just lost a friend, a loss made even more poignant by Sir Nicholas's uncompromising control that showed no sign of abating. Far from offering her a chance to discuss what had been said in the inn, which he must have known concerned him, he appeared to take it for granted that an explanation had been given and accepted. He would neither add anything to it, nor gloat, nor ask for her reaction.

His sternness unsettled her as much this time as it

had before and did nothing to convince her of Lady Celia's statement that he was in love with her. If this present attitude was a sign of it, then the lady was obviously in possession of some evidence that she was not. Twice in the last twenty-four hours, Adorna had been advised to trust him, yet in his present mood he appeared to be quite indifferent to the chance of any change in her opinion of him.

She watched him silently checking the gelding's stirrup-leathers, girth and bridle with sure strong hands, pulling at the forelock to tidy it. He was dressed in workmanlike clothes, but no less elegant for that, buff-coloured suede breeches that ended below the knee, a brown leather doublet under a padded buff jerkin, a white shirt, open-fronted. She tore her eyes away as he suddenly confronted her.

'Now,' he said, skimming her bare neck with a cool appraisal, 'we can catch Sir Thomas's party if we get a move on.'

Instantly, his tone rubbed her up the wrong way. She had a right to be consulted. 'I do not intend to catch my father up, sir,' she said. 'I am going my own way.' She gathered the reins up into her left hand.

'You are going my way, mistress, like it or not.'

'Sir Nicholas, I cannot imagine how I have managed these last twenty years without your interference, but I shall keep trying. Now, will you please help me to mount, if that is what you intend to do, and then leave me alone.'

'Very well, let's see how far you get before you come back.'

Taken aback by his sudden reversal, Adorna swallowed her sudden misgivings. She had intended to show some appeasement, but he was giving her little chance in this matter of where she should go. She allowed him to help her into the saddle and then, with a curt nod of thanks and farewell, signalled Maybelle to follow her away from the inn in the opposite direction from that taken by Lady Celia. She had not gone more than twenty paces along the busy street when a distant whistle made the gelding's ears swing wildly backwards and forwards. He stopped dead in his tracks and turned about to face the way they had come, despite all she could do to stop him and move him forward.

'No!' she shouted, kicking with her heels. 'What's the matter with you? Get on...this way...stupid horse!' But he snatched at the bit and trotted disobediently back to the inn, ignoring every one of her commands and oblivious to her humiliation. Sir Nicholas was mounted, waiting for them. 'You wretch!' she yelled. 'This is your doing!'

'Stop fighting him or he'll throw you off. Come on. I told you. We go my way.' Quickly, he leaned and pulled at one of the gelding's glossy ears. 'Well done, boy,' he said, laughing.

Adorna was close to tears. 'I don't *want* to travel with my father,' she snarled. 'We're looking for Cousin Hester, and we're just beginning to enjoy a taste of freedom. If Lady Celia can be allowed her freedom, why can't I?' She knew the answer before she asked it. Lady Celia was running because she had courage: she herself was running because she was afraid. She had yet to discover the exact reason for Hester's escape.

'Then I'll help you to taste it. How will Aylesbury do for a start?'

She had no idea where Aylesbury was except that there were ducks there, but the temptation to reject his suggestion was by now almost second nature. 'No,' she said, knowing that he would ask for an alternative.

'Then where?'

'The Thames,' she said, on impulse. It was the river that flowed through Richmond. 'I intended to follow the River Thames to home.'

'Then it's a good thing you didn't get far just now or you'd have been in Scotland before you realised it.'

'Don't exaggerate!'

'All right, so we'll pick up the Thames and follow it to Richmond. We should be home by about Christmas.'

Now that *was* an exaggeration, and well he knew it, but it made the two men and Maybelle smile. It did not, however, make Adorna smile. 'Sir Nicholas,' she said, low-voiced.

He noted the lingering uncertainty, the one glistening teardrop clinging to her lower lashes, the top lip pulled in and let go, and he guessed what had taken place with Celia in the inn room. They were both remarkable women; their conversation would have reflected that. He moved away to one side, leading her horse. 'What is it?' he said, knowing what it was.

'It was Cousin Hester I came looking for,' she said.

'Yes, and it was you I came looking for, as you know.'

'Do I?'

'You know you do. But there's no need to continue the search for Hester, because I happen to know that she is not alone, or lost, or in any danger.'

'What? You know where she is?'

'I didn't say that. I made some enquiries before I left and now I have a reasonably clear picture of what's happened. She's with somebody.'

'An admirer?'

'Yes.'

'She's been abducted? Merciful heavens!'

'On the contrary, she's been planning this for some time. And that's all I shall tell you except to say that by the time we reach home, Hester and her companion will probably be there, or in London. Now stop worrying about her moral welfare. She's not nearly as helpless as you appear to think.'

'But she *is*! She's—'

'No, she's not. I've known her longer than you. She's as tough as old boots. Naïve, I grant you, but she'll be a bit more worldly by the time we catch up with her.'

'You mean…? Oh, dear, I should never have allowed her to run off like that.'

'Look, clear your mind of this business once and for all, Adorna. What she saw had no bearing on what she decided to do, I tell you. I'm quite convinced she intended to make a run for it well before that.'

'How d'ye know?'

'I know. And now your search for her has developed into something else, hasn't it? A few days of freedom, eh? Without me to curb you?'

She stared hard at the glossy mane before her and felt the shift of the horse as he changed his resting-leg. 'I was enjoying myself,' she retorted. 'I need to be alone, to sort myself out without—'

'Interference?' He smiled wickedly at the thought. 'Well, that's something you're going to have to put up with, because we made an agreement, remember, which you have already broken.'

'Which I suppose puts me at a disadvantage again.'

'It puts you, Adorna, in the position of being my wife for the purposes of this journey, at least. Unless, of course, you prefer to be known as my mistress? I have no objection to that. You understand what I'm saying?'

Their eyes met at last, each reading the other, hers in bright sunshine and his in the shadow of his black velvet cap, but as compelling as that first day by the Thames when he had told her that there was nothing here that a little gentle schooling could not cure.

She knew what he was saying, and the hair prickled at the back of her neck. Her eyes lowered meekly as she nodded, an almost imperceptible movement that belied the defiant set of her mouth.

'Lady Adorna,' he said. 'Sounds good. Looks good, too.' He viewed with some appreciation the countrified dress which, although full-skirted, was clearly not supported by the rigid whalebone bodice she usually wore. Now, her beautiful contours filled the soft fabric with the natural lusciousness of young womanhood and her neck, without a lace ruff to hide it, had begun to soak up the sun and the breeze.

Flustered by her new status and by his scrutiny, she tucked stray wisps of hair back into her caul and wished she had paid more attention to her toilette.

'One more thing before we go,' said Sir Nicholas. He passed her a small velvet bag. 'Find a convenient moment to put that on some time today. It will avoid the need for explanations.'

She took it without question, for she recognised the bag as belonging to Leicester's Men, having worn its contents in her role as Beatrice when she had married Benedict. 'I hope Master Burbage won't mind,' she said, attempting to make light of it. But the situation had become almost too serious for quips and, as they moved off at last, it escaped neither of them that they presented a perfect picture of a genteel married couple travelling with a maid, a squire, a groom and a pack-horse, apparently at peace with each other and the world.

Although this was a development she had not anticipated, it took only a mile or so for her to admit that having men in the party made a vast difference to their comfort. Fellow-travellers instantly moved to one side of the track instead of forcing them off; no one made ribald remarks, asked them where they were going, or suggested that they might need company. One look at the men's array of scabbards hanging from belts made the deference due to a lord and his lady a foregone conclusion. She felt as safe and protected as she had when she had ridden pillion behind him only a few days ago.

On the other hand, their relationship had now entered a new and potentially conclusive stage, for he was clearly expecting from her a commitment she had never faced before, the giving up of something she held dear, claimed by a man used to winning. Understandably, she was worried and apprehensive, despite Lady Celia's second-hand revelation that he was in love with her, which came without any form of guarantee. One worry was out of the way, however; the problem of Lady Celia herself was now over, their friendship understandable, acceptable, and in no way threatening. In fact, Adorna mused, their meeting had been a godsend.

It was late in the day when they emerged from the woodland below Woodstock and came at last to the top curve of the River Thames where the water level was low enough for them to wade across to the opposite side.

'Not far now,' Sir Nicholas told them.

'How far is not far?' Adorna said, wearily.

'Another mile, that's all. There's an inn at Wytham.'

Nestling on the edge of the great wood at Wytham, the White Hart was small but welcoming, the landlord overjoyed to see prestigious travellers on his side of the river. 'They usually choose Oxford on the other side, m'lady,' he said to Adorna. 'Never enough bridges, that's the problem. Come inside if you will, sir. My goodwife will show your lady to the rooms. Clean sheets on all the beds. No need to share. This way, m'lady.' His shining bald head led them to the small but clean parlour where the goodwife curtsied, tying on a clean pinafore.

There was an aroma of new-baked bread in the creaking oak-lined passageway, the faintest whiff of woodsmoke along the staircase, and newly cut rushes in the small bedchamber. The goodwife opened a small window just above floor level, letting in the distant sound of a mill-wheel slowing, then stopping. 'Ye can have both rooms up here, if you wish,' she told Adorna, patting the blanketed tester-bed. 'This one is the biggest. The two men can sleep above the 'osses in the stable. Now, what'll you have for your supper, m'lady? We have roast pigeons, pickled beef, mutton pie, a cheese and egg pasty and new bread. Or perhaps you'd prefer a chimney-smoked gammon with garlic and turnips?'

'No garlic,' said Sir Nicholas, entering the room unexpectedly.

Adorna smiled at the goodwife's astonishment. 'The men will be hungry by the time they've seen to the horses,' she said. 'I dare say they'll make short work of whatever you have. We'll be down presently.'

She bobbed another curtsy, looked sideways at Sir Nicholas, and closed the door mumbling, 'No garlic! Tch!'

'Where's Maybelle?' Adorna said. 'I need her.'

The room was not as large as the goodwife had implied, the oak beams only just clearing Sir Nicholas's head and allowing the canopied top of the tester-bed to fit cosily between two of the great timbers. He ducked, cautiously. 'She's chatting up Perkin still,' he said. 'They're getting on rather well, hadn't you noticed?'

'Then there's going to be trouble; there's a young man called David at the palace.' She turned away, suddenly confused by his nearness.

'David has gone back to France with his master.' His voice dropped to a whisper. 'Speaking of which—' he came to stand behind her with his arms enclosing her shoulders '—don't get any ideas about Belle sleeping in here. This is where *your* master sleeps.'

She stopped his caressing hands with her own. 'Hasn't this gone far enough, sir?' she whispered, hearing him smile.

'Good try,' he said, kissing her sun-warmed neck. 'But no, it hasn't. Not nearly far enough.'

With determination that he clearly did not expect, she lifted his arms and shook herself free. 'No,' she said. 'No!' She turned to face him, looking everywhere except into his eyes. 'This is *not* how it should be.' Her voice wavered, searching uncertainly for the words.

He took her face tenderly in his hands as if it might break and held it until her gaze settled upon him at last. 'Tell me,' he said softly. 'Tell me how it should be.'

'I swore…' she began as if reluctantly parting with a secret.

'Yes?'

'I swore I'd make it hard for you.' She took his hands away and held them together before her. 'And now…look at this…' Her eyes skimmed the room. 'Look at me…cornered! Trapped!'

'You think it's been *easy* to get you this far, lass? Take my word for it, it hasn't.'

'I don't know. All I know is that I've ridden dutifully with you all day and now I'm expected to eat dutifully with you downstairs and make dutiful wifely conversation and then come dutifully back up here and let you…dutifully…' Tears brimmed, squeaking the words. 'And that's *not* how it should be. If I have to give myself to you, I'm damned if I'll give it to you here…' she glared at the bed '…where everyone knows what's happening. What choice do I have?' she croaked. 'Four walls. A locked door. How difficult will *that* be for you? Have you ever had it easier?'

He would not give her the answer to that. Not yet. 'Don't say any more,' he said, keeping her hands. 'I understand. What we need, I think, is some exercise. We'll take a walk after supper, shall we? There's still some hours of light left.'

Adorna nodded, breathing out at last. 'Yes.'

'And you can lead. And I'll follow.'

'Yes.'

'And you can be as bloody difficult as you like. Yes?'

A huff of laughter escaped as she brushed a tear away. 'You're not supposed to understand,' she said. 'You're a man.'

'I'm sorry. I'll try harder next time.'

So after the roast pigeons, the new bread, the cam-
embert cheese, baked apples, cream and ale, but no
garlic, Adorna excused herself and left the parlour.

'Should I go with her?' Maybelle asked Sir Nicholas.

He rose to his feet. 'No, go to bed, all of you.
There's a fair way to go tomorrow.'

But beyond the garden and the dovecote besieged
with plump white pigeons, Adorna crossed the wooden
bridge over the stream into the meadow where a path
ran along the riverside. The innkeeper had mentioned
an abbey; Godstow Abbey, ruined for many years;
they would have passed it and seen it but for the trees.
The grass here was already shin-high, waiting for hay-
time.

The trees soon enclosed her again, shading the river
with black shadows, and soon the stone walls of the
old nunnery appeared as if by magic in a sheltered
clearing, massive foundations rising up steeply to tow-
ering reminders of security and peace. How ironic,
then, that she should seek her last vestiges of freedom
in such a place where nuns had forfeited theirs. Each
for their own reason, as Lady Celia had said.

Slowly, she picked her way over wide rubble-filled
walls now level with the grass and smoothed with
time, moss and lichen, shading her eyes as the low sun
shafted orange light through branches and pointed
arches. She stood to listen to the last call of the birds,
comparing this new tranquillity to the last frenetic

weeks, to her most recent burst of anger and resentment, and to her apprehensions which seemed now to have lost their sting. *There's nothing to fear with Nicholas*, Lady Celia had told her.

Beyond the ruined eastern end of the scattered conventual buildings was an open space, part enclosed by a stone wall where ridges of once-cultivated ground showed that this had been a small garden. It was private, secluded, warmed by the sun, where wild roses flung themselves about in heaps and overpowered the leggy mallow, one of whose pink flowers she plucked and held to her breast. Then she stood by a large stone and waited. This would be the place and no other.

He must have been watching from close by for he appeared almost immediately, like a moving shadow, slowly, as if half-expecting her to leap away like a doe in a clearing. He stopped a few paces from her. 'Now, my beauty,' he whispered, 'is this to be the place?' He moved slowly towards her. 'Perfect for wild creatures, eh, lass? Stand still…softly…' He reached out a hand and pulled at the open-mesh caul that held her hair, shaking it loose in a white gold flood down one shoulder to her waist.

She knew he would have seen the mallow flower trembling in her hand, but there was no trace of frivolity in his manner nor even of the harshness he had brought to their meeting earlier that day. The quaking flower was removed from her fingers and its stem was woven amongst the strands of gold. 'There,' he said, taking her hands and kissing the knuckles, 'you'll need these, I think. What do you remember, I wonder? Anything?'

'Very little,' she said, speaking to his hands, 'except the headache afterwards.'

He smiled at that. 'Shall I tell you what I remember?'

'Best not to,' she said, looking away.

His knuckle brought her back to face him. 'I remember the most stunningly beautiful and headstrong woman I've ever met,' he said, softly, 'lying by my side after an evening of opposition and showing me a part of herself that she'd tried hard for a long time to convince me didn't exist. Yet I knew it did, and I wanted to prove it to her. And I find she doesn't remember much, which is just as well because now...' he lifted her into his arms '...I can prove it to her all over again.'

He placed her in a shadowy corner of the garden upon a soft mossy bed warmed by the sun, and it was here that their kisses, held off for so long, came together like a star-burst in which all their doubts, misunderstandings and schemes faded, replaced by sensations that had been left starved and wanting till now. He had intended gentleness; she had feared revenge for his waiting; yet what emerged in the blind heat of their union was an amalgam of all this and so much more that Adorna's fears became joys, his intentions merely preludes to the next fiery duet. As with their dancing, they partnered each other in a perfect accord that neither of them could have predicted.

Once, at the beginning, she took hold of the hand

that untied her laces, delaying its investigations. But his lips on hers diverted her while he proceeded, skin touching skin, fingertips, palms, lips, teeth and tongue, her breasts coming alive with an urge that touched chords in every part of her being. 'Nicholas!' she cried. Just that. But the birds in the trees above fell silent, listening.

The wide expanse beneath his shirt would alone have been enough for an afternoon's exploration but, combined with her own body's new experiences, the excitement drew her on faster, ever faster. When his hand slid down over her hips and groin to the warm cavern between her legs, a vague memory of fear dissipated in a groan of ecstasy. Her hands on his back curled into claws that dug into his firm flesh, and she arched against his searching hand, turning her face into the tumbled mass of her hair. Panting, she cried out to him, 'Nicholas! I want you…now, now!'

Her legs opened as he nudged them apart with his knee. 'Lift them, sweetheart. Wrap them round me, that's it…easy.'

She was moist and ready, but had not been prepared by anything her mother had told her for the almost frightening experience of having another body so close to that most isolated of all parts. She cried out, not with pain but with shock as she felt the gentle invasion, the insistence, the first surging thrust, the incredible locking, the hunch of his body over hers, the tender male weight of him, his restricting arms, his pulling her into him with a hand under her back. His control. Her breathing shuddered to a stop.

'Sweetheart, I hurt you?'

'No,' she said, getting her breath back.

'You cried out.'

'Did I? Is this it, Nicholas?'

He smiled and began to move, heady with victory. 'Yes, my beauty. This is it.'

Her mother, come to think of it, had missed out so much of the whole business of loving that Adorna, lying quietly in his arms afterwards, felt bound to mention the uselessness of similes as opposed to hard facts. 'Rather like a warm bath, she told me. Really!' she said, combing his chest with her fingertips.

'And was it? Like a warm bath?'

'Nothing at all like a warm bath unless you take one in the middle of a blizzard, just for the excitement.'

He raised himself onto his elbows to look down on her, 'Well, it can be, if you want it to. Every time is different, or it should be, if the man is doing his job properly. And that was quite exceptional.'

'Was it? For you, too?'

'Unbelievably good. As I knew it would be. So now we could go back to the inn and try that warm bath experience, if you like.'

'In bed?'

'Just for comparison.'

Later, as they strolled back through the darkening meadow, he teased her just a little. 'And *are* you going to be bloody difficult, or was that as bad as it gets?'

'I'm saving it,' she said, perversely, 'for tomorrow.'

'Forewarned is forearmed then, my lady.'

For the rest of that night, she was more than willing to be led and to be introduced to the slow and leisurely loving of Lady Marion's—probably recent—experience that verified Sir Nicholas's assurance that the variations on the theme were endless. In the warm and comfortable darkness without a shred of clothing to inhibit them, they used their heightened senses to discover what had previously only been hinted at. Hands caressed and fondled to the brink of rapture and beyond, the control that Adorna had balked at now so sweet that there was no part of her that she would not allow him to explore. That alone, she told him shyly, was sheer bliss, not having believed it could be so exquisite.

He raised his head from her breast. '"And so my love protesting came, but yet I made her mine,"' he quoted, 'but not without a fight. Perhaps that should have been written on the other side of the roundel.' He resumed his teasing of her other nipple.

'You are bragging,' she warned. 'And pride cometh before a fall, sir.'

Inch by inch his mouth moved upwards until it reached her mouth. 'I have your measure, my lady,' he growled. 'I can handle you.' His kiss was both commanding and possessive, meant to show that, even in teasing talk, she had capitulated and he was the winner. Her silence confirmed his claim. 'Good,' he whispered. 'Open your legs.'

Excited as much by his fierce command as by the hard bulge of his muscular shoulders, she received him willingly yet tried to remain passive and unresponsive in the face of his boast. It did not work, for his exceptional tenderness was the last thing she had expected from him, and soon she was drawn like a reluctant dancer into the rhythm of his body, sharing every moment, following his lead, crying out at the gathering speed that only he could control.

It burst upon her without warning, whirling her away into space and keeping her breath deep in her lungs as the beat slowed and swirled away into her thighs. Dizzy and exhilarated, she lay beneath him as the warm flood of exhaustion overtook her, and she rocked him in her arms as his exceptional vigour ebbed into deep languor. Seamlessly, sleep overtook them.

Waking at intervals during the night by the strangeness of the large male body at her side, Adorna asked herself over and over why she had wanted to evade him and how strong were her reasons. The main stumbling block had been dealt with in one chance meeting that very morning, and she had been urged to trust him. But did she dare? Had he threatened her with exposure if she didn't co-operate? She knew that he had not, though he had gone along with her pretence because it suited him to. And she had proposed it because, in her heart, she wanted an excuse to surrender. And now she had surrendered, what would be the outcome? Abandonment and disgrace? Or life with the only man she had ever wanted?

She turned to him and snuggled deep into him, marvelling at the unaccustomed hardness of his welcom-

ing arms, plotting the rise and fall of his powerful
chest under her hand. What if she bore his child?
Would that be enough to keep him? Had other women
had the same ambitions? Well, if this was what she
wanted to hold for life, and it was, then she would
have to make sure of keeping his interest. Not too
pliable.

'You knew of the White Hart Inn beforehand, Sir
Nicholas?' Adorna said as they rode away next morning. She tried, unsuccessfully, to keep the extra curiosity out of her voice.

His mouth twitched but his eyes looked straight
ahead. 'This area belongs to the Earl of Leicester,' he
said. 'Near here is another inn called the Bear and the
Ragged Staff. His arms, you remember. And at nearby
Cumnor is the house where he and his first wife lived
until her death. I've visited all his lordship's proper-
ties, for one reason or another.'

'For one reason or another?'

He caught her eyes and held them, amused rather
than critical. 'Yes, lady. On my lord's business. Anything else?'

'And now we head for…where is it? Abbey?'

'Abingdon.' His smile broke as he recognised her
train of thought. 'We pass through Radley where Lord
Thomas Seymour lived.'

Adorna remained silent. She had heard tales of Seymour, Lord High Admiral, the Queen's handsome and
foolish late uncle. Everyone had. Poor young Eliza-

beth. Her love life in ruins, despite all Leicester's attempts.

Sir Nicholas's observation regarding Maybelle and his man Perkin had not been exaggerated, the young man's interest in the vivacious maid being every bit as keen as hers in him. The development suited Adorna well enough, for it kept Belle's curiosity about her mistress well in check. Young Perkin, a solid, bold and efficient man, was well able to make best use of his time with Maybelle and to keep her occupied while his master and Lady Adorna went off on their own with Lytton, the squire, to hold the horses.

Their journey to Abingdon took them along the riverside path through woodland and lush meadow, past thick hedgerows, wading knee-deep in fallen blossom, buttercups and meadowsweet. But his authority still caused Adorna some contradictory emotions, for while she loved his masculine assuredness, she did not care to be anticipated on every point, nor for him to know what she wanted better than she knew herself. Not even her father went so far. Last night, that had been close to the truth, but telling her that she would like Abingdon was stretching her new-found compliance too far. She would *not* like Abingdon. She had no intention of liking it. She told him so.

'I don't know why we're here at all,' she said, crossly, pulling the bay to one side as an ox-team and waggon lumbered past without any apparent form of steering.

'We're here,' Sir Nicholas said, 'because you wanted to follow the Isis all the way to Richmond.'

'I didn't want to follow the Isis,' she snapped. 'I wanted to follow the Thames. How could you—?'

'The Isis *is* the Thames, woman!' he snapped back. 'It's called the Isis on this stretch of Oxfordshire. And pull your horse out of the middle of the road.'

'But we've been heading west for the last half-hour. Look at the sun.'

He groaned. 'Well, that's because the river doesn't flow in a straight line like a Roman road,' he said, pulling at the bay's bridle. 'Come. If you don't want to stay here we'll move on down the river, though what's wrong with Abingdon I can't imagine. Sounds like a clear-cut case of that bloody-mindedness you promised me. Is it?'

Denying him an instant confirmation, Adorna had already taken a route away from the track and was following the river southwards which, she mumbled under her breath, since they couldn't go east, was better than going west. Suspecting that he knew at least one good reason for her rebelliousness, Sir Nicholas rode alongside her without comment for a mile or so until, quite out of the blue, she spoke to him in a low voice. 'I'm sorry. There's nothing wrong with Abingdon. It's just…' she shrugged her shoulders '…I don't know.'

'I think I do, though,' he said, smiling.

She glanced at him and saw the laughter in his jasper eyes, a look that sent waves of pink upwards into her cheeks.

'It's all right,' he said. 'You're allowed to take the reins occasionally.'

'As long as it doesn't interfere with your plans.'

'Easy, my lass. Easy,' he whispered.

Nevertheless, she could not help thinking that, on this matter, she had taken the reins into her own hands only to ride along his chosen route by default, for the small village of Kings Sutton, which lay less than two miles south from Abingdon, was owned by Sir Nicholas's father, Lord Elyot. The manor house there was kept in a habitable state for his periodic use and, as they arrived, only the steward, the bailiff and a handful of servants were there, as delighted to see Sir Nicholas and the lady as he was to find somewhere, at last, which she appeared to like.

In all conscience, she could not have objected to the delightful old place where buildings had once been erected to provide a retreat and convalescent home for monks from Abingdon Abbey. The old Abbots' House had been their country retreat set in a secluded garden bordered by limes, elms and yew. The ancient church stood beside what had now become the manor house.

'Will this do for the night?' he said, lifting her down from the saddle.

'Better,' she said. 'Much better, I thank you.'

But although the fine oak-panelled chambers lacked nothing in comfort, it was to the scented and well-tended garden that Adorna went alone after a private supper when Sir Nicholas believed she had gone upstairs. The sun touched the horizon in a ball of fire, and the tall trees awaited with open arms for the last crows to settle into their lacy spaces. In the mirrored pond the lilies had closed for the night, and a lone blackbird warned its mates from a rosemary bush that something was astir. Adorna felt it, too.

'You,' she said to the shadowy figure that approached, soundlessly.

'There was a time,' he said, reaching her, 'only a few nights ago, when I stood in the paradise at Kenilworth Castle to wait for a certain woman who declined to come to me.' He took her hands in his. 'And I have an inkling, just an inkling mind, that this certain woman…'

'Who shall be nameless.'

'…who shall be nameless, may be trying to put that right by coming to this private monks' paradise, and to the nuns' paradise at Godstow, to wait for *me*. I wonder if that's what could be happening.'

It was still light enough for him to see her smile at that. 'You may wonder, sir, if you wish, but the woman may have quite a different reason for drawing her lover into such a place.'

'Is that so? Will she tell me, d'ye think?'

'Eventually. If all goes according to her wishes.'

'Ah, so she has wishes, does she?' He pulled at her hands and held her close. 'So I must try not to divert her, is that it?'

'She would prefer to be humoured on this, I believe.'

'This is indeed gentler talk, lady. There was also a time when she would have insisted, stridently. She would have flayed me with her tongue, told me that she didn't care one way or the other.'

'She cares, sir,' she said, breathing the words on to his cheek like a kiss.

He seemed to hold his breath and let it out so carefully that she could not tell whether it was a sigh or a gasp. His arms tightened about her like the approaching darkness. 'Again,' he said. 'Tell me again.'

She lifted her arms to caress his wide shoulders, her hands skimming his hair, his ears. 'She cares, Nicholas. How could she not care?'

'Sweetheart.' His kisses rained on her face and throat, bathing her in his delight, while she marvelled that he should be so affected when her words were still so minimal and when he must have received the unqualified adoration of many another woman.

He carried her at last through the hall of the timber-framed house where an old servant ignored them, up into their chamber. With barely enough light from the pale glow in the sky, Nicholas unwrapped her as if she were the most precious and delicate parcel, slowly prolonging the discovery of her body as if for the first time, caressing each beautiful limb and mound.

Wrapped only in her hair, she stood naked before him, melting at his touch and vaguely recalling the time when, in her room at Richmond, she had imagined this occasion without knowing anything of its realities. Deftly, her fingers went to work on his fastenings, each revelation punctuated by her lengthy examination of his magnificent body, an examination that involved lips as well as hands. She had never known that a man's body could be so comely, so well proportioned or so impressively virile, nor had she understood that the mechanics worked so obviously fast until now. Overawed, she hesitated as the phenomenon was revealed, not sure how to continue.

'I could make love to you with my boots *on*,' he offered, pushing at his knee-length breeches, 'if you wish.' He pulled them off and threw them aside in a tangle, reaching out for her in one smooth movement.

But she held him off, laughing at his impatience. 'I thought one of us,' she said, holding his hands, 'had unlimited control. I thought...'

'Correction,' he whispered, lifting her off the floor, 'one of us has more than the other, but only at certain times. And this is—'

'Not one of—?'

'Those times.' He placed her on the bed, but already the waiting had stretched beyond breaking-point and, making up for every moment when they had each burned for the other, their consummation could be delayed no longer. She was as fierce as he, urging him on with a relentlessness that brought them both to a shattering release even before the linen sheet had been warmed by their bodies.

Groaning, he lay softly upon her, still throbbing and as amazed by her fervour as by his own sudden inability to prolong the act. 'What have you done to me, woman?' he said. 'That's not happened to me since I was sixteen.'

Adorna lay smiling into the smooth warm patch of skin behind his ear, and he took her silence for exhaustion. Which was not entirely the case.

*   *   *

By early morning they had left behind the idyllic manor and paradise at Kings Sutton to follow the winding river eastwards through Appleford. From here, they cut across a loop of the river and left the horses with young Master Lytton to climb to the top of a hill where a clump of beeches huddled together. 'Like a tuft of hair on a bald man's head,' Adorna said, merrily. Hand in hand, she and Maybelle were pulled along by the two men, preventing them from lifting their skirts, tripping them into the long grass from where they had to be hauled, speechless with laughter. Sheep stared, then walked away, munching. The top of the hill gave them panoramic views across a plain ridged with small hills, and the river like molten silver weaving through them.

'Over there, to the right. See,' Sir Nicholas said, 'in the distance, that's Wallingford.'

Adorna shaded her eyes. 'I wonder where Hester is,' she murmured. She had had her hair plaited into one long rope that hung to her waist, and she wore another simple gown of dusky rose pink, already tasting the freedom she had once been sure she would lose by accepting Sir Nicholas's escort. She could never have travelled like this in her father's company. Or Peter's. Maybelle had remarked on her mistress's new vivacity, but she herself was in love and had found a new sparkle for her laughing eyes. The separate rooms had allowed them little time together to explore the consequences, yet here on the hilltop they

both saw an opportunity at last. 'I think it's time we
had a dip in that water,' Adorna said. 'Can we escape
them, d'ye think?'

An hour later they came to a secluded bend in the
river, sheltered on one side by trees where the sun had
warmed slow-moving pools. Rocks and sandy slopes
provided little bays for undressing, and it was here that
the two women left their clothes and entered the tepid
brown water, gulping and puffing at the coolness that
crept upwards and clung to their bodies. Further in,
they pirouetted and splashed, rubbing themselves
down with handfuls of moss, then floating down on
the slow current to the bend, protesting mildly at the
change in temperature. They turned to go back, but
Maybelle touched Adorna's arm, signalling her to silence and patting the water. 'Keep down,' she whispered.

Looking in the direction of Maybelle's wide-eyed
stare, Adorna saw that, further round the bend and
hidden from their own entry into the river, the heads
and shoulders of two people were clearly visible,
closely entwined beneath the water and quite oblivious
to their amazed audience. A man and a woman, shining and sleek as fish.

But for their overpowering curiosity, the two
women would have quietly departed, but the intimate
scene held them transfixed as the woman's arms
wrapped and clung. She threw her head back in ecstasy as the man's dark head bent to her throat and

then, with her straddling him like a child, he carried her to the shallows and lay upon her.

Adorna and Maybelle turned at once and waded back to their clothes, their hearts beating like tabors. 'It's Mistress Hester,' Maybelle said. 'I'd swear it.'

'With Master Peter Fowler,' said Adorna, grabbing at her petticoat. 'Master Peter Two-faced Fowler and Cousin Oh-so-shy Hester. *Well, well!*'

Chapter Eleven

'**Y**ou knew!' Adorna scolded, sitting under a tree to have the tangles combed out of her hair. 'You knew it was him, so why could you not have told me?'

Bare to his waist, Sir Nicholas removed the comb from Maybelle's hand and signalled her to go. 'What good would it have done? Would it have made you any happier to know?' he said.

'That's not the point.'

'Then what is the point? He's an ambitious young rascal, but if he's what Hester wants, then where's the problem? She doesn't require anyone's permission, not even Uncle Samuel's. She can do as she likes.'

'She has no *experience* of men.'

'Well, she has now.' He grinned. 'What exactly *were* they doing?'

'Oh—men!' She snatched her hair away and held him off. 'Trust a man to miss the point entirely. He's taking advantage of her, can't you see?' She tried to evade him, but his arm across her shoulders threw her sideways into the grass, and she was caught beneath him with her damp hair like a veil of gauze over her face.

He held her hands away, enjoying her anger. 'While you, my fierce little filly, saw nothing amiss in taking advantage of Hester's inexperience, did you? Or of Fowler's so-called protection?'

'What do you mean? Let me up!'

'No. You'll stay here till we've had this out.'

'I shall not say a word, damn you.'

'Yes, you will. Now, what's all this righteous indignation about, eh? You're hopping mad because you tried to manipulate Hester and she decided to manipulate herself instead. Is that it? You tried to use Fowler to keep me at a distance and, when it didn't have the desired effect, he didn't stay around to mope for you as you expected him to do, but went dashing off after a more lucrative prize instead. So now you're mad at him, too, for being so quick off the mark. Did you really expect them to ask your permission, lass?'

'I'm not! I didn't!' she yelled. 'I don't care a damn what they do. They can do it on horseback for all I care, but why did they have to be so deceitful about it? Why did Hester make out she was interested in *you*? Why did Peter—pretend?'

'Why did either of them pretend?' he said, removing a strand of her hair to reveal an angry eye. 'Because they balked at telling you they didn't like your plan, I expect.'

'There *was* no plan!'

'Of course there was. D'ye think I don't know how you and Lady Marion tried to pair me off with Hester?

Or how you steered her in my direction and groomed her to try to make her more interesting? Then it began to get out of hand, didn't it?'

'That's most unfair! We wanted to help her to be more comfortable with our guests. All of them. She wasn't at ease in crowds.'

'Well, that's not changed, by the look of things. She couldn't wait to skip off alone, in spite of your help. And that's exactly what *you* wanted to do, isn't it?'

'On my own, sir, not with a lover. Not with anybody.'

'Which is what you've always done,' he continued, ignoring her interruption. 'Run away and hide when the going gets rough, when a man shows too much interest. Panic. Run home. Surround yourself with family and safe things so that you can avoid making any kind of commitment. Eh?'

'It's not like that,' she whispered, turning her head away, furious to be so misinterpreted. Yet how could she tell him that it was not simply a case of avoiding a commitment but evading men she didn't want to be with for more than an hour or two? Until now. To explain that to him, she would have to confess at least some of her feelings for him, and that was something she had no intention of doing. How could she, without first knowing for sure whether his pursuit of her was a temporary or a permanent one? She had watched his farewell to Lady Celia in the paradise at Richmond, and could share the woman's pain as if it had been her own.

'It's *not* like that,' she repeated, rounding on him.

'What d'ye think I've been doing these last few days if not making a commitment? You've had three whole days of my company, which is something no other man has ever had, and you were glad enough to take advantage of that, so it seemed. Yet now we have to wail about Hester's delicate feelings instead of mine. Well, go and *find* her!' She pushed at him in fury. 'Get off me! Go! She didn't look as if she was suffering too much when I saw her.' Angry tears stung her eyes as she struggled against him.

'So why do *you* think,' he said, holding her wrists, 'I came after you when I was needed at Kenilworth? Well, I'll tell you, woman. Because this is one dash for freedom you're not going to complete. You put yourself in my power and now you'll stay in it, not for three days, which for you must seem like a lifetime, but until you get the message that I'm in control. You've met your master, my beauty. Did I need to tell you that?'

'Leave me *alone*!'

'Not on your life! You've led me a merry dance since the beginning, and you've had Hester and Fowler and half the men at Court dancing to your tune, but no more, sweetheart. There's no one to run to out here and nowhere for you to hide, and we've got quite a way to go before we reach Richmond.'

She gave up the unequal struggle, his strength being far too great for her. 'I *hate* you!' she said, weeping. 'I could never expect you to understand.'

'Shh! Easy now. I understand far more than you think.'

His lips on hers suggested that he expected no reply, and certainly his kisses distanced her thoughts from Hester and Peter as nothing else could have done. Gradually, she softened and, while not returning his caresses, lay quietly while he brushed away her tears of vexation. He helped her to her feet and, while she watched the muscles of his chest ripple under the dusting of dark hair, he licked a handkerchief and wiped her face. 'Did you two actually get round to washing yourselves?' he said, sternly.

Suspecting that Adorna was not eager to meet Cousin Hester and the dastardly Peter at Wallingford, Sir Nicholas decided that this would be a good time to sleep under the stars. It was a balmy night, and they had enough food with them for at least two meals: bread, cheese, fruit and ale. Perkin's expedition into the town produced hot pies, roast chicken and flasks of wine, which they shared in a warm corner of a cattle-shelter where there was still enough hay for the horses.

With never enough house-room for servants, high or low, the men were not unused to such primitive accommodation and knew how to make themselves comfortable with only the barest essentials. The two women treated it as an adventure, though Adorna was noticeably subdued.

The distant bridge at Wallingford provided a focal point as she and Maybelle sat together on the river-bank, sharing the kind of silence that holds distant sounds only half-observed. Jumbled thoughts of the past and future combined in Adorna's mind with the doubts she hoped had faded, though they had not.

'He doesn't understand,' she whispered to Maybelle. 'What's a woman supposed to do when she doesn't want a man's company? Stand still and smile and let them believe she does?'

Maybelle threw a stick into the water and watched it swirl away. 'The problem is,' she said, 'that you've always had more than your fair share of men to seek your attention, so it's natural for you to have found places where they couldn't go. If you'd been Mistress Hester, you'd probably have been quite glad of their company. And I dare say she's accepted Master Fowler because he was the first man she was introduced to at Richmond. Do you remember?'

'Yes,' said Adorna. 'I do. I *do* remember. It was at the dinner party. They talked about—'

'Her father, Sir William.'

'That's right. So you think that's when it began?'

'Sure to be, but Mistress Hester's never had to find places to hide because, for one thing, she was hidden already and for another, no one went to look for her. With her new wealth it really doesn't matter whether she leaves the Queen's progress or not because she'll be seen to be like her father, an eccentric. He was, wasn't he?'

'He certainly was, likeable but quite strange. But why doesn't Sir Nicholas tell me what he has in mind for the future, Belle?'

'Because he's proud, I suppose. He may be waiting

for you, too.' She threw another stick into the water.
'Maybe it's up to you now.'

'And you, Belle? What about you and Perkin?'

'Oh…' she laughed, blushing a little '…we know
where we are. He loves me and I love him, and that's
all there is to it, really. We'll probably make babies
together, I expect.'

'Babies?'

'Yes. You know, those little mewling things that
come looking like screwed-up badly dyed leather.
They're called babies, love.'

The description fulfilled its purpose in making
Adorna smile but, all the same, it set her thinking
about her mother's advice, which had come too late
to be of much use, and the possible manufacture of
one of those screwed-up leathery things.

As night descended, she lay in her lover's arms in
a distant corner of the shelter on a thick bed of hay
and cloaks and thought about that conversation and
Maybelle's advice which, in the past, had not always
been entirely appropriate.

'Have you thought,' she said ambiguously, 'what
might happen if—?'

'Yes, sweetheart. Often,' he murmured.

She sighed and withdrew her hand from his chest,
but he caught it and kept his hand over hers. 'I want
it to look exactly like Lady Adorna Rayne,' he said.
'Unless it should turn out to be a boy, of course.'

She sat upright with a jolt to stare down at him in
the gloom. 'How did you…?'

But again he pulled her back to him. 'Go to sleep,' he whispered. 'I told you I understand more than you think.' The next moment he was sound asleep, and her well-planned questioning had been disposed of in one quick riposte. Damn the man! Nevertheless, she fell asleep with a smile on her face for the third time in three nights.

During the night, however, she came half-awake to the unusual surroundings, the close hoots of owls, the breathing of the river, the warm bulk of the man she had come to love too quickly for comfort. Drowsily, she lifted herself over him, reminding herself of the taste of his chin, the contours of his cheeks, chin and brow. Her fingers burrowed seductively into his hair.

Without a word, he awoke and lent himself willingly to her investigations until, with an arm under her back, he reversed their positions in one quick flip that astounded her by its suddenness. She enveloped him with her legs and took him into her, hungrily and with a sudden urge that flared with a wild spontaneity like a forest fire. He responded like one who meets his mate in the still dark night and takes her, and satisfies her, and falls asleep again in her arms till dawn. Silently.

He was missing when she awoke and she lay for a moment or two, wondering if she had dreamed it, and what the day would hold for them. Maybelle came to her with a beaker of ale. 'He's exercising the bay,' she said. 'Come and see.'

In total concentration, the gleaming bay gelding and its rider executed manoeuvres similar to those they had performed at Kenilworth before the Queen, this time before an admiring audience of four. Sitting perfectly still in the saddle, Sir Nicholas guided the bay through its precise paces, moving sideways, crossing legs, pirouetting and dancing daintily, reminding Adorna of their partnership in quite a different setting. He dismounted and came to her, smiling. 'Your turn,' he said. 'Come on. A few basic moves to start with.' His eyes held another message that made her blush, but she did as she was told and discovered that under his guidance, she could manage many of the simpler movements. He corrected her; the horse obeyed. 'Well done,' he said, lifting her down. 'You learn quickly. We'll take that other palomino in hand when we get back home.'

She made no reply to that, for she had recently begun to take a perverse kind of pleasure from his authoritative manner, appreciating once again the sweetness of handing the reins to a capable and decisive man, following his direction and knowing that it was sure to be hers also.

They reached Pangbourne by evening and bathed amongst the swans in the River Pang, half-hidden by a bank of alders. The cygnets were curious, the parents protective and suspicious of the two humans who lingered in the warmest pools, quietly preening each other's plumage. Later, the two walked hand in hand through a field of poppies to join some late hay-

makers, sharing their ale like country lovers for the
price of some help with the raking and the loading of
carts. They stayed at an inn with the sign of a swan
above the door, and made love with renewed passion
well into the night.

By dawn, they were away again, heading eastwards
at last.

Reading was a pleasant and bustling abbey town
where they bought food but did not stay: there was,
Sir Nicholas told her, a far prettier place than this a
mile or two further on. He was right; Sonning-on-
Thames had everything, including a village wedding
which, by the time they arrived, had been in full swing
all day and looked set to continue well into the night.
Drawn into the festivities as anonymous guests of the
happy couple, they ate, drank, and slept once more
under the clear night sky along with many others who
made their beds where they fell.

It was nearly noon when they crossed the bridge at
Sonning and continued along the Oxfordshire side as
far as Henley-on-Thames, crossing back again into
Berkshire over the river. 'We could make it as far as
Bisham,' Sir Nicholas said, after a stop to rest the
horses, 'if you want to go on while it's still light.'

'Whatever you say,' Adorna replied, blowing down
the open front of her bodice.

'May I help you with that?' he said.

'If you wish.'

He did, then looked at her intently. 'We've come a

long way, my lass, have we not? Is the lady tamed, then?'

'Will you still want to know in a year's time?'

'Probably not. I shall be able to answer it myself, by then.'

They cut across a loop of the river to arrive at Bisham Abbey by dusk, staying with Sir Edward and Lady Hoby. In return for tales of the Queen and her Court at Kenilworth, the Hobys showed the two lovers round their beautiful home, pointing out the huge bay window specially built for Her Majesty's visit some years earlier. Taking Adorna's apparent marriage in their stride, they asked no awkward questions but wished the couple good fortune and a large brood of children, which Sir Nicholas endorsed with a squeeze of her hand.

In the late evening, Adorna lured him into the private garden that had once been the monks' paradise, in some strange way connecting a mental image to a physical one that had something to do with his constancy. She could define it no more clearly than that, though she suspected by the way he smiled and indulged her that he knew what was passing through her mind.

From Bisham, they cut across to the little village of Cookham, where there was a smithy for the horses, and at Maidenhead they bridged the river again and came, in only a few more miles, within sight of the huge white towers of Windsor Castle like icebergs on the horizon.

They had come so far without needing to explain their new and unexpected espousal. The Hobys had accepted it without question and, so far, they had met no one who might do otherwise. But Windsor was a different matter, for here Sir Nicholas was known, as was the lovely daughter of Sir Thomas Pickering. According to Sir Nicholas, it was time for another decision.

'What kind of decision?' said Adorna, throwing crumbs of bread to a gaggle of ducks. They sat on the riverbank at Eton with the castle in the distance and, behind them, the open fields where Maybelle, Perkin and Lytton played a noisy and unruly game of football with an old pig's bladder they had found. The evening was not altogether peaceful.

'A decision, my lady,' Sir Nicholas said, lifting her left hand, 'concerning this.' He twisted the borrowed ring on her finger. 'This is all right as a temporary arrangement, but now I think it's about time we had something more convincing for nearer home, don't you? Unless you prefer to arrive at Richmond in two days' time as seemingly chaste as when you left?'

The breath tightened in her lungs and, still unsure of him, still half-expecting the worst to happen, she removed her hand from his, took the ring off and held it out to him. She did not know exactly what he meant, nor did she have the courage to ask him. 'There,' she said. 'Of course, you're right. I don't want my mother to see me wearing it after all that advice about the sanctity of marriage. You keep it. It may come in handy.'

He studied the distant expression on her face, folding her fingers over the ring. 'Adorna,' he said, 'what are you saying to me? What is it you think I'm saying to you?' His voice, full of concern, almost broke her heart.

'I don't know,' she said in a small voice, her words tripping up over a sudden need to weep. 'I don't know what you're saying, Nicholas, but if it's what…what I fear it might…be, then don't say any more. I cannot bear it.'

'Still so distrustful, after all this time?'

'I'm not distrustful, just…'

'Just unsettled? Unsure? I should have said it sooner, sweetheart.'

'Don't say it, please.'

'What, don't say that I love you? That I've loved you for weeks? Ached for you? Don't say that I want you to marry me? Is that what you don't want to hear, sweetheart? Come, my lass.' He pulled her into his arms and lowered her backwards on to the grass, his face close enough for her to feel his words. 'What did you think these last few days have been about, then? Did you really think I'd bed you all the way to Richmond then say thank you and goodbye and don't let your mother know? Is that what you thought?'

Tears had gathered in the corners of her eyes. 'I don't know…didn't know…what I was supposed to think,' she said, touching a scratch on his cheek. 'I hoped…I wanted you to say…but you didn't. How was I to know?'

'Ah!' He sighed. 'Would you believe that men can

be so careful that they sometimes get the timing wrong? Do you remember the first time I told you how lovely you are?'

'Yes.' She smiled, sniffing.

'And how you reacted to my poor timing?'

'Yes.'

'Because you'd heard it all before? And how many times have men told you they love you? Dozens?'

'Boys and old men,' she said. 'No one I could have loved in return.'

'So I thought you'd not want to hear how I felt about you for a while. I thought that if you wanted to know you'd ask me. Or perhaps tell me how you feel about me. And—'

'Shh!' She moved her finger to his lips. 'Then let me tell you how I feel. Let me tell you how I adore you. I've loved you from the beginning, Nicholas.'

'You mean it, sweetheart?'

'I mean it, truly. I thought it was hate. It's very confusing, isn't it?'

His kiss kept her mouth occupied for quite some time, during which she began to make some sense of their misunderstandings, the resulting confusion, and her own fears which had been left to grow for far too long.

'Very confusing,' he agreed 'And now?'

'I feared what you were doing to me,' she whispered against his cheek, 'and what you *could* do to me, if I let you. I've never loved before, you see, and it scared me, and I was madly jealous of all the others, even though I had no idea who they were.'

'So tell me again. I want to hear it at least twenty times a day.'

'I love you, Nicholas. Even when you were horrid to me, I loved you then, too.'

'Little snarling she-cat,' he grinned.

'I'm sorry.'

'Don't be. I loved it. I'd not want to marry a woman who couldn't stand up to me.'

'But what about Hester?'

'What about her? She was never in the running. She knew that.'

'I thought…' She bit her lip.

'I think you and she have a few things to discuss, don't you? There's more to Mistress Hester than meets the eye, obviously. She may not have been too sure about what she wants, but she certainly knows what she doesn't want. She has the Pickering trait, too.'

'What's that?'

'She's a fast learner.'

Their intimate laughter was brought to a sudden yelping conclusion by an inflated pig's bladder bouncing hard off the back of Nicholas's head, only to be retrieved by two lusty howling men who apparently lacked any respect, at that moment, for their master or his mistress.

Laughing, he helped her to stand. 'You've not replied to my proposal, I notice. Have you got used to the idea of being Lady Adorna Rayne, yet?'

She watched the three footballers chase away, Belle with her skirt pulled up between her legs. The idyll must be prolonged as it was, for two more days, at least. 'I think,' she said, 'I'll give you my answer at Richmond. Can you wait?'

'I can wait. And I think I know where I'll be when I wait.'

'Shh!' she said, smiling. 'Meanwhile, put this ring away and give it back to Master Burbage. It's fulfilled its purpose, but now I have to be myself or there'll be far more questions than I can answer.'

'Is your mother going to be shocked, d'ye think?'

'Slightly confused, more like, after all the protesting I've done.'

In the warm haven of his arms in a little inn at Eton, there was another matter to be attended to, though the answer was no more than a formality. 'Nicholas, would you really have told anyone about me taking Seton's part in the plays?'

He turned to her, stroking her hair and almost laughing. 'Think about it, sweetheart. Who would I tell? The earl? He'd be more than grateful to you, I should imagine, as Master Burbage and Seton were, as the rest of the company would have been, if they'd realised. They'd not want to be disbanded, would they? Your father would hardly shout about it, with his own family so closely involved, and any scandal involving the earl and his players would involve me, too, one way or another, as his servant. So I'd not want to put him in an embarrassing position either. Besides, I'm loyal. It makes no sense at all, my sweet, does it?'

'Yet you went along with the whole idea,' she said, trying to sound indignant.

'So I did.' He smiled. 'Who wouldn't? And we have Seton's nerves and wobbly voice to thank for it, and his most courageous sister. That took some doing, my love. I hope he appreciates what you did as much as I do.'

'I didn't really have much choice,' she said, knowing that he knew the truth of the matter as well as she did.

If they had not lingered in Windsor market, or played tennis at Hampton Court Palace, or met friends, or made a lengthy visit to one of Nicholas's brothers at Kingston-upon-Thames, they would certainly have reached Richmond sooner than they did. As it was, it was almost mid-afternoon when they wound their way up Paradise Road towards Sheen House, far more reconciled to each other than when they had set out. Their arrival was not far behind that of Sir Thomas Pickering and the Queen's Wardrobe, Leicester's Men, and the whole enormous slow-moving paraphernalia of baggage that beat them by less than an hour from a more direct route.

The courtyard was still teeming with men, horses and luggage, amongst which Sir Nicholas's small party made very little impression until the bright silvery toss of Adorna's hair caught the Master of Revels in mid-sentence. 'What…! What the *devil*?' he cried. 'Where have *you* come from?'

It took some time to explain. Seton joined in, as incredulous of his sister's sun-bronzed and unladylike appearance as of her obviously radiant happiness.

Lady Marion didn't care about the route they'd taken, which was all that interested the men, but about the daughter from whom she had had no news for well over a week. Close to tears, she hugged Adorna, leaving questions about her happiness to answer themselves. 'Hester arrived yesterday,' she said, wiping her tears. 'She's around somewhere.'

'Hester came back *here*?'

Her mother wobbled her head. 'Don't ask me,' she said, as confused as Adorna's prediction. 'I've no idea what's going on. I think your father is the only one so far who's come back the same as he went. Even Seton's got a new voice. Just listen to him.'

'Did Hester tell you what happened?'

Lady Marion rolled her eyes. 'You know what Hester's like. It'll be at least a month before we discover what she's been up to.'

In fact, it was nothing like a month, though it was not Hester, of course, who enlightened her cousin. But although Hester was unused to having to explain herself to others, there were certain things Adorna needed to know rather more urgently. The two hugged like sisters, too happy with the outcome of their own affairs to be affronted by the petty deceptions of the past.

Nevertheless, Hester was surprised by Adorna's appearance. 'Then you must have followed us…er, me,' she said, retrieving herself.

'Well, of course I followed you. You left rather abruptly and I was concerned. I thought you must have been upset by what you saw.'

'In your chamber? Oh, no. I went to tell you what I'd decided to do, but I didn't know Sir Nicholas was with you, so when I saw you were…er…busy, I left and went to find…er…to make arrangements. I wasn't upset at all.' She coiled her long brown hair into a rope, worn loose like a maiden, and taking at least five off her twenty-one years. Like Adorna, she was sun-browned and sparkling with health and now, having discarded her stays, there was an elfin quality about her which had not shown itself before. 'Oh, dear,' she said, as the implications dawned upon her, 'did you think I was upset over Sir Nicholas? Yes, I can quite see that you would. It's all been a bit of a mix-up, hasn't it?'

'Hester,' Adorna said, tired of beating around the bush, 'I know that you travelled with Peter, and I don't mind. Really. I don't. Did you think I'd be annoyed about it?'

Hester stared. 'You *know*? I told Lady Marion I'd travelled with friends from the palace.'

'Of course. I told you, I followed you.'

'What, so close? You saw us?' The horrified expression grew.

It was time for some diplomacy. 'We caught sight of you in the distance—oh, I can't recall where it was—but Sir Nicholas had made enquiries before he left Kenilworth and he knew that you were in good company.'

'Oh, he's been so very kind.'

'Who, Peter?'

'Well, yes, but I meant Sir Nicholas. He promised

Uncle Samuel he'd keep an eye on me while I was here. Did you know that? I had it in one of my aunt's letters. I suppose I should have let him know where I was going, but when I saw that you and he had become friends at last, I realised I wouldn't have to pretend any more, so I forgot.'

'Pretend what, Hester?' said Adorna, noting the lack of regret.

'Well, pretend to be interested in him. You and Lady Marion were rather set on the idea, weren't you? And I felt obliged to make an effort. I thought I was doing quite well at one time when I saw that you were looking quite convinced, even though I knew it was a waste of time. Sir Nicholas has never seen me in *that* light, you know.'

So, it was as Sir Nicholas had said. Hester was so obliging. 'I see, so you and Peter found mutual comfort in each other.'

'Not exactly.' Hester smiled, suddenly coy. 'I think there was something between us at our first meeting, but at that time he was your friend, Adorna. He's *so* interesting though, isn't he? So dependable. It must have been Fate that sent me here to Richmond, don't you think?'

'And was it Fate that made you fall off your horse that day at the hunt?' Adorna could not resist the teasing laugh which Hester had the grace to echo.

'Oh, dear,' she said, twisting madly at the rope of hair. 'You realised that I was shamming, did you?'

No, Adorna had not, until now. 'So what was all that about?'

'Peter's idea. He thought that if I had a good reason to return home, your father would agree to let him escort me. But Sir Thomas didn't, so we just had to wait for another chance, and if we'd left it any longer Peter would have had to go on up to Staffordshire to check the security. I would have told you, Adorna, but I thought you'd be angry at me going with Peter. So we thought it best just to go and say nothing. Peter met me beyond the gate. It was so exciting. Neither of us could bear any more of that socialising, especially me. I thought it would have been fun, but it was such hard work. Our journey back was simply heavenly.'

'And the letters?'

'Oh, the letters. Well, it was the only way we could communicate, really, with so many people watching. Especially after I was confined to my room.'

'But what about Peter's position in the Queen's service? Surely he'll lose it?'

'Oh, that doesn't matter too much. We have all the money we need to live off without him having to earn anything. We'll probably travel to Italy soon.'

Well done, Peter, Adorna thought. Certainly this was a few steps up from Gentleman Controller of the Queen's Works. Yet it was only to be expected that, having had no reason to think about anyone except herself in twenty-one years, Hester would display a singular lack of interest in any doings except her own, and it was not long before Adorna realised that hers and Sir Nicholas's affairs were only relevant insofar as they affected Hester. Italy, she thought, would be about far enough.

It didn't seem to matter for, once the shock of having dozens of extra mouths to feed had passed, Lady Marion played hostess to the merriest crowd of people that either Adorna or Seton could remember. Young Adrian could not hear enough about his elder brother's performances before the Queen while congratulating him on the acquisition of a fine new baritone voice. Adrian, however, was ecstatic when Master Burbage, his hero, persuaded Sir Thomas to allow him to take over Seton's former role as principal female actor with the company. It was the only time any of them had seen Adrian speechless.

Seton would have wept, but found himself suddenly and inexplicably unable to. Instead, he clung to Adorna and shook with relief. 'Thank you, dear one,' he said for her ear alone. 'Thank you. I am the happiest man alive.'

This sentiment was contested later on after Sir Nicholas, in a rare moment of privacy, managed to corner Sir Thomas to ask him formally for the hand of his daughter in marriage, after which he no longer had to wonder which side of the family Adorna got her unpredictability from. Sir Thomas's exact reply was unrepeatable but, according to Sir Nicholas, contained the overtones of a command to the effect that he had bloody well taken the goods first and asked afterwards, so now he'd better be sharp and give a name to the bairn he'd no doubt spawned.

To Sir Nicholas's reminder that they had actually agreed at Kenilworth on a certain line of action—which dumbfounded yet another of the Pickering siblings—Sir Thomas replied that he had not believed it remotely likely that anyone would bed his daughter before her marriage, least of all Sir Nicholas to whom she seemed particularly ill disposed. He had, he said, agreed to him wooing her, not to getting her pregnant as fast as possible. Which was another good reason for the high good humour and air of complacency displayed by the Deputy Master of Horse as darkness fell over the garden at Sheen House.

People wandered quietly amongst the arbours and terraces or stood in shadowy chattering groups around the banqueting house as Sir Nicholas took Adorna's hand and caught the smile on her face. 'What?' he said.

'I'd not have believed I'd be won over either,' she said. 'Especially not by you.'

'Ah, then it's just as well I believe in myself, isn't it? Yet I'm not convinced that you didn't believe it. You kept it hidden, that's all.'

Unable to contradict him, for it was true, Adorna led him away from the garden, along the paved walkways, down steps and out beyond the house to Paradise Road where, in the wall along the grassy verge there was a door leading into the old friary paradise at the side of the Queen's palace garden. Past gnarled fruit trees and blowsy roses, straggling honeysuckle, golden-rod and fragrant lavender, she brought him to a stand where once he had waited for a woman while Adorna had watched, aching with envy and longing.

'Here,' she whispered. 'It was here, wasn't it?' She stood apart from him, hoping that he would know what she wanted. He did.

Stretching out his hands, he went to meet her and pulled her into his arms, enclosing her with strong hands whose warmth she could feel through the thin linen bodice. 'I knew it,' he whispered, kissing her eyelids. 'The paradise at Godstow nunnery, then at Kings Sutton, then at Bisham, and now here at Richmond. And this is where I tell you again that I want you to be my wife, the mother of my children, my companion, friend and lover. My adored Adorna. I want to keep you, protect you, give you my name. Will you be mine, sweetheart?'

For an answer, she quoted Beatrice's beautiful confession. '"Now I am persuaded to accept, to love, to be no more aloof, to say that what was mine shall now be yours, forsooth." Take my heart and my promise, beloved. I *am* yours; all of me. I think I always was since I first saw you just on this spot. I wanted you then so much. I willed you to come to me.'

His mouth roamed over her face as he spoke. 'And I would rather anyone had seen that farewell kiss but you. Saints, woman, I've never felt about another living soul as I do about you. Shall we have bairns, sweet lass, to give others the same sweet torment?'

'Bold, tenacious lads like their father?'

'Wilful Water Maidens like their mother. Tempestuous, passionate women that will test a man's resolve. We'll have a family of beauties, shall we, love?'

There were plenty of dark out-of-the-way corners amongst the old overgrown plots of the friary garden, places where they could lie on sun-warmed chamomile and clover to make urgent love as though time was running out on them instead of just beginning. Vaguely, they heard the chime of the clock over in the palace courtyard, the distant call of guests from Sir Thomas's garden and the faint laughter of lovers in the Queen's. But for them, the sweetest sounds were of their own soft moans of joy. Safe in his love and sure of his devotion, Adorna led him to paradise at last and herself to the mastership of the only man she had ever wanted, though it had taken her long enough to admit it.

They chuckled, remembering their first watery meeting. 'You were so unmannerly,' she said, sprinkling his chest with her hair. 'So high-handed. I think I hated you then.'

'You feared me. And you could hardly wait to hare off to your father's office, could you?'

'Where you barged in while I was trying on that ridiculous dress. Ogling me.'

His hand moved possessively over her naked breast. 'It was a rare sight. I saw far more than I could have hoped for. You didn't like my net, though. Did you?' He laughed softly, caressing her. 'How you fought me, eh?'

She turned her head into his neck. 'Shh! Don't remind me. It was shameful.'

'Not a bit of it! It was my triumph.' His hand stopped, and he lay over her, seeing the last glint of light in her eyes. 'And there was not a man in the hall who didn't envy me with Mistress Adorna Pickering in my arms. Netted. Well, I have you now, my beauty.'

'Here in paradise, for ever, love.' She smiled.

Adorna and Nicholas were married on August 5th, 1575, at Sheen House in Richmond in the presence of the Queen and the Earl of Leicester. Their first boy was born the following May in London, followed by two more boys and then a girl.

Author's Note

As the story states, Sir William Pickering was in fact a one-time contender for the Queen's hand. He was a brilliant eccentric who had a daughter named Hester to whom he left his entire fortune and his house in London. Nothing is known of this lady, or of her mother, but one lady about whom far more is known was the Countess of Essex, otherwise known as Lettice Knollys, to whose home in Staffordshire the progress moved from Kenilworth. The earl's long-standing love affair with the countess caused even more scandal when, shortly after her widowhood, they married in secret—an act of betrayal for which the Queen never forgave either of them.

Sir Christopher Hatton, Sir John Fortescue, Dr Dee, the Hobys and James Burbage are all real characters in history, and all the places mentioned in the story are real except Sheen House, which is imaginary. There was, however, a Sheen Manor, which the Queen gave to a former lady-in-waiting, the Swedish Marchioness of Northampton. Kings Sutton is now known as Sutton Courtney, and Kenilworth Castle is now a ruin. The Tudor Palace of Richmond covered about ten acres of land from what is now Old Palace Lane to Water Lane, but the only parts now remaining are the pink brick gateway into the Great Court and behind it, in Old Palace Yard, some original brickwork of the Tudor period which was once part of the Wardrobe. This was reconstructed in the early eighteenth century.

Queen Elizabeth I died in Richmond Palace in 1603, after which it declined in favour and was eventually demolished along with the remains of the old friary. We have seventeenth-century drawings of Antonis van Wyngaerde and Wenceslaus Hollar to show us what the buildings looked like.

However, the modern town of Richmond in Surrey retains names that remind us of its more serene past. Names such as Old Palace Lane, Water Lane, Friars Stile Road, Orchard Road, Manor Road, Vineyard Passage and, of course, Paradise Road, where, at Eton House, numbers 18 to 24, is situated the UK Head Office of the publisher of this book, Harlequin Mills & Boon, Ltd.

The excerpts from Seton's plays, read by Adorna and Sir Nicholas, are purely the invention of the author and are not taken, directly or indirectly, from anything written by anyone else, real or imaginary. Beatrice and Benedict may also have been Seton's own invention as borrowing, now known as plagiarism, was common and not illegal in Tudor England. And, since young William Shakespeare was open to all influences, this may have remained in his mind until he wrote *Much Ado About Nothing* in 1598/9. Similarly, Ovid's 'Titania' and the Germanic mythical 'Oberon', of the thirteenth-century romance *Huon of Bordeaux*, translated into English in 1534, were fair game for any author to use, as many did in later years. Shakespeare borrowed them both for *A Midsummer Night's Dream*.

* * * * *